A FEATHER TO FLY WITH

A Regency Romance

By

Joyce Harmon

A Feather To Fly With

Published by Joyce Harmon at Amazon

A FEATHER TO FLY WITH
By Joyce Harmon

ONE

Lady Sefton saw the new arrival being bowed into the ballroom at Almack's by Mister Willis, and turned to her fellow patroness Lady Jersey. "Winton is here," she said complacently.

Lady Jersey rolled her eyes in mock despair. "My dear, I do not care! The man is hopeless!"

Felicity Harwell, in her first season and only her second appearance at Almack's, was already well on her way to being toasted as the season's Incomparable. She had just shaken off her admirers for a time to engage the patronesses in conversation, and looked with interest at this hopeless man. "Why, what is the matter with him, ma'am?" she asked politely. "Is he a great rake?"

The man who had just entered did not bear the appearance of a rake, though Felicity wasn't sure that she would recognize such a man if she saw one. But this Winton bore no outward marks of dissipation. He was neatly dressed in the required knee-breeches, with neither the excruciating exactness of dress that proclaimed the dandy, nor the casual negligence that was the mark of the buck.

His coat was well-tailored, but a modest blue. His hair was light brown, worn in a sensible crop, and his features were pleasingly regular. Only one ring graced his hands, and it a signet. His eyes were gray, and his air was that of mild abstraction. He was perhaps a year or two shy of thirty.

Lady Sefton tittered. "A rake? My dear, of course His Grace is not a rake."

His Grace? Suddenly Felicity was listening keenly; this was no longer idle conversation, but vital information. So the mysteriously hopeless gentleman was a duke, was he? A young lady in this society had one task – to marry, one ambition – to marry well, and one secret dream – to marry brilliantly. And there was no match so brilliant as a duke.

"Would that he were," Lady Jersey said. "Rakes at least have been known to reform."

"More do not," Lady Sefton replied darkly.

The two ladies began to delve into a comprehensive catalogue of rakes they had known, detailing which ones had reformed and which ones had not.

"Oh, but ma'am!" Felicity pleaded. "If he is not a rake, in what way is he hopeless?"

Lady Jersey patted her hand and broke the news. "My dear, he is a scholar!"

***

Arthur Ramsey, sixth Duke of Winton, surveyed the room with a dismay he was too well-bred to show. How they stared! From across the room, a deep jolly voice called, "Winton!" and he was relieved to see his best friend waving at him.

He made his way around the perimeter of the room to join the Honorable Justin Amesbury at the refreshments table. Justin was a tall well-built man of thirty, equally at home in the ballroom or on the hunting field. The Amesbury property adjoined the Winton estate, and the two had grown up together. They were nothing alike, but both men were tolerant enough to enjoy their differences.

"You here?" Justin greeted him, deftly snagging a glass of Almack's despised lemonade from a passing waiter. "I thought you fixed in the country."

"I had to come to Town," Arthur explained. "Gould will be speaking at the Royal Society on planetary orbits."

Justin's eyes twinkled. "You obviously couldn't miss that."

"No, I couldn't," Arthur said earnestly. "Justin, he's *wrong*."

"Well then, well-met, whatever the reason. What do you say to a hand or two of piquet?"

"I can't." Arthur sipped his lemonade and moodily surveyed the room. "I must mingle and dance. I promised Mother."

"Oh, indeed? And how is the dear Duchess?"

"Fretful," Arthur said. "She rang a fair peal over me, I must admit, over my duty to the family."

Justin was surprised. "Aunt Phyllida never struck me as a managing sort of female."

"She isn't, really," Arthur said fairly. "But she's experiencing anxiety, you know, with Charley in the Peninsula."

4

"Ah," Justin nodded. "I see. So with Charley risking life and limb, it's up to you to assure the succession."

"Something of that nature. She can't say she's worried for Charley's safety, she's far too much the Spartan mother for that. But that worry has to come out somehow, so she's deflected it onto my single and childless state."

"Which explains His Grace's presence at the Marriage Mart. You should have followed my example. Note how cleverly I timed my birth order, leaving it to George to play the family patriarch and hopeful father of a large brood, while yours truly remains unattached and free to follow my own inclinations."

"Alas, my infant self did not think that far ahead," Arthur said with a laugh. He turned and faced the assembled multitude, and then turned back to Justin, daunted. "How does one go about this?" he asked.

"Come now!" Justin admonished. "Surely you recall when Clara was fired off. You were down from Cambridge by then."

"Oh, yes." Arthur thought back to his sister's debut. "I seem to recall a great deal of to-do about clothing. But I'd just got my telescope, you see."

"Indeed, I do. Earthly concerns were doubtless the furthest thing from your mind. Well. This will be a challenge. Tell me, what sort of female are you looking for?"

"A duchess," Arthur replied simply.

"My dear fellow! They don't come that way! You must find a likely candidate and make her a duchess."

"So you must suggest some likely candidates."

"I will do nothing of the sort!" Justin pulled Arthur to an alcove, gesturing to a passing waiter and claiming more lemonade. He sat down and said, "Let's work this through."

Arthur meekly took a seat, ready to be instructed.

"Your first step will be to meet a wide variety of females," Justin said. "From those, you can determine a smaller group that you find most appealing. You pay more attention to this group, and eventually you will form an attachment to one specific female."

Arthur nodded approvingly. "It sounds very scientific. Have you followed this procedure?"

"Not at all, for I'm fine as I am. I enjoy the ladies. They like my company and I like theirs. But I'm not in the market for leg-

5

shackling just yet. Now, for your case. Almack's is an excellent place to begin. Our indomitable patronesses has already done the work of winnowing the ineligibles for us, so that every single young lady here is potential duchess raw material. I would suggest that tonight you dance with five or six different ladies. Only one dance apiece, since you're just meeting them, and two dances would be considered too particular. You are a duke, after all, and that makes the quizzes interested in everything you do."

"Five or six." Arthur agreed. "That sounds quite feasible." He scanned the crowded dance floor and then remarked plaintively, "I don't know any of these people."

"They've none of them written scholarly papers; that explains it," Justin said briskly. "Do any of the young ladies strike you as attractive?"

After a moment, Arthur said, "The tall brunette looks rather... regal."

Justin followed his gaze and shook his head. "Miss Jennings. No, she won't do for you."

"What's wrong with her?"

"Nothing in the world. It's merely that she's musical. Very musical."

"I like music," Arthur protested.

"As do I," Justin agreed. "But not that much music. Earlier in the season, I'd thought to attach myself to her court, but there are limits. She plays the pianoforte and the harp, and she sings. Her family is forever attending the opera and hosting musical evenings at home. Unless you are a genuine music enthusiast..."

"No," Arthur said. "Only moderately interested."

"But, I say," Justin went on. "Perhaps Miss Harwell might do for you. Just out, but she's certainly taken. She'll be the belle of the season."

"Which one is she?"

"Over near the refreshments table. The little blonde there in that peach satin?"

Arthur examined the little blonde. She was undeniably beautiful, with gold ringlets artfully tousled, and a trim little figure. She was waltzing with a young man in regimentals and laughing up at him.

"She's rather jolly," Justin said. "I've decided to make her my main interest this season."

6

Arthur turned to him with concern. "Oh, then I'll not cut you out."

"Nothing of the sort, my dear Arthur," he was assured. "I escort the dears. Send them flowers, walk with them in the park, dance with them at the balls. It keeps me in fashion. By now I bring them into fashion. Once she attaches her prize, I'll attend the wedding and send a lovely gift. Think nothing of it. But Miss Harwell is a nice girl. Good-humored, good dancer, fun to be around. And her mother is less terrible than most. Why don't I introduce you?"

The dance ended as the two men made their way around the ballroom, and Miss Harwell joined several other young ladies. "Excellent," Justin murmured to Arthur. "More subjects for the Winton experiment."

***

Felicity was having a splendid evening. Her dance card was full, her partners were both charming and eligible, and all strove to fix their interest with her. In the interval between dances, she took a moment to catch her breath and compare notes with Lillian Dumphreys and Marianne Keene, her great friends from Miss Frobish's Select Academy. Lillian and Marianne were also well pleased with their evening and the gentlemen they were meeting.

When they saw Mister Amesbury coming toward them, Felicity was able to tell them that the young man accompanying him was the Duke of Winton, feeling well up on every *on dit* in Town.

But when the Duke was presented to them, Felicity realized that her social success could pose a problem. "Winton is determined to dance," Amesbury told them, "so I hope you ladies will all favor him with a dance."

Lillian and Marianne could easily comply, but Felicity replied with a look of dismay. "Oh dear, I am sorry," she said, "but I'm afraid all my dances are taken."

"Easily mended," Amesbury assured her. "I greedily claimed two dances, so will nobly forfeit one. But not the waltz. I insist upon the waltz." He quickly made the change to Felicity's delicate ivory dance card.

Amesbury couldn't recall when he'd last spent a more amusing evening at Almack's. Never, most likely.

Following a quadrille, Arthur returned Miss Dumphreys to her chaperon and then made his way to Amesbury. "Well?" Justin asked, observing the little redhead whispering excitedly to her duenna.

"She seems a pleasant enough girl, as far as I could tell," Arthur admitted.

"As far as you could tell?"

"The figures of the dance make conversation a most disjointed affair," Arthur complained. "It seems irrational that dancing should be the order of the day if the goal is for young men and women to become acquainted with one another."

"Perhaps it isn't the most sensible way to go about it," Amesbury had to admit. "But it is a start. And you did manage snatches of conversation, surely."

"Yes, snatches."

"And what did you glean from these snatches?"

"That she is finding her season vastly amusing. That she quite dotes on the novels of Mrs. Radcliffe. That her brother will take her up in his phaeton tomorrow, allowing her to display a new carriage gown that is simply ravishing."

"Clever girl," said Amesbury with an appreciative chuckle.

"Clever?" Arthur looked perplexed.

"Yes, for she's ensured that if you wish to encounter her again, you'll know where to be."

"I do?"

Amesbury listed the clues. "Brother? Tomorrow? Phaeton?" Seeing Arthur's continued incomprehension, Amesbury gave up and spelled it out for him. "Hyde Park at five," he said pityingly.

"Oh? Oh! I see," Arthur exclaimed. "Why didn't she just say that?"

"Because then she would be stating clearly that she hopes you will encounter her again."

"Well, doesn't she?"

Justin couldn't help laughing out loud. "There's the cotillion just starting," he told his friend. "You mustn't leave Miss Keene waiting."

Following the cotillion, the Duke found his way back to Amesbury, looking perturbed. "I may have offended Miss Keene," he said. "But I'm not sure how."

Mild-mannered Arthur offending a young lady at Almack's? Greatly amused, Justin asked for specifics.

"I don't understand it," Arthur told him. "When she mentioned her father's country estate, I simply asked if he encouraged his tenants to follow the principles of scientific farming."

Fascinated, Justin asked, "And her reply?"

"She asked how I imagined she would possibly know such a thing. The question seemed to put her out of humor."

"I shouldn't let it concern you," Justin advised. "Farming methods might not be considered strictly within the purview of female concerns, but if that's going to offend her, she's far too starchy for you to consider."

"Perhaps I'm too eccentric?" Arthur suggested.

Justin chuckled. "Nonsense. You could be a pure bedlamite; so long as you are His Grace of Bedlam, you must always be acceptable to society."

"That doesn't seem rational," Arthur protested.

"Rational or not, it's the way of society," Justin assured him. "Now go dance with Miss Harwell before I reclaim the dance I forfeited."

Amesbury's information on the next dance came from Miss Harwell herself. Following the dance, Justin lost track of Arthur, but soon presented himself to Miss Harwell and claimed the waltz. As they danced, Miss Harwell asked him hesitantly, "Is His Grace perhaps a poet?"

"Great heavens! Wherever did you get such a notion?" Amesbury asked her.

Miss Harwell nodded toward a row of gilt chairs and Justin saw Arthur there, busily writing in a small notebook with a stub of pencil.

"He talked with me during our dance about planets," the beauty told him. "And then he got a faraway look in his eyes, and once the dance was over he escorted me back to my mother, and then pulled out that little book and began to write. He seems lost to the world."

"And you assumed he must have been inspired to write you a poem?" Amesbury asked, his lips quirking involuntarily.

Miss Harwell looked momentarily confused but then chuckled. "Oh dear, how conceited that sounds." After a moment, she added, "But if I've become conceited, I must lay the blame on you London

9

gentlemen, who tell a green girl such extravagant compliments that she becomes quite puffed up about her charms. I gather that His Grace is not a poet?"

"I'll tell you the unvarnished truth, Miss Harwell," Justin replied. "I fear that you have inspired – an equation."

***

In the carriage returning to their townhouse in Mayfair, Felicity was quizzed by her mama about the evening. Usually these sessions covered the entirety of her dance card, but this evening, Mrs. Harwell had only one subject in mind – His Grace the Duke of Winton. While Felicity had never heard of him before today, her mother certainly had.

"Fabulously wealthy, a family that can trace itself back to the Conqueror, and still unattached! He is rarely seen in society, which perhaps explains how he has escaped thus far. Oh, my dear, if you could only succeed in attaching him! The houses, the carriages, the clothes you would wear!"

Mrs. Harwell sat back and fanned herself vigorously for a moment, overcome by these delightful visions. Then she sat up and returned to the interrogation.

"How did he like you? Did he seem interested?"

"I scarcely know," Felicity admitted. "His conversation is not what I am used to."

"He didn't go beyond the line, I hope?" Her mama's eyes narrowed.

"Oh, no!" Felicity hastened to correct her. "But I found him difficult to understand."

"How do you mean?"

"He spoke of planets and their orbits around the sun. He told me that there is a planet that no one had ever seen before, despite its vastness, because it is so far away. He has seen it, he assured me, through his own telescope."

"Ha," said Mrs. Harwell in wonder. It was difficult to interpret these words as the raptures of a lover.

"And then perhaps he saw how bewildered I felt, because he brought the conversation back to earth. Quite literally, because he talked of farming."

"Farming!" Mrs. Harwell marveled. "What has a duke to do with farming?"

10

"He seemed quite taken with it," Felicity told her. "And spoke quite favorably about something he called crop rotation."

"Nonsense," her mother snapped.

"He did!"

"You must have misunderstood him, silly girl. If one rotated a crop, its roots would be in the air, and how that could be said to be a benefit is quite beyond me. No, you misheard him."

For the remainder of the ride, Mrs. Harwell enumerated the locations and sizes of His Grace's properties, which seemed to Felicity to be vast indeed.

***

The clock in the hall of the Grosvenor Square mansion had already chimed past three when Phyllida, Duchess of Winton heard the front door open. A murmur of voices as her son was greeted by Tolliver the butler, and then soft footsteps ascending the stairs. The Duchess picked up the novel on the table beside her chair and opened it. Her son entered the drawing room to find his mother engrossed in a book.

She looked up as he entered. "Arthur? Gracious, what time is it? Sophronia vowed I would find this book enthralling, and indeed I have lost all track of time."

Arthur dropped into the divan across from her and gave her an amused look. The Duchess was a small woman, with light brown hair now liberally streaked with grey and enclosed in a foolish lace cap. Her comfortable old round gown was so plain that she might be mistaken for a housekeeper. Her consequence was something she could don and doff like a cloak. "You don't deceive me for a moment, Mama." He gestured at the book in her hands. "*The Hungarian Brothers?* You read it last summer and proclaimed it a farrago of nonsense."

The Duchess closed the book with a sound of exasperation and replaced it on the table. "I should have known better," she said. "Must you notice everything?"

"I can't seem to help it," he said apologetically.

"Then you must learn not to mention it," his mother told him sternly. "Especially if you wish to take your place in society, where there will be many things you will notice that should not be mentioned."

Tolliver entered the room, bearing a tray that held a decanter and elegant little glasses. "Sherry!" the Duchess exclaimed approvingly. "Much too late for tea. Thank you, Tolliver."

As the butler made his stately departure, Arthur rose and poured them each a glass. He handed his mother her glass and resumed his seat. "You waited up for me," he said.

"And if I did?"

"Were you worried about me?"

"Let's say curious, rather." The Duchess leaned forward. "So? Did you enjoy your excursion into society?"

Arthur frowned thoughtfully. "It was interesting, certainly."

"Did you meet some young ladies?"

"Yes, quite a few. Justin introduced me to several and then Lady Jersey presented me to several more."

"How did you go on?"

"I wish I knew," Arthur confessed. After a moment, he added, "I wonder if I've been too greatly indulged and allowed to follow my own inclinations without regard to my station."

"Arthur! Are you accusing me of being a bad mother?" his mother teased.

"Of course not," he replied with a smile. "And yet... It's hard to explain. Justin moved through those rooms like it was second nature to him, because it was. But I? I felt as if I'd been set down in a tribe of Esquimaux, with no knowledge of their customs and habits."

His mother considered this for a moment. "Think of it this way," she suggested. "What would you do if you were indeed set down in a tribe of Esquimaux and had to make your way among them?"

Arthur nodded his comprehension. "I would study them and their ways until I could pass among them as one of their own."

"So you see, then," the Duchess told him. "It's merely a new field of study."

Arthur felt in his pocket and removed a small notebook and pencil. "I should make notes of the customs," he decided. "Justin told me that Hyde Park is the place to walk, ride and drive." He flipped through the book, murmuring to himself. "That's my rebuttal of Gould's equations, that's my requirements for a duchess..." He found a fresh page and began to make a note, but his mother interrupted him.

"Go back," she said. "Your requirements for a duchess?"

12

"Oh, yes," Arthur flipped back to the page in question. "I've determined that I want a lady of good birth, naturally, reasonably attractive and good natured. She would need to be intelligent and it would be best if she came from a large family, indicative of healthy childbearing."

The Duchess waited, but Arthur seemed to be done with his requirements list. "Are you sure that's all?" she asked patiently.

"Have you other suggestions?" Arthur waited, pencil poised.

She sighed. "Oh, my dear. Remember that you will live with this woman for the rest of your life! So surely it must be a requirement that you at least like her!"

"Excellent point," Arthur told her, and made a note of it.

The Duchess sat up long after Arthur had gone to bed. Staring into the fire, she came to the conclusion that she too had been too self-indulgent. She had cultivated her own society of close friends and virtually ignored the larger society. Well, that was about to change. Since her son was in the market for a wife, she needed to be out there, monitoring the ladies who put themselves forward as potential duchesses.

She was not a snob, she told herself, and not a meddling mama. But Arthur, in his expedition among the Esquimaux, could easily fall prey to a scheming miss. The Duchess was determined to ensure that the chosen bride would be a wife to make him happy. If she were to cede her title to the newcomer and assume the aging title of Dowager, at least she wanted to give way to a worthy successor.

With a fond smile, she remembered a time over twenty years ago. They were at Winton Court, and a noise in the entrance hall had drawn her out of her morning room, to greet the sight of her son being towed up the stairs by a scolding Nanny. Five year old Arthur had been covered with mud and slime, his hair adorned with water weeds. But he pulled away from Nanny to lean over the railing and call down to her exultantly, "Fish breathe through their necks! I know, for I have seen it!"

How many young Society damsels would have been able to see past the mud to appreciate the keen thrill of discovery underneath? The new Duchess of Winton would be one who could, or the Dowager Duchess of Winton would know the reason why.

TWO

Pelton went softly up the back stairs dreaming dreams of glory. His Grace had gone to Almack's! The word among the upper servants was that the Duke was in the market for a wife. His valet hoped it was so.

Pelton had been born into service at Winton Court, and following a career beginning as boot boy, ascended to footman, becoming the Duke's valet when His Grace came down from Cambridge. While Pelton would never think of seeking another position, and while his status among the upper servants at his favorite drinking establishment was solidly entrenched, valeting for such a studious young gentleman gave very little scope for the flashes of genius which Pelton was sure that he possessed. His peers were able to speak of their gentlemen's fashionable triumphs and mad starts. There were only so many ways to work a "His Grace" into these conversations.

The Duke patronized Weston for his coats, but merely because his father had done so, and not for any preference of his own. And even then, he refused to allow Weston to make them so tight that they could only be donned with assistance. He remained in the middle range of what was fashionable, and that only because Pelton took care to see that he was. But as for setting fashion, His Grace was simply not interested. Pelton, however, was interested on his behalf. It was all well and good to invent an ingenious method to drain standing water from low-lying fields and transport it to fields where it was needed, as the Duke had done. No doubt very useful and admirable. But couldn't he take just a bit of that massive intellect and invent a new way of tying a neckcloth that all the dandies would seek to emulate? Couldn't he allow the barber more scope with the scissors to give him a distinctive style?

Pelton dreamed of the day when men of fashion would tie their neckcloths in a Winton Fall, while their heads sported the Winton Crop. It seemed a foolish dream, but now it was revived. For in Pelton's experience, there was nothing like a young lady to drive a young gentleman to the pursuit of fashion.

He approached his master's chamber entranced by golden visions; riding dress, ball dress, opera dress, clothing for morning calls, for promenades, for evening illuminations. So it came as a sad blow to enter the Duke's chamber and find himself confronting a familiar old enemy. For His Grace, at nine in the morning after a late evening, was already up and dressed.

"Oh, Your Grace, not the brown coat! That shabby thing!" he was startled into exclaiming.

Arthur held up an arm and examined the sleeve, answering mildly, "If it were actually frayed, I would have it disposed of. But as it is, it is well enough for a morning walk."

For the Duke was a tireless walker. A habit perhaps tolerable in the country, but in Pelton's eyes greatly to be deplored in Town.

"Walk if you must," Pelton said resignedly. "But must you wear that coat? It makes you look like a clerk!"

"No one will see me," the Duke told him patiently. "Or no one to signify. I don't walk down the main thoroughfares of Mayfair, you know, and it's too early for the fashionable to be abroad anyway."

"Your Grace should walk in the Park," Pelton insisted. "That's what it's there for!"

But Arthur shook his head. "You know I gave up walking, or rather sauntering, in the Park long ago, Pelton. What with the morning riders and the bowing to acquaintances, and stopping to exchange greetings, one is unable to get a sufficient exercise. I must greet them or they take offense, you see."

"It's sufficient exercise for every other gentleman in society," Pelton argued. "Unless they box at Gentleman Jackson's, or ride a horse. Forgive me, Your Grace, but walking is common." But it was a losing battle and he knew it. And indeed, the Duke was shaking his head, unoffended but unpersuaded.

"You know how out of sorts I become when I miss my walk," Arthur told him gently. "I am persuaded it is healthful, and it helps me think."

He moved to the door, saying over his shoulder, "Have hot water for me in an hour's time. I'll not be taking a country walk, just enough to get the blood moving."

Alone in the room, Pelton snorted. "Helps him think!" he grumbled. "Why does a duke need to think? He's got people for that."

***

The Duke strode briskly down the street, allowing his thoughts to wander. He knew from experience that it was a pointless endeavor to attempt to force inspiration. But if he was patient and allowed his thoughts to wander where they would, eventually inspiration would come. In what form it would come, and on what topic, he couldn't say. It might be the perfect mathematical expression to expose Gould's folly. It might be a decided preference for one of the young ladies he'd met the previous evening. It might be something altogether new. But it would come, so long as he exercised his limbs and his stamina.

It was a mild day in early spring, and he was soon out of Mayfair and well into the genteel but unfashionable environs of Hans Town when the Duke took note of a young lady coming toward him. He was too unschooled yet to recognize that her blue kerseymere pelisse and matching bonnet were several years out of fashion.

He noted that her hair and eyes were both a dark brown, so dark as to seem almost black, though the sunlight brought glints of red when it struck her curls. She was, he thought dispassionately, a remarkably pretty young lady, though a sweetly retrousse nose and a mischievous glint in her eyes barred her from being considered a classic beauty. But it was not her prettiness that drew his attention. It was the fact that she was carrying a large and unwieldy bundle and seemed to be in some difficulty with it.

As he came abreast of her, he stopped and tipped his hat. "Pardon me, miss," he said. "Might I be able to assist you with that?"

"Thank you, but I can manage," the young lady said, as she too came to a halt. "And I perceive that you are in a great hurry and would hate to make you late for an appointment."

"Not at all," Arthur assured her. "I am merely walking for exercise and can just as easily walk toward your destination and carry this for you." Without further debate, he took the bundle from her hands. It was heavier than he expected. Remembering the habits

16

of the laborers on the home farm, Arthur slung the parcel onto his shoulder and turned back the way he'd come. "Shall we?"

"Are you certain you don't need to be somewhere soon?" the young lady asked, matching his stride. "You were walking at such a great rate."

"A brisk pace is necessary to gain the benefits of it," Arthur told her. "I believe it's considered eccentric of me, but I am convinced it is healthful and nourishes the brain."

"Indeed? How interesting, to be sure. If I were to walk briskly every day, would the added nourishment to the brain make me more clever?"

"I don't believe the point has been put to scientific test," Arthur admitted, "but I feel certain that it must be so for everyone."

"I will have to make the attempt," the young lady said thoughtfully. "Though I believe that I am already quite clever, I might of course be wrong. And surely there is no such thing as too much cleverness."

Arthur was much struck by this. A young lady admitting to being clever was not a usual thing. "Perhaps I should add weight carrying to my daily practice," he suggested. "But shouldn't you have brought a footman along with you to assist in this?"

"And so I would have," she said decisively, "had I but known he would be needed. My errand, sir, was to buy ribbon! But my atrocious little brother prevailed upon me to pick up his package since it was on my way, with no warning that it would be such a great monstrous thing." She saw in his eyes the question he was too polite to ask, and added, "It's bird seed. My brother is a great bird fancier."

"Ah." Arthur had begun to feel uncomfortable conversing with a young lady who had not been presented to him, so he said, "I'm Winton, you know." At her uncomprehending look, he added, "Arthur Ramsey."

"Then thank you very much, Mister Ramsey," the young lady said. "I'm Cleo Cooper and I will be certain to tell Han to whom he owes the debt of gratitude for preventing me from becoming more vexed with him than I already am."

Mister Ramsey? Arthur saw that he'd made a mull of the introduction and wondered if he should correct it. He realized ruefully that he had never before needed to puff up his consequences

17

since so many were ready to do the deed for him. But he decided that it didn't matter. This neighborhood, while genteel, was scarcely fashionable; the odds that he would ever encounter Miss Cooper again were small indeed.

She came to a halt at the steps of a neat and well-maintained townhouse. "Here we are," she said with satisfaction. She ran lightly up the steps to ring and then returned to the pavement. Arthur slung the seed package from his shoulder to the doorstep.

The door was opened by an elderly butler of such fearsome dignity that even Tolliver would be quite overshadowed. "Miss Cleo?" the butler asked.

Miss Cooper turned to Arthur with a smile. "Thank you again, Mister Ramsey," she said, and extended his hand. Arthur shook it and prepared to be on his way. The old butler moved the package indoors and as the door closed behind them, Arthur thought he heard the young lady say, "Thank you, General."

General? Pondering this little puzzle, Arthur continued his interrupted walk.

***

In the front hall, the butler stooped to pick up the bird seed bundle. Cleo stopped him. "Just leave that for Han," she advised. Removing her bonnet and pelisse, she moved into the front room. It was a room of moderate size, overwhelmed by several large paintings of classical subjects on the walls. Near the fire, Miss Merrihew bent over a piece of sewing. She was a plump, gray-haired woman wearing a neat morning dress of dark green and an air of gentle abstraction. Lounging in the chair across from her, a lanky young man dressed as a footman leafed idly through a ladies fashion magazine.

"I was just chided for not having you along with me," Cleo told the young man.

He looked up, his eyes crinkling with amusement. Leaning over to the sewing table, he picked up the scissors by the blades. With a languid turn of the wrist, he held the thumb-hole to his eye in imitation of a quizzing glass. "My dear girl," he drawled, "I hope you have acquaintance in Town of whom I am unaware, because I should not like to think of you entering into conversation with chance-met strangers on the street."

18

Startled, Cleo gave a spurt of laughter. "Oh my goodness, do they really sound like that?"

Miss Merrihew was nodding approvingly. "Quite like that. Very good, Peter, very good indeed. And Peter's right, dear. You shouldn't be talking to strangers, it simply isn't done."

Cleo waved a dismissive hand. "Oh, stuff. A nice gentleman gave me assistance with Han's bird seed, which turned out to be an enormous thing that I could barely carry. I think he was a lawyer."

"How so?" Peter asked.

"He spoke of exercising for his brain," Cleo said. "So what else could he be?"

"You should have asked for his card," the other woman said darkly. "We might have need of a lawyer."

Cleo leaned over and gave her an impulsive hug. "We've never needed one before. Dear Merry, have more faith in me."

"You've never gotten up to your tricks in England before," Miss Merrihew pointed out.

"I'm sure it's much like any other place," Cleo argued. She joined Miss Merrihew on the settee, adding with a frown, "And yet..."

"And yet?" Miss Merrihew prompted.

"I don't know," Cleo admitted.

"It's opening night nerves," Peter said knowledgably. "Our moment on stage has almost arrived."

"It's the plan," Cleo said at last. "We have two avenues into society and they both need to work, yet I see weaknesses in both."

"Perhaps we could correct the weaknesses," Miss Merrihew said mildly. "What are your concerns, dear?"

"There's Peter as young man about Town," Cleo began.

Peter elaborately mimed outrage. "My dear Miss Cooper! I've been studying the role for six weeks. More than that, since I've practically memorized *Debrett's*."

"I don't doubt your ability to play the role," Cleo hastened to assure him. "But studying at Almack's?! Surely everyone in society has seen you there."

"Ah, that's where you're wrong," Peter replied. "I've been completely invisible. No one in society ever looks at a waiter."

Cleo looked doubtfully at Miss Merrihew, who nodded.

"I've studied their voices, their vocabularies and their mannerisms," Peter went on. "And more than that, I've listened. I know who's ruralizing, who's been sent down, who's been rolled up. Once I'm on the toddle and dropping names and *on dits*, people will come to believe I've been there among them all along."

"I feel sure he can do it," Miss Merrihew said. "What was your other concern?"

"The Countess of Dorwood," Cleo said. "Aunt Lucinda. Why would she want to help us?"

"It's been over twenty years," Miss Merrihew admitted, "but I remember Lucy and she was a very sweet girl."

"She was a Bufford," Cleo said. From her tone it was obvious that being a Bufford was a very bad thing indeed.

"My dear," Miss Merrihew said, "if anyone knows members of a family, surely it would be their governess. Your mother's parents were cold, proud people, and their son most disagreeable, but your mother and aunt were the dearest girls! Your mother was always livelier and more headstrong than Lucy, but both girls were so warm-hearted and made me feel quite valued, like family."

"We shall see," Cleo said, unconvinced.

"By the by," Peter said, picking up the magazine he'd been browsing. "This copy of *La Belle Assemblee* is over two years old."

"Of course it is," said Cleo with a shrug.

"You should have gotten newer copies," Peter told her. "If you're following the guidance here, you'll not be in the first stare of fashion."

Miss Merrihew looked at her sewing with dismay. "Oh, dear…"

Cleo patted her shoulder. "It's fine, Merry."

"Oh, but perhaps…"

"It's fine." Cleo turned back to Peter. "I don't wish to be in the first stare of fashion, or even the second stare."

"You don't?"

"Of course not. You must be, of course, because you have your own position to establish in the fashionable set. But as for me, and Han and Merry, that's a different story. We don't want to be impossibly dowdy, of course. But bang up to the mark? No."

Peter deployed the sewing scissors quizzing glass and said affectedly, "I confess myself baffled."

"Consider," Cleo said. After a moment's thought, she went on, "You remember the story of the prodigal son?"

"Of course."

"Imagine, though, if the son, after being cast out, returned to his family in a fine carriage and sumptuous clothing, obviously fat and sleek and prosperous. Do you suppose he would have been welcomed back so whole-heartedly?"

"Of course not," Peter admitted. "How insufferable that would be."

"That's our position," Cleo said. "A generation removed. It's a very fine line. We don't want to look entirely indigent, or so hopelessly gauche that the Countess will not want to recognize us as kinfolk. But nor do we want to appear so well-heeled and fashionable that she can obviously do nothing for us. A few introductions, a few hints as to how to go on, and her ladyship can feel the glow of charity with very little effort on her part."

Peter bowed. "I stand corrected. If there were only a science of human behavior and manipulation, you would be its master."

The front door slammed open and feet thundered up the stairs. The residents of the front room listened as the footsteps continued, all the way to the roof. After a few moments, the footsteps returned, and a young boy presented himself in the doorway. "She's back!" he announced proudly. "Twenty miles this time. What a champion!"

"Han, your shirt!" Miss Merrihew said in reproachful tones.

Han looked down at his shirt. He was a handsome boy of twelve, with honey-colored hair and eyes between grey and blue. He looked down at his shirt, where the seam was separated at the shoulder. "Oh, that," he said with a shrug. "I caught a ride at the back of a cart and the carter didn't half create when he discovered me there, but I shook him off easily."

"I'll mend that for you, Han," Cleo told him. "Go change and give this one back to me. But don't change into your best shirt, remember we're making a morning call tomorrow."

Han waved an impatient hand. "Presently," he said, and subsided onto the floor. "What are you discussing?"

"Our plans for London," Cleo answered.

"Good," Han said. He looked at her for a long moment.

"What?" she finally asked.

"Here we are in England," the boy said. "So what are we going to do to find the scoundrel who swindled Papa?"

Cleo sighed. "Han, we've been over this before. It's hopeless."

"He was an Englishman," Han pointed out.

"Yes, but he used a false name. Once I obtained a *Debrett's Peerage* and realized that there was no such person as Baron Marcuse, I knew it was a lost cause. As for him being English, why so he was. But we met him in Venice, and he claimed to be going to Sicily, though he never arrived there. He could be anywhere in the world."

"We ought to do something!" her brother insisted. "All those ducats! Papa worked over a year on those frescoes. And nothing to show for it."

Cleo shook her head. "If I knew where 'Baron Marcuse' could be found, rest assured I'd be after him in an instant. But think, Han. How can we find a man when we don't even know his real name?"

Han scuffed the carpet with his feet. "I suppose you're right," he said at last. "But I don't like it."

***

"Arthur! You come for breakfast?"

Amesbury lived in comfortable rooms in the Albany. His front room served as combination sitting room, breakfast room, and office. The small table was cluttered with invitations, writing paper and a riding crop, all pushed to the center to make room for Amesbury's meal.

Arthur looked dubiously at the slab of ham Amesbury was addressing, and shook his head with a smile. "I've already breakfasted, thank you." He took a seat across from Amesbury at the breakfast table and examined his friend. "Is that... thing you're wearing fashionable?"

Amesbury regarded his dressing gown, an eye-catching silk of red and yellow. "It is now," he said casually. "Duddy Wainwright saw it last week and determined that he must have one too."

"If you can bring that into fashion, Brummell had better look to his laurels," said Arthur, much impressed.

"So what can I do for you today?" Amesbury asked.

"I'm here for more tutelage," Arthur admitted. "I've met young ladies, I've danced with them. What comes next?"

"You've sent flowers, of course?"

22

"What? Flowers? No. Was I supposed to?"

"Certainly. You don't wish to be behindhand." Amesbury pulled a paper toward him across the clutter of the table.

"But I haven't settled on a particular female yet," Arthur protested.

"Not to worry," Amesbury assured him. "Flowers are not a declaration. They merely express appreciation. So, who should receive your flowers? Pick two or three young ladies."

Arthur pondered for a moment. "Miss Harwell, of course."

"Excellent." Amesbury made a note.

"And I suppose Miss Lassiter and Miss Meadows."

"Lady Jersey's introductions. Very good. Unexceptionable, amiable girls."

Justin scratched at the paper for several moments and then rang the bell. When his man answered, Justin handed him the paper. "His Grace wishes flowers sent to these ladies, Gordon. Please see to it, won't you?"

Gordon bowed silently and withdrew. "Wait," Arthur said. "The cards?"

"You've have expressed all the appropriate sentiments," Justin told him. "Admiring, but not overwhelmed with passion."

"I suppose you'll let me know when I must be overwhelmed with passion," Arthur said, feeling a flicker of resentment.

"Not at all," Justin laughed. "I'll let you determine that. This afternoon, we will walk in the park."

"But I've already walked," Arthur protested.

"Not this sort of walk," Justin corrected. "You performed one of your absurd forced marches. This will be the walk of a civilized man among civilized people. That is the way to meet and become acquainted with young ladies."

"As it happens, I met a young lady on my walk this morning."

"You did?" Justin looked interested. "There's hope for you yet. Pretty?"

"I believe so," Arthur said. "She was carrying a bundle and I helped her get it home."

"Oh, Arthur! We're not dallying with the serving girls now, are we?"

"Not at all! She was unquestionably a lady. It was obvious in her voice and manner."

"Ladies don't carry bundles," Justin argued.

"It was a commission for her brother," Arthur explained. "And she didn't expect it to be so large or she would have brought a footman."

"Oh, well then. Where was this?"

"On Upper Wimpole Street."

"Hans Town? Oh, my dear Arthur, no," Justin replied in a dampening manner. "You don't find duchesses on Upper Wimpole Street."

"Fortunately, I didn't propose to her," Arthur said.

"Then let's hear no more about it," Justin said dismissively. "Upper Wimpole Street indeed! Now, return here at four, and I will teach you how to walk in the park."

***

"Why are we here?" Arthur asked Justin, following him into Twomey's Gallery on Bond Street. "We were to walk in the park."

"And so we will," Justin assured him. "As soon as I complete a commission for my mother." He stood just inside the door, scanning the art on display in the first of several gallery rooms. "She requires a painting for the dining room, over the sideboard. A still life or a landscape."

Arthur thought back to his memory of Amesbury Hall. "But there's already a painting over the sideboard," he protested.

"Not anymore," Justin said. "Not since Davey shot it."

"Ah, I see. Is your nephew in serious trouble?"

"Surprisingly little, actually," Justin said. "My mother always hated that painting, refused to sit facing it. It was the one of game, if you recall. Mother said she didn't want to look at dead rabbits until Armand had worked his magic on them in the kitchen. And my brother is actually rather proud of the young ruffian. He potted both rabbits neatly in the head, you see."

"So his demonstration of skill obviated the original offense."

"That's about the size of it. The plasterers have been and the wall is repaired, so now a replacement painting will make it ancient history." He scanned the paintings. "A still life of flowers and fruit is Mother's preference."

"Quite unexceptionable," Arthur agreed. He scanned the paintings as well. "I've never been in here before," he admitted.

"Are you interested in art?"

24

"Not at all."

"That's why, then."

"Where do they get all these paintings?"

"This is the first stop of choice for families who are run off their legs," Justin explained. "Take the horses to sale at Tattersall's, and the paintings to Twomey's. Ah, there's Twomey in the far room. Look around, I won't be long."

He returned a few minutes later to find Arthur staring at a landscape and clapped his friend on the back. "Grapes and roses," he reported. "A better match for the new draperies than those dead rabbits and pheasants, so it all works out for the best. What do you have here?"

"I'm going to buy this," Arthur said.

Justin turned to study the painting that had caught Arthur's attention. It was a landscape at night. Most of the canvas featured a starry sky, while a small figure stood silhouetted against the sky atop a craggy hill, a firearm over his shoulder. The small plaque beside it informed the viewer that it was "The Hunter".

"The Hunter?" Justin said. "More like The Poacher, out at night as he is."

"Not that hunter," Arthur chuckled. "This hunter." He extended a finger and outlined the stars over the tiny figure's head.

"You're buying a painting for the stars?"

"It's not just that there are stars," Arthur explained. "It's that they are the right stars. I've never before seen a painting that treated stars as anything other than random blobs of light in absurd patterns never seen in the night sky. But look here." Again he traced the stars in the painting's center. "Orion. The Hunter."

"Ah." Justin nodded.

"And here is Aldebaran, and here are the Pleiades, and they're where they're supposed to be," Arthur said approvingly. "This will fit nicely into my study." He turned to the hovering sales clerk. "Have this delivered to Winton House, Grosvenor Square."

"Yes, Your Grace," said the clerk, bowing obsequiously.

"And now," Arthur turned back to Justin. "You've promised to teach me the walk of a civilized man."

***

25

The afternoon was fine and mild, and all of fashionable society seemed to be in Hyde Park that afternoon, passing in front of one another's eyes.

Mrs. Harwell, walking with Felicity, encountered her great friend Mrs. Ainsley along with her youngest, Dorothy. "So young Winton is on the market now!" Mrs. Ainsley marveled.

"He was certainly dancing, which I'm told is well-nigh unheard of," Mrs. Harwell replied complacently.

"And of course our Felicity took his eye," Mrs. Ainsley gushed. "I always said your girl would take. And that she would find favor among the highest. You see how right I was. The Ramseys of Winton! They can trace their lineage back a thousand years and have become only richer in every generation. A duke! I'm so pleased for you, my dear."

"Ma'am, you refine too much on one dance," Felicity stammered. "Recall that he danced with many other girls."

"Oh, other girls," said Mrs. Ainsley with great humor. "I snap my fingers at them, and am convinced I will soon be wishing you well. 'Your Grace!' I'm only vexed with the man for deciding to settle this year rather than last. I daresay my Sarah might have interested him. And alas, our Dorothy here is but fourteen."

Miss Dorothy made a rude noise. "Oh, poo to any old duke," she exclaimed. "Sally's Robert adores her and she is fine as she is. As for me, I care nothing for dukes. Is he a poet, is he a soldier? If not, what a poor creature indeed."

The Ainsleys went on their way, Mrs. Ainsley scolding Dorothy for her taste in novels.

Watching them go, Mrs. Harwell said, "Just a bit... vulgar, don't you think, dear? All that exclaiming over rank and fortune."

"Mama, how can you?" Felicity replied. "Why, when all the way home from Almack's, all you could think of was Winton's rank and fortune."

"Among family, dearest."

On another path in the park, Amesbury and the Duke stepped back from the Dumphreys' phaeton and watched it continue on its circuit. The Duke looked at Amesbury. "Well, what do you think?"

Justin clapped him on the shoulder. "What I think is immaterial, my good fellow! You're the one who must live with your choice. What do you think?"

Arthur said hesitantly, "You are more familiar that I with the manners of the ladies of society, but I have to say that Miss Dumphreys strikes me as… quite silly."

"Aha! I think you've hit on an important point," Justin replied. "Yes, Miss Dumphreys is silly. Sillier than most, I must admit. I'm sure she'll make a fine wife for some man of fashion, but not for such a long-headed chap as yourself."

They continued on their way. After a moment, Arthur heard a loud, "Ahem!" He turned back to find Justin quite a distance behind him. "Notice my pace, old man," Justin said. Arthur waited for him and then matched his speed.

"It seems so dawdling," Arthur complained.

"Get used to it," Justin advised. "Remember, it is not our objective to cover territory rapidly."

"The exercise value must be minimal."

"Nor is it exercise. This is a social activity. Mind your pace."

They came to a place where paths joined and saw the Harwells mother and daughter approaching them. Justin murmured, "Here we go. Social, Arthur, social!"

Then he raised his hat. "Ladies! The flowers bloom early this spring!"

Mrs. Harwell beamed. "How you do go on!"

"Winton, may I present Mrs. Harwell?" Justin said smoothly. "I daresay you'll be stunned to hear that this lovely creature is not our Miss Harwell's sister, but in fact is her mother. Ma'am, His Grace the Duke of Winton."

Mrs. Harwell curtsied. "Your Grace."

Winton bowed. "Ma'am." He bowed to Felicity. "Miss Harwell."

"Your Grace," with a sweet little curtsey. "Your flowers were lovely." She blushed prettily.

"I glad you enjoyed them," Arthur said awkwardly.

Felicity shot a quick look at Justin. Was that reproach he saw in those lovely eyes? Then he realized – he'd been so busy seeing to Arthur's floral offerings that he'd forgotten his own. Justin mentally kicked himself. But perhaps it was for the best. He wasn't looking for a wife, after all; Winton was.

The silence stretched out. The Harwell women were too overawed by Arthur's rank to converse easily, and Arthur… well,

Justin thought, Arthur was just hopeless. "I've been teaching Winton how to take a walk like a civilized man," he offered.

Felicity gave a startled giggle. "Oh, Mister Amesbury, what nonsense you talk!"

"Alas, it's quite true," Arthur told her. "Amesbury assures me that my stride is much too rapid for society and I must relearn my paces. I walk for exercise, you see."

"Indeed." Felicity found this incomprehensible. "Do you enjoy riding?"

"It is enjoyable, certainly," Arthur said, "but I would not call it exercise. For the horse perhaps, but not for the rider."

"May we expect to see Your Grace at Lady Castlereagh's ball?" Mrs. Harwell asked.

Arthur hesitated. Did he get an invitation? He had no idea. Justin stepped in. "Of course you will," he assured the ladies smoothly.

After a few more minutes of elegant commonplaces, the two parties went on their way. Arthur turned to Justin. "I don't even know that I was invited to Lady Castlereagh's ball!" he protested.

"Of course you were," Justin assured him. "Ask your secretary. No doubt he sent the usual polite refusal, but such a response can always be rescinded."

***

On another path in the park, Lord Wainwright strolled along, lost in thought. He knew himself to be complete to a shade, from his fashionable Brutus crop to the tips of his polished Hessians. His coat was a blue superfine, his breeches fawn, and not a wrinkle disturbed the elegant lines. Wainwright, christened Gerald but nicknamed Duddy in his school days for reasons no one could now remember, was torn. On the one hand, he approved of the new understated elegance that Beau Brummell's influence had brought to male attire, and had to admit that the fops who ignored the Beau's strictures in matters of color and extravagance looked absurd. But on the other hand, he felt a yearning for bright colors and eye-catching patterns that modern fashion did nothing to quench.

Last week, following a convivial evening during the course of which he'd forgotten his way home, Wainwright had spent the night on the sofa in Justin Amesbury's rooms. The following morning, he discovered the solution to his sartorial dilemma. Dressing gowns!

Never worn in public, but confined strictly to home wear, a dressing gown could be as lushly extravagant as one pleased.

The Baron quickly set about acquiring his own magnificent dressing gown, and was delighted with its silken stripes in plum and cherry. But now he wanted more. An entire wardrobe of dressing gowns, a veritable rainbow of colors. He'd sent to the drapers for color samples and now was pondering combinations. Straw and celery? Cerulean and jonquil? Evening primrose and pomona green? The possibilities were endless! And perhaps a fuller skirt, a broader lapel and collar?

"Lord Wainwright!"

Wainwright turned toward the voice. A young man approached him. Obviously top drawer. Coat unmistakably Weston. Boots, Hoby. Shirt points moderate and cravat elegant. An expression of modest friendliness enhanced a pleasing countenance. He was several years younger than the Baron, and unless Wainwright's memory was more deficient than he realized, a complete stranger.

The young man had reached him now. "Forgive me, sir, we've never met, but I was at school with David. Peter Barton." The men exchanged bows and Barton continued, "I was hoping you could provide me with David's direction. I'm just arrived in Town; he promised me some prime larks when I managed to come here."

"Devilish sorry to have to tell you," Wainwright replied. "But my foolish brother is quite run off his legs. In dun territory. Not a feather to fly with."

"I'm sorry to hear that," replied Barton with dismay. "Poor old Duffy. But perhaps I could pay him a call?"

"Not here, y'see. Outrun the constable. He's in Dorset, dancing attendance on our grandmama. Nonsensical notion of his, she'll never frank him, but I suppose he must ruralize somewhere after all. I don't expect to see him in Town till after quarter day, if that. Got in devilish deep, you know."

"Oh. Well, thank you so much…" Barton made to move on his way.

"Say, though," Wainwright said. "Why don't you come round for dinner this evening? Me and a few fellows, just a plain dinner, crack a few bottles, maybe wander round to the club later? Since David promised you some larks, we must see what we can do."

"Sir, that would be most kind!"

Wainwright provided his new friend with his address and they parted and went their separate ways.

THREE

As the Dowager Marchioness of Woolston was shown out of the drawing room, Lucinda, Countess of Dorwood dared to hope she was the last morning caller. Sylvia had enjoyed the call, certainly. The two of them had had a splendid coze, ripping up the character of any young lady too pretty, too wealthy, or too happy to suit their strict standards of propriety. But Lucinda was relieved when the old harridan finally took stately leave of them.

The Countess was a good-humored matron dressed in the forefront of fashion. She had reached the age of forty, but looked younger. Her sister-in-law, Lady Sylvia, was approaching fifty but looked older. The differences in their circumstances and in their personalities perhaps accounted for the discrepancy, because Lady Sylvia, for all the advantage of noble birth, was the poor relation here. A less tolerant woman than the Countess might have found accommodations for her in a cottage on a remote estate, as Sylvia was difficult to live with and even more difficult to like.

Now Lady Sylvia was gathering up her oppressively ugly needlework and stowing it in her workbag. It was her custom to retire to her room for a rest before tea. But the knocker sounded. "Drat," said Lady Sylvia.

"You needn't remain," Lucinda told her.

"Don't think I will," Sylvia replied and moved toward the door.

But before she could make good her escape, Bannister the butler threw open the drawing room door. "Miss Cooper, Master Han Cooper, and Miss Merrihew," he announced grandly.

Lucinda stood with a blink of surprise, for the party ushered in to her drawing room were strangers. A lovely dark young woman, a handsome little lad, and an older woman.

But something sparked a hint of recognition. Lucinda took another look at the older woman. Then, with an unladylike shriek of "MERRY!", she ran across the room to give the visitor a hug.

After a few moments of laughter and incoherent exclamations, Lucinda stood back, clasping Miss Merrihew's hands. "But Merry, I looked for you! After I married my dear Harold and had my own

31

establishment, I tried to find you. I truly did. But you'd vanished without a trace. Where did you go?"

Miss Merrihew chuckled. "Where did I go? Everywhere."

Lady Sylvia's eyes had widened and then narrowed as she recognized the visitor. Now she stumped forward. "Merrihew. I wouldn't have expected you to find another position after the Buffords dismissed you without a character."

"You *must* be Lady Sylvia." This from the younger lady. At Sylvia's look of haughty surprise, the minx sketched an ironic curtsey and said sweetly, "I've heard so much about you."

"And who might you be?" Sylvia demanded.

"Gracious, where are my wits?" said Miss Merrihew. "Lucy, or rather Your Ladyship I suppose I must say, and Lady Sylvia, allow me to present Cleo and Han Cooper."

Lucinda turned to her other guests. "Cooper?" She looked first at Cleo and then at Han. Her hand went to her mouth as tears filled her eyes. "Can it be? You must be Belle's children." Overcome, she found her way back to a chair, gesturing them to take seats.

The Coopers smiled uncomfortably under their aunt's gaze. She stared, first at one, then the other, in the grip of some powerful emotion. Finally she said to Han, "You're the image of your mother, you know."

"So I've been told," he replied, squirming on the slick silk of the chair.

Lucinda turned to Cleo. "And you, my dear, you've the look of your father that is quite extraordinary."

"Bad blood." This extraordinary pronouncement, in the voice of doom, from Lady Sylvia. She still stood by the door, scowling.

Lucinda gasped. "Sylvia, I can't allow you to insult my company."

Sylvia snorted. "If you actually mean to receive these... persons, think I'll go to my room." She called sharply, "Hector!"

An overweight elderly pug emerged from a low basket by the fire and waddled over to his mistress. The two made their departure and the door closed behind them. Lucinda turned back to the visitors, red-faced with embarrassment. "My dears, I am so sorry."

Cleo looked curiously at the closed door. "Mama described Lady Sylvia to us, but ma'am, why is she here?"

Lucinda sighed. "She had nowhere else to go. I suppose you know that your Uncle William is dead?"

"We had heard that," Miss Merrihew said.

"He left nothing," Lucinda said. "Absolutely nothing. He'd lost the Grange and died deeply in debt."

"Blew his brains out, in fact?" Miss Merrihew asked.

"We did try to hush that up," the Countess said. "An accident cleaning his gun. But yes. So here is Sylvia, and we just have to make the best of it."

She looked back at her niece and nephew. "Dare I hope your papa is in Town with you? I was so sorry when I heard about Belle, and sorry I'd never got to see her after she left home."

"Papa's dead!" Han blurted.

"Oh, my dears!"

"Yes, Papa died last year," Cleo said. "He always wanted us to return to England, so here we are."

"Though how can you return to a place you've never been?" Han added.

"Never been to England?" Lucinda asked in astonishment. "Why, where have you been?"

"A lengthy itinerary," Cleo answered. "Italy, for a number of years. Austria, for a time. Sicily. Even Egypt. An artist can work anywhere."

"I want to hear all about it!" the Countess exclaimed. "Where you went and how you lived, and Belle and your papa."

"The entire history might be too involved for a morning call," Miss Merrihew pointed out.

"But you're not callers, you're family!" Lucinda protested. "Surely you've come to stay."

"Stay?" Cleo asked, astonished. "Oh, no, ma'am. We have rented a townhouse. We wouldn't dream of imposing on you so."

"You're on your own?" Lucinda asked.

"We have Miss Merrihew," Cleo pointed out. "She's given us a solid grasp of English propriety. We only hoped that you would acknowledge us and we could get to know you. We've lost the family we once had."

"Well, I won't press you just now," Lucinda said, dissatisfied. "But I'll want to see your accommodations and we might have a brangle about it yet. How old are you, dear?"

"I am two and twenty," Cleo replied.

"And out, I suppose?"

Cleo laughed. "I don't think I could ever have been said to be in, in fact."

"We must see about introducing you to the people who matter," Lucinda declared briskly. "And shopping, of course."

The conversation continued until Miss Merrihew, at the correct thirty minutes, stood and announced they must be going. In the interim, the Coopers had learned that they had three cousins, all boys, two at Eton and one at Cambridge, and none of them, according to their doting mama, apparently learning a thing, and that Aunt Lucinda's 'Dear Harold', the Earl of Dorwood, was involved with the Foreign Office and often abroad. The Countess learned that her newly discovered niece was a very decided and self-assured young lady who'd been mistress of the family establishment since her mother's death almost ten years ago. And that Miles Cooper, while perhaps artistically successful, had never attained much in the way of financial success. "He never became fashionable," Cleo explained sadly.

They parted with Cleo determined to maintain their Hans Town townhouse, and the Countess determined to persuade her newly discovered kinfolk to make their home with her, and an agreement that she would call on them tomorrow.

After the Coopers departed Lucinda went up the stairs to examine several vacant bedrooms, in the hopes that she would prevail and convince them to move in. The guest bedroom known as the Rose Room would be ideal for Cleo, she thought, and the children's floor had a room that ought to suit young Han.

As she left the Rose Room, she encountered Sylvia. "They gone?" Sylvia asked.

"Yes, I'm calling on them tomorrow. I'm hoping to convince them to move in here, but young Cleo seems determined to maintain a separate address."

"Just as well," Sylvia said. "They'll not do you credit, you know."

"They were charming! And perfectly well-mannered," Lucinda protested.

Sylvia snorted. "Raised by a silly young chit with no more principles than to run off with the drawing master? Oh, I know you had a *tendre* for Miles Cooper yourself."

"I was thirteen!" Lucinda said hotly.

"Girls are never too young to make a fool of themselves over a handsome face," she was told.

"Belinda and Miles were in love," Lucinda said. "And they never would have had to commit the offense of an elopement if Mama and Papa had been reasonable and not so determined to marry Belle off to that old man. The very idea of a seventeen year old girl being wed to a widower with five children!"

"She would have been mistress of an enviable establishment and never wanted for anything in her life. Instead she ran off with a penniless nobody whose own family had turned their backs on him, and lived who knows how. A less tolerant man than Dorwood might have thought twice about allying himself with a family with such connections."

Lucinda took a deep breath. "I'll not quarrel with you," she said evenly. "The Coopers have as much right to my home as you do, and I intend to do everything in my power to see that they accept it."

***

In the hackney returning home, the Coopers and Miss Merrihew discussed their visit.

"Was I right?" Merry asked smugly.

"You were right," Cleo admitted. "Aunt Lucinda is everything that is amiable."

"Too amiable, I'd say," Han added. "Cleo, we can't move there!"

"Of course we can't," Cleo told him.

"She sounded quite determined," Han said dubiously.

"It would certainly be more correct for an orphaned young niece and nephew to move in with their aunt," Merry said. "Two and twenty is not considered by society to be entirely on the shelf, so you will find the proprieties stricter for you."

"We must discourage the notion somehow without giving Aunt Lucinda a disgust for us," Cleo said thoughtfully.

"I have some ideas," Han said. But he refused to elaborate.

***

Arthur would always remember Lady Castlereagh's ball as a blur of satin, lace, pearls, and ivory. And young ladies. A bewildering abundance of them, all being presented to him by beaming mamas, grandmothers, and aunties. A few dances at Almack's and a stroll in the park, and the message went forth — Winton is in search of a bride!

He dutifully danced with many of the young ladies, but took a break to escape to the garden to blow a cloud. Arthur seldom indulged in tobacco, but it made an excuse to break away from the besieging lovelies for a time, and to escape from a room brilliant with candlelight and redolent with a hundred different perfumes.

Justin found him pacing among the roses. "Is there a problem?"

"Not yet," his friend replied. "But I'm sure there will be tomorrow and thereafter, when I will be considered to be snubbing the young ladies I've met tonight and will have no memory of tomorrow. Justin, there are so many of them, and they are all so similar! Pastel and pearls and simpering smiles. How the deuce am I supposed to keep them sorted out in my head?"

"That is a problem," Justin admitted. "Too many at once. You're just so dashed eligible, you know. Perhaps now you could just dance with the young ladies you've already met."

Arthur nodded with relief. "I've already danced with Miss Harwell, I was so relieved to see a familiar face. A second dance would not be out of order, would it?"

"No, but not a third."

"I'll try for the supper dance," Arthur decided.

***

Felicity was trying not to become conceited, but it was hard. Her debut season was already an unqualified success and she knew herself to be a Toast. And she could not deny that Winton had been very happy to see her tonight. He had claimed a second dance, and the supper dance at that, so she went down to supper on the arm of the eligible young duke.

She saw her mama smiling and nodding at her from a gilt chair among the chaperons and knew that her mother's joy surpassed her own. At supper, she considered Winton and concluded that he was the most suitable of all her court of admirers. In addition to the things that impressed society, the title and the wealth, he was also handsome (though his friend Amesbury was handsomer, she had to

36

admit). And he was a genuinely nice man. He was not a rank snob, as many of the nobility could be toward an untitled country squire's daughter. Nor was he arrogant, condescending, indifferent or cruel. He did not drink to excess and according to all reports, didn't gamble at all. He was entirely ideal. Felicity only wished she understood what he was talking about.

By the time Amesbury joined them (with Marianne Keene on his arm, Felicity noted with a twinge of pique), the tablecloth sported a model of the solar system constructed of hothouse grapes orbiting an orange. "Haven't you outgrown playing with your food?" Amesbury asked, seizing a grape and popping into his mouth.

"You just ate Mars," Felicity told him.

Amesbury surveyed the ravaged solar system. "Lady Castlereagh won't thank you for turning her elegant supper into a schoolroom," he chided the Duke. "Honestly, my dear fellow, have you no small talk at all?"

"It seems not," Winton replied ruefully.

Fortunately for frivolity, Amesbury's arrival improved the small talk quota for their table. He really was the most amusing rattle, Felicity thought. Winton listened to his sallies with close and careful attention, almost as if he were studying them.

Felicity knew not to expect another dance with Winton; no gentleman would dance more than twice in an evening with a young lady unless they were engaged to be married. She did have a dance with Amesbury, who was always an amusing partner. Tonight, rather than flirting with her, he told her childhood stories about his friend. Felicity found the information both humorous and alarming – what kind of ten year old would try to invent a flying machine?

Emboldened, she confessed to Amesbury, "The Duke seems all that is amiable, but half the time I don't understand him."

"Don't fret about it, my dear," Amesbury reassured her. "I don't either. No one understands him. Except perhaps for a few old gentlemen of the Royal Society. But I assure you, he's the best of good fellows."

It was the first time Felicity could recall that she'd danced with a man who spent most of the time talking about someone else, rather than speaking of her in flattering terms and of himself in a manner to make her appreciate his own good qualities. It dawned on her that Amesbury was not really interested in her romantically, but was furthering his friend's prospects. She felt mixed emotions about this realization. On the one hand, it was surely significant that he was promoting her interest in the matrimonial catch of this or any other season. But on the other hand, it was a comedown to realize she had not attached Amesbury himself.

Felicity told herself sternly that she didn't need every man in society to be in love with her, and Amesbury was an amusing and pleasant friend.

***

The Duke gave Amesbury a ride home from the Castlereaghs in his carriage. "Well?" Amesbury asked comprehensively.

"I see that I must work on my small talk," the Duke told him. "You needn't coach me on flowers; I think I have that now. But must one always send flowers? Are there not other ways to show admiration?"

"Oh, certainly," Amesbury told him. "You can always send a young lady a gift. No jewelry or clothing, of course. But a book or a fan is always unexceptionable."

"A fan?" Winton asked. "A cooling device? This early in the year? Wouldn't that more appropriately be a summer gift?"

"A fan is an elegant accessory, which the young ladies wield with devilish skill. I'll help you pick one out, if you wish. And surely you've noticed how overheated a ballroom may become. Enough candles to provide the necessary brilliance must also produce a goodly amount of heat. Add in the crush of bodies and the exertion of dancing, and a fan is quite welcome."

"Welcome in a ballroom perhaps. But would not a bonnet be more universally useful?"

Justin, who'd been lounging back against the carriage's velvet squabs, bolted upright in alarm. "A bonnet?! Heavens, no!"

"Whatever is the matter with you?" Arthur asked.

"My dear fellow, a bonnet is not a signifier of honorable intentions, not at all! Save the bonnets for your chere amie."

"I don't have a chere amie," Arthur said testily.

"Then you've no call to be giving bonnets. Honestly, old man, Miss Harwell would think you were offering her a slip on the shoulder."

"Such an unequivocal message? From a hat? Surely not!"

"I assure you, it is so."

The carriage slowed and pulled to a stop at the entrance to Amesbury's rooms. Amesbury leaped down, and then turned back, "We're clear on this, aren't we? No bonnets."

"No bonnets," Arthur replied.

"There's a good fellow! And after all, you'll have a lifetime of buying bonnets once you've got your duchess."

He trotted up his front steps and the carriage moved on. Leaning back against the squabs, Arthur nodded thoughtfully. "A book or a fan," he told himself. "Surely a book would be sufficiently uncontroversial."

Back at Winton House, the Duke found his mother in the drawing room with a book. "Another absorbing read keeping you up late, Mama?" he asked.

"I was waiting up for you, to hear how you got on at Lady Castlereagh's," she admitted, putting a bookmark in the volume. "But I shall take this book up with me tonight, for it's quite captivating."

"More castles and monks and secret identities, I suppose?" Arthur asked.

"Oh, no, it's quite a modern story," the Duchess told him. "About a shabby-genteel family with five grown girls to dispose of. I thought it might bring me up to date on the sort of tricks these chits get up to, but it's quite a humorous read in its own right."

Arthur took the book and opened it to the cover page. "*Pride and Prejudice*," he read aloud. "By the author of *Sense and Sensibility*."

"And *Sense and Sensibility* is by 'A Lady', which tells one nothing because of course a man could not have written these. So absurd. But never mind that, Arthur – the ball!"

Arthur handed back the book. "I wish I'd had you for moral support, because I was besieged by mamas."

The Duchess nodded. "I suppose that was only to be expected, now that you're going to social events and dancing. I'm furbishing up my wardrobe and will be joining you shortly. All my ball gowns are five years out of date, and you wouldn't want me to look a quiz."

"As if you could," Arthur said fondly. "But I will welcome the reinforcements, because I felt like prey."

"Ah, but look at the bright side," said his mother, standing and gathering up her book and her work basket. "At least these Esquimaux are not provided with harpoons."

FOUR

When Cleo came down to breakfast the next morning, she found a large black mastiff asleep at the foot of the stairs. The creature raised its head as she stepped over it. "Good morning, Vulcan," she told it.

In the breakfast room, she was greeted with a flurry of chirps from two canaries in a cage by the window. Puzzled, she made her way back to the kitchen, where Mrs. Mimms was assembling breakfast. "Good morning, Mrs. Mimms," she said. "Why is Major Davies' Vulcan in the front hall? And the Misses Peabodys' canaries in the breakfast room?"

"You'll have to ask Master Han about that," the stout cook said grimly.

"Oh, so it's Han, is it? I'll ask him, then."

As Cleo left the kitchen, Mrs. Mimms called after her, "*And* the goat in the back garden!"

By the time Miss Merrihew joined Cleo in the breakfast room, Cleo was looking pensively at a slice of ham.

"Are we dog-tending today, dear?" Merry asked.

"I had no idea," Cleo answered. "It's some project of Han's. He seems to have collected all the neighbors' pets."

"I wonder what he's up to?"

Thundering footsteps announced Han's arrival, and the boy breezed into the room, mounded a plate with food, and joined the ladies at the table. "Good, you're up," he said.

Vulcan had followed him into the room and now sat by his chair, looking meaningfully at his plate.

"Explain, please?" Cleo asked her brother, pointing a fork at their guest.

"Oh, this?" Han said. He slipped a sausage to the massive beast. "Our beloved dog? That our sainted papa gave to me when he was but a puppy and I a tot in leading strings?"

"Han!"

Han sighed. "You did say you wanted to discourage Aunt Lucinda from her plan to move us to her house, didn't you?"

"Oh." Cleo nodded in comprehension. "So if she wants to take us, she also must take Vulcan."

"But of course," Han said. "You can't separate a boy from his faithful dog, can you?"

"That's a good thought," Merry said. "Especially with Lady Sylvia having that fat little pug. I doubt they'd get along at all."

Han nodded and swallowed a large bite of ham. "And you know, I've been thinking. It was wrong of me to give up my music practice when Papa died, don't you think?"

Cleo chuckled. "I was never more relieved than when you abandoned your music, but just for today, I think perhaps you're right."

So when the elegant Dorwood town coach pulled up at the Coopers' townhouse on Upper Wimpole Street, the neighborhood was flooded with the sound of a violin being played with more enthusiasm than artistry. The Countess paused for a moment on the front steps, head cocked to one side. The tune was almost recognizable, but hovered just on the brink of memory. Every few seconds, the notes turned into a screech that punished the ear, and through it all the violin was accompanied by basso-profundo howls.

"Tell Han that Aunt Lucinda is here," Cleo told the butler who had ushered the Countess into the morning room. Then to Lucinda's relief, a blessed silence fell. Lucinda had just seated herself and was asking Cleo's impression of London when Han entered and made his bow.

"That was much better, Han," Cleo told him approvingly.

"But you must practice every day," Merry added.

Lucinda suppressed a shudder. Her elegant townhouse in Grosvenor Square was certainly large, but not large enough to escape that caterwauling. She wondered if Master Han could be discouraged in his pursuit of violin mastery.

She felt a warm moist breeze on her ear and turned to find herself staring into the eyes of a large black beast. She leaped to her feet with an unladylike yelp.

"Vulcan!" Cleo chided. The beast lowered itself to the ground. "Oh, do be seated, Aunt Lucinda," she urged. "He's really the gentlest creature in nature."

The Countess carefully reseated herself, keeping an eye on the massive dog. "He quite startled me," she said with a nervous titter. "He's just so large!"

Han flung himself on the floor and threw a possessive arm around the dog.

"I don't think Papa realized how large he would grow," Cleo confessed.

"Might have known," Merry said with a snort. "When a pup's got feet the size of soup platters, you should realize it's going to do some growing."

"Dear Papa wasn't always very practical," Cleo admitted.

Which gave Lucinda the opening she was looking for and allowed her to delicately inquire how Miles Cooper had left his family situated financially.

"Oh, well enough," Cleo replied with a maddening lack of precision. "We won't be able to do more than one season in Town, I don't suppose, before we must look for a modest place in the country."

"One season ought to be sufficient," Aunt Lucinda told her briskly. "With my sponsorship, we should be able to see you quite creditably established."

"But it's Han who concerns me," Cleo began.

Merry cut her off. "She means married, Cleo."

"Oh!" Cleo gave her aunt a blank look.

"Of course, married," the Countess laughed. "Whyever else come to Town? We'll get you a fresh new wardrobe and take you about. You're quite lovely and conversable, you should do very well."

Cleo opened her mouth to protest, but caught Merry's frown and subsided. "Perhaps you're right," she said meekly.

"A season is quite an undertaking," the Countess continued. "Don't you see, my dear, how much more suitable it would be if you moved in with me?"

But here Cleo would not budge. "Oh, dear Aunt Lucinda, that is so sweet and generous of you, but can't you see how impossible it is? With Han's pets, and the staff we've had for years, we could hardly turn them off, they're like family."

Pets, plural? Lucinda thought with dismay. Aloud, she said, "But Cleo, dear, a debut from Hans Town?"

43

Cleo took a deep breath and appeared to come to a decision. "I quite understand," she said sadly. "Think nothing of it. It's very good of you to offer to sponsor me, dearest Aunt, but I can't allow you to risk your own standing in society on our account. We shall have to make do on our own. And I assure you that if you find yourself unable to recognize us in public, we will quite understand and bear you no malice. Our mother burned her bridges, and some actions can't be undone."

The Countess of Dorwood listened to this speech in growing indignation. Now she burst forth. "I assure you, young lady, *my* credit in society is not so precarious as to be unable to survive a niece in Hans Town!"

"Oh, now I've offended you!"

Lucinda took a calming breath. "Not at all, my dear. No, if you insist, remain here you will. And present you to the Polite World I will! Hans Town is unfashionable, not completely ineligible. I'll simply drop a hint here and there that coming from abroad, you couldn't be expected to know better." She looked around appraisingly. "And other than the address, I see nothing here to give one a disgust of the place."

Her appraisal brought her eye to the large portrait between the windows. "Gracious!" she exclaimed. "Is that Belle? Why is she wearing that helmet?"

"That's Mama as Athena," Cleo explained. "Papa always said Mama was too wise to be merely human. He took such fancies. There's me as Artemis over by the bookcase."

Lucinda stood and moved over to examine the portraits. "He really was a superb artist," she admitted. "A shame he never took." She turned and drew on her gloves. "Well," she continued briskly. "We're settled. Tomorrow, Cleo, I must take you shopping for a new wardrobe." Seeing her niece about to protest, she hurried on. "I insist. And I'll stand the business. I have an absurdly generous clothing allowance and never had a daughter to dress. It will be delightful."

"Yes, Aunt Lucinda," Cleo said meekly.

"I believe I can manage vouchers to Almack's," Lucinda went on. "Several of the patronesses are good friends of mine, and several of the others owe me favors. Is Cleo your full name, dear, or is it short for Cleone? Clothilde?"

From the floor, Han gave a shout of laughter. "CleoPATra!" he crowed.

Lucinda blinked. "Oh, my dear. Is he joking?"

"Sadly, no," Cleo told her. "My full first name is Cleopatra." She scowled at Han. "And Han's is Hannibal."

Unabashed, Han stuck out his tongue. "Elephants!"

"Cleopatra no doubt had elephants as well," Merry pointed out.

"I think perhaps we'll just go with Cleo," Lucinda suggested diplomatically.

After Lady Lucinda had taken her departure, Han scrambled to his feet. "I saw what you did there with Aunt Lucy," he said. "It was brilliant. By pretending to believe she couldn't launch you from Hans Town and being so understanding about it, you as good as challenged her to prove you wrong."

"I'm glad you approve. Now get all this livestock out of our home."

Han grinned and went off to comply.

Merry said, "It was quite clever of you, dear. But have you ever thought..." She trailed off.

"What?" Cleo prodded.

"You're going to allow Lucy to believe you're seeking to establish yourself in the usual manner with an advantageous marriage. Why not actually do so? Might not that be a better way of achieving our ends?"

Cleo snorted. "What, put myself at the mercy of some man I haven't met yet? Who would control all the money? That might establish me, if I were willing to sacrifice my freedom, but what about the rest of us?"

"The law favors the gentlemen," Merry admitted, "but women are not entirely helpless. There are marriage settlements."

"Do you imagine that a young lady with no fortune and dubious parentage would receive a settlement sufficient to provide for the whole of us? You and Mrs. Mimms and the General? Not to mention Han. I must establish Han as a gentleman; you know how like Papa he is. He's far too impractical to have to make his own way in the world." Cleo strode vigorously around the room as she spoke and shook her head. "No, I can see no advantage to the marriage option over our original plan."

Merry cleared her throat and said hesitantly, "Well, dear, it would be legal."

Cleo laughed. "If that matters to you."

In a soft voice, Merry replied, "I confess that it does." She turned in her chair to face Cleo. "Oh, my dear, it is just so much more *comfortable* to have no reason to fear the authorities!"

"I daresay it is, when one can afford it," Cleo replied. She leaned over the back of Merry's chair to give her a reassuring hug. "You poor thing, life in the Cooper household must have been a constant source of anxiety for you. Never fear, one last big score and I'll become a perfect pattern card of rectitude. I promise."

After Cleo left the room, Merry stared after her, troubled. "I fear you would find being that pattern card of rectitude sadly flat, dear Cleo."

***

Mrs. Harwell was already at the breakfast table when Felicity came down. She looked remarkably self-satisfied when Felicity joined her at the table.

"Have you looked at your offerings this morning?" she asked.

Felicity felt a twinge of guilt as she looked at the floral displays on the side table. "How spoiled I've become, Mama! Only a few weeks ago, it seemed remarkable and thrilling that so many gentlemen were moved to send me flowers. Now it seems commonplace."

"Never mind that, silly girl. Flowers are only your due. You've taken! But it's not only flowers today. There's a package as well."

"There is?" Showing that she was not completely jaded by her success, Felicity rose eagerly from the table and went to retrieve her package.

"It's from Winton," said her mother complacently. "A book, from the size and shape."

Felicity regained her seat, bringing the paper-wrapped parcel with her. The Duke's calling card was tucked under the wrapping string.

"Poetry, I'll be bound," Mrs. Harwell said, crunching on her morning toast. "I do hope it's not Byron. He's all the rage, of course, but to my mind, his work is a bit too warm to be considered a suitable gift for a single young lady."

46

Felicity unwrapped the book, for indeed it was a book, and opened it. She paged through it with increasing perplexity.

"Oh dear, is it Byron?" her mother said. "Well, never mind, dear. Young men in the first flush of infatuation can't always be expected to consider the delicacies."

Felicity laughed rather hysterically. "Byron? No, it's not Byron. And I don't think it could be considered improper."

"If not Byron...?"

"Newton!" Felicity flipped back to the title page. "*Mathematical Principles of Natural Philosophy*," she read.

Mrs. Harwell sat back in her chair. "Extraordinary!" she finally said.

"I can't make heads or tails of it," Felicity said. "And oh, Mama, there are *diagrams*!"

"Gracious!" her mother said faintly.

"What on earth shall I do with it?" Felicity asked.

Mrs. Harwell rallied. "You will place it on the table in the drawing room. You received a book from the Duke of Winton, after all. Is there an inscription?"

"Yes." Felicity opened the front cover of the book and read aloud, " 'I hope you find this as useful and instructive as I', and it's signed Winton."

"Well, then! Definitely, the drawing room."

"But, mama! Am I expected to *read* it?"

"Skim over it until you find several sentences and phrases that appear to be key," Mrs. Harwell advised. "Memorize them and have them ready to produce when the subject arises. That's what I did with *The Corsair*."

***

They had been shopping for hours and Cleo was tired and bewildered. No, she was past bewildered and rapidly approaching aghast. The amount of clothing that Aunt Lucinda considered indispensable for a debut season seemed absurd. And a different costume for every activity, it seemed. Visiting in the evening required different clothing than visiting in the morning. Riding in a carriage did not call for the same dress as riding on a horse.

Cleo had listened to her mama's stories and read the English periodicals and felt she was prepared. She knew that living in London was grander than living in a decaying villa on a

Mediterranean island where she would end the day wearing the same clothing she'd donned in the morning, even hiking up her skirts to ride the pony down the hill to the fishing village. She expected a grander and more formal lifestyle. But the reality surpassed her imagination.

Fortunately, her advanced age protected her from the insipid pastels that were the common lot of most debutantes. Aunt Lucinda decreed brighter colors and more jewel tones. "You're not seventeen, after all," she said, adding in a lower voice, "and just as well; with your coloring, those colors would make you look sallow."

But finally they were finished for the day. The dresses would be made to Cleo's measurements and delivered to her townhouse. "Tired?" Aunt Lucinda asked.

"Exhausted!" Cleo confessed. "I consider myself hardy, but this…"

"You're unaccustomed to it," Aunt Lucinda told her. "Let's stop at Gunter's for ices."

As they sat on a bench outdoors spooning their ices, Cleo watched in amazement as Gunter's waiters dodged traffic to take orders and deliver ices to an al fresco clientele. "I've eaten outdoors when traveling," she told her aunt. "But why do so in the heart of London?"

"It's the fashion," the Countess said. "And a young lady can be in the company of a young gentleman here without compromise, so that makes it attractive."

Every society had its own rules for what was permitted and what was not. Cleo hoped she would learn the rules of this society before she innocently put a foot wrong. But there were so many of them!

Coming toward them now was a fashionable young goddess, walking with an older woman. The two were attired in what Cleo's newly educated eye recognized as walking dresses. "Maria!" Aunt Lucinda waved to the older woman, added to Cleo in an undertone, "Maria Harwell, was Maria Climpson. She was a great friend of your mother. This season she's presenting her daughter, who is doing quite well."

"Good afternoon, Lucy," Mrs. Harwell said, eying Cleo with undisguised curiosity.

48

The Countess saw the curiosity and immediately alleviated it. "I'd like you to meet Cleo Cooper," she said, adding with a note of triumph, "my niece."

There was a pause as Mrs. Harwell did a rapid mental survey of Lucinda's siblings. Then her eyes widened. "Cooper?!"

"Belle's daughter!"

Mrs. Harwell gave a gasp, hand to her throat. "Belle! Oh, my dear, how I missed your mother when she left us."

"I'm presenting Cleo this season," the Countess said. "We must see that she is accepted as her mother was not."

"Oh, without question!"

Felicity had been smiling silently, hoping someone would soon explain to her this midday drama. Her mother turned to her. "And this is my Felicity," she told Cleo. "You'll be seeing a lot of one another, as she's just out and making quite an impression on the young men."

"Mama!" Felicity protested with a faint blush. "You always warn me about boasting."

"Boasting about oneself, certainly. Boasting about one's children, that's another kettle of fish." To Lucinda, "Winton is paying her attentions, you know."

"Indeed!" Lucinda said approvingly.

"He sent her a book!"

"Mama!"

"Never mind, dear. Miss Cooper's mother was my best friend in school. You must show her how to go on. Why don't you girls take a turn around the park?"

The two young ladies obediently moved away, Felicity murmuring to Cleo, "Let's give them some privacy; they want to gossip."

Cleo was startled. "Perhaps they do," she agreed. "And you can explain to me, who sent you a book?"

"The Duke of Winton," Felicity replied with modest pride. "It's by Newton, the strangest business. His Grace is very scientific, you know."

"I didn't know," Cleo admitted. "I'm new here and unfamiliar with society."

Felicity felt intense curiosity about this poised young woman, obviously years older than the usual debutante. "I haven't seen you before," she ventured. "Is this your first time in Town?"

"My first time in Town and my first time in England," Cleo told her.

"Gracious! I've never been anywhere but Sussex, Bath, and London," Felicity said. "I think I'd like to see more of the world. Well, perhaps the more comfortable parts of it."

Cleo chuckled. "A great deal of it is uncomfortable. Or at least very different. London seems quite strange to me. I hope Aunt Lucinda isn't taking on too much, presenting me to society. There's so much I don't know."

"But you must know a great deal!" Felicity protested.

"But not to our current purpose," Cleo said. "I know how to hire a camel caravan in the Levant. Or how to recover a stolen goat in Sicily without setting off a vendetta. But those skills perhaps don't translate to social success in London."

"Social success doesn't seem too complicated," Felicity assured her. "Everyone is so agreeable and affable."

"But I suspect it is easy for you," Cleo said. "You look like an illustration from *La Belle Assemblee*."

Felicity blushed and shook her head, though she was secretly flattered. And intrigued at the artless comment coming from a woman otherwise so worldly and knowledgeable. "I'm sure we'll be seeing a lot of one another," she said. "And you'll see, it's not really that difficult."

They were completing their circuit now, and approached their sponsors, to learn that the older women had decided that the two of them should walk in the park the next afternoon. "I look forward to it," Felicity said sincerely.

As the Dorwood carriage went on its way, Felicity and her mother continued their walk. "Well!" said Mrs. Harwell. "So that's Belle Bufford's girl."

"She seemed quite nice," Felicity ventured.

"Two and twenty!" her mother exclaimed. "And just now to be presented to society. A scrambling business."

"But she's just now in the country," Felicity said. "So she couldn't have been presented sooner."

"I suppose not."

"Tell me about her mother," Felicity asked. "Why was she not accepted?"

"Oh, my dear!" Mrs. Harwell replied with a pleasurable shudder. "Such a scandal it was! She eloped, you know. With the drawing master!"

"Really!"

"We girls were hard pressed to blame her, so handsome as he was, and so gentlemanlike."

"Gentleman*like*?"

"Well, that was the thing, don't you know? Miles Cooper was quite well educated and well spoken, but not really a gentleman. From some merchant family, I believe."

"But mama! Is not Lady Fenshire from a merchant family?"

"Ah, but with money," her mother explained. "Sometimes when an old family is run off its legs, these matches are necessary. Unfortunately for Belle, Miles Cooper had neither family nor fortune. His own family cast him out for choosing art over business, so he had to make his own way. You can be assured that he wouldn't have been giving drawing and watercolor lessons to a bunch of silly girls if he hadn't needed the money. And that's how he met Belle."

"Was he... a fortune hunter?" Felicity had been warned often about the wiles of fortune hunters.

"Not at all, for Belle had no fortune to hunt. The family was a moderately well-to-do county family then, but nothing to tempt a fortune hunter. No, it was a true love match, but how improvident! If he'd even been a younger son of good family, I suppose Belle's family might have accepted them eventually. But a Cit, and a penniless Cit? They weren't received, you know, and soon went abroad."

"How sad," Felicity said. And thought, but didn't say – how unfair.

***

His Grace was not present at Lady Willoughby's drum, but his friend was. Felicity, though quite amply attended by her devoted court, was pleased to observe her most amusing courtier and her most distinguished suitor's best friend, and admired how adroitly he cut out young Willoughby to claim the supper dance.

After a few elegant compliments delivered during the figures of the dance, Justin remarked, "That silly chub Winton! Fancy missing this for a fusty bunch of scholars!"

"Indeed?" Felicity prompted. "What scholars are those?"

"Oh, the Royal Society, of course. We're to meet at Watier's later so that I might hear all about his triumph."

"Is this about those orbits His Grace frequently discusses?"

"That's it," Justin agreed. "And however right he might be, I can assure you that tomorrow not a soul that you know or I know will have heard of it or would care about it they had."

"And yet, His Grace cares very much," Felicity pointed out.

"That's certainly true," Justin admitted. He continued broadmindedly, "Ah well, it's a harmless pursuit, that wastes neither his health nor his wealth. Oh, that telescope that he installed at Winton Court was a bit of an extravagance, but nothing compared to a yacht, or a bird..."

He broke off, suddenly remembered who he was talking to. Felicity gave an enchanting giggle and completed the sentence for him, "... of paradise!"

Justin looked around quickly and hushed his partner. "You'll have the old cats believing I'm corrupting you."

The music ended and he extended his elbow to Felicity. She took his arm and walked with him toward the supper room. "Mister Amesbury," she chided. "Do you think we young ladies would not know of such creatures if you didn't tell us? We see them in the park every day!"

"Where I hope you pretend not to notice them," he advised.

"Of course," she replied, wide-eyed.

Attaining their plates and a table, Felicity brought up a new subject. "Have you read Mister Newton's book?" she asked.

Startled, Justin answered, "Heavens, no!"

"Ah, I see." After a moment, she added, "I was hoping you could explain it to me."

"Not a prayer of that," he said. "I read classics at Cambridge and remember precious little about them. But why?"

"His Grace gave me a copy, and I hoped to gain at least a few facts from it."

Justin stifled a sigh. Oh, Arthur, he thought with exasperation. Yes, he had suggested a book, but surely even Arthur would know...

"The silly gudgeon," he said lightly. "I shall have to take him to task for such a dry offering."

"Oh, pray do not!" Felicity said. "After all, it's meaningful to him. And surely he must consider me intelligent to give me such a thing, so you see that it's quite a compliment."

Justin thought savagely that if he had the courting of a lady such as this, she would not have to tease out his compliments by inference. But it was after all Arthur who was in the market for a wife, and surely a little occasional bewilderment was a small price to pay for the advantages that would accrue to the Duchess of Winton. And there wasn't an ounce of harm in the fellow. Miss Harwell could certainly do worse.

***

Nonetheless, when the Duke hailed him in the lobby of Watier's, eager to go into incomprehensible detail of how he had routed Gould with charts and equations, Justin interrupted him with a quizzing look and said, "Arthur, really, my dear fellow! *The Principia?*"

Arthur, deep in a complex sentence that somehow involved ellipses, came to a halt. "No, these were my own calculations."

"I wasn't referring to the Society, you lobcock! Miss Harwell's gift!"

"Oh. That."

"That."

"But I didn't give her *The Principia*!"

"You didn't? But surely, Newton's book..."

"I gave her the English translation," Arthur said virtuously. "I know how few young ladies receive any schooling in Latin."

Justin sighed and gave it up. He clapped Arthur on the shoulder. "Lead me to dinner," he said. "Lady Willoughby provides a lean table."

FIVE

Over a fine beef roast and a finer wine, Justin listened with patient incomprehension as Arthur described the meeting of the Royal Society.

"You see?" Arthur said at last.

"Devil a bit," Justin replied cheerfully. "But I know you'll soon burst if you're not allowed to explain it to someone. Might as well be me."

"But it's so clear!" Arthur said. All their lives, Arthur had been telling Justin how clear and how simple something was. Justin no longer bothered to challenge the assertion. The beef at Watier's was extraordinarily good.

Arthur seemed to be finally winding down his account when the two men were hailed by a newcomer to the room. "Amesbury!" It was Baron Wainwright, accompanied by a young man dressed in the first stare of fashion. Unceremoniously, Wainwright pulled a chair up to their table, gesturing his friend to do likewise. "I must tell you my scheme for a new dressing gown."

Belatedly, he remembered his manners and introduced Peter Barton. "A school chum of Duffy's," he explained. "Duff is ruralizing, so I'm showing Barton the sights. Now, Amesbury, what do you say to this?"

With a pencil stub, he began to sketch on a linen napkin a complicated arrangement of frogs and braiding. Arthur looked at the newcomer, frowning slightly.

"Haven't we met?" he asked at last.

"No, sir, I'm sure we haven't," Barton told him.

"But I'm sure I've seen you before." Arthur leaned back in his chair, thinking. After a few moments, he sat up straight. "I have it!" he said. "Almack's. The lemonade."

Barton made hushing motions. Looking over at Wainwright and Amesbury, he saw that they were still deep in design. He scooted his chair closer to the Duke and lowered his voice. "I say, old fellow, not so loud please. You'll get me into the most fearful trouble."

"How so?" asked Arthur, puzzled.

"It was a bet, you see," Barton explained. "That I could serve as a waiter at Almack's without being recognized. No one ever looks at waiters, you know, not really looks at them. Well, other than you, I suppose."

"I see." Arthur was not surprised. He knew that placing absurd bets was a commonplace in modern society. "But how would you get into trouble?"

"I won the bet, don't you see? And now you've recognized me. But the bet was already settled, and I'm afraid," here Barton gave a deprecating laugh, "well, I'm afraid I've already spent the money."

Arthur gave the matter careful thought. At last he said, "But as I didn't recognize the waiter as Peter Barton, but only later recognized Peter Barton as the waiter, I think your victory still stands and the money is yours by rights."

"I'm relieved to hear that," Barton said with a smile. "And yet, I would prefer you didn't mention it. Some of the fellows might cut up rough about it. Right or wrong, they could be unpleasant."

"I see no reason to mention it," the Duke assured him. "The bet is settled, the matter is closed."

Across the table, Wainwright folded the napkin and, careless of the expropriation of Watier's property, stuffed it into a pocket. Justin told him, "You must show me the finished product. Perhaps an all-night card party with dressing gowns?"

"Splendid idea!" Wainright agreed. "Won't the others look all anyhow when they see our gowns?" He slapped the table. "We came here for whist. Would you gentlemen care to join us?"

Receiving a polite refusal, he collected Barton and the two strolled off to the card room. Watching them go, Justin remarked idly, "The dressing gown promises to be beyond brilliant. Searing, I should say."

"And yet, I'm the eccentric one, as least in society's eyes," Arthur said.

Justin grinned at him. "But society is composed of some very silly people."

***

The first of Cleo's new wardrobe had arrived, and she was pleased to go walking in her new walking dress. Aunt Lucy had emphasized speed to the modiste and instructed Cleo under no circumstances to be out and about in the fashionable districts until she had the new wardrobe items to match the occasion. So as yet, Cleo felt the only thing she could do was walk. She joined her new friend Felicity in the park, feeling complete to a shade in her jaconet muslin high dress and cerulean blue spenser.

She was pleased that Felicity complimented her walking attire, saying that it exactly suited her.

"Thank you," Cleo said. "But tell me this. Suppose I were dressed in this costume, but instead of walking with you and your abigail, I were –" she looked about and pointed at a passing carriage. "Suppose I were riding in that curricle."

Felicity looked at the curricle and gasped. "Oh, you mustn't! Not with Lord Salford!"

Cleo looked at her in astonishment. "Salford?"

"He is the most awful man, truly!"

Intrigued, Cleo asked, "How is he awful?" She watched the young man trotting past them. He did have a dissolute air about him, to be sure.

"I don't actually know," Felicity admitted. "But when I was newly come to town, Mama pointed him out to me and told me to be sure to have nothing to do with him. He isn't received, despite the title, and you won't find him at Almack's or the better houses. Sometimes one seems him in public places like Vauxhall or the opera, usually with some dreadful creature on his arm. He is dangerous, Mama says."

Cleo shrugged. She rather thought that dangerous in England meant something milder than the dangerous men she had encountered in the past. "Some other curricle, then," she said. "The driver doesn't matter. I'm riding in the park, wearing this. What would be the reaction?"

Felicity pondered this. Her new friend had a tendency to ask difficult questions. "I suppose," she said at last, "that people would assume that you didn't know any better."

Cleo nodded. "That's interesting. What if it were you in the curricle, wearing your walking dress?"

The hard questions just kept coming! Felicity hazarded, "They might think that for some reason I had been summoned so urgently that I had no time to change?"

Cleo pointed at a dashing young woman driving by in a high perch phaeton. "What if she were wearing a walking dress?"

"Oh, that's easy," Felicity said, relieved. "That's Lady Alice Broome, and she will do anything to confound society and cause people to talk about her."

"But they would mention it? And everyone here in the park would recognize the costume as walking dress?"

"Of course."

"And would no one among them say 'what difference does it make?'"

The two paced in silence for a moment, until Felicity said, "Perhaps the Duke might say such a thing. He has a very scientific frame of mind."

"This is your noble suitor? I think I should like to meet him."

Felicity looked ahead and chuckled. "That's fortunate, because you're about to meet him now." She nodded to the path ahead of them, where Cleo saw two men approaching them. A tall self-assured dark-haired gentleman, and with him –

"Why, that's Mister Ramsey!" Cleo exclaimed.

Felicity shook her head. "No, that's Mister Amesbury with the Duke."

Walking in the park with Justin, Arthur thought he was becoming accustomed to this pace. At least he didn't have to pay attention to his stride so constantly.

"Ah, here comes Miss Harwell," Justin said. "Remember, this is the park, not the Royal Society. Lightly, dear fellow."

Arthur looked ahead and saw Miss Harwell approaching. "She's walking with Miss Cooper," he said.

"Who?"

"The young lady I told you about, with the bird seed."

"Ah, yes," Justin said dismissively. "Hans Town."

The young ladies approached and the gentlemen tipped their hats. "Miss Harwell, Miss Cooper," said the Duke.

Felicity, prepared to perform introductions, said, "Oh, you've met?" just as Cleo said with a smile, "How do you do, Mister Ramsey?"

Self-consciously, the Duke corrected her. "I'm afraid I made a mull of my earlier introduction," he said apologetically. "I am Arthur Ramsey, Duke of Winton."

Cleo was so astonished that she blurted without thinking, "A duke! I thought you were someone useful!"

A profound silence fell. Her hasty exclamation had carried beyond her small group, bringing the sociable park traffic to a halt. Seeing Felicity's mortification, Cleo blushed, knowing that she'd stepped out of line.

Justin was too astonished to speak. Arthur, though, was deep in thought. At last he responded, "But surely, ma'am, one's usefulness should be measured by what one does, rather than by who one is."

Gratefully, Cleo smiled and nodded. "I'm sure you must be right," she said weakly.

Felicity slipped in with her fine social instincts. "And the Duke must certainly be considered useful with his scientific pursuits. Tell Miss Cooper about your new planet, Your Grace."

Arthur nodded to her. "Neither mine nor new, but discovered fairly recently," he corrected. Glad of a topic he excelled at, he was off, describing Sir William Herschel's telescope in Bath, and the faint light in the sky whose very name was in dispute.

Society, realizing that what had looked like a promising scandal had devolved into a scholarly lecture, moved on. "Shall we proceed together?" Justin suggested. "We block progress as we stand here."

The quartet moved on down the path, Arthur and Cleo deep in debate. "How contentious must scientists be that they can't even agree on a name for the thing!" she said.

"Herschel named his discovery Georgium Sidum after the king," Arthur explained. "But foreign scientists find that too British and prefer the name Herschel, though others are adopting the name Uranus, which is more in keeping with the classical origins of the names of the other planets."

Felicity and Justin strolled behind them, listening with bemusement on her part and amusement on his. "How clever she is!" she murmured.

"Is she?" Justin answered skeptically. "I doubt she even realizes that he could have ruined her by taking offense at her extraordinary comment." After a moment he added, "And I don't suppose he realizes it either."

"I am glad he took no offense!" Felicity replied. "Miss Cooper is unused to society and it would be infamous to cast her out before she has a chance to learn how to go on."

Justin quirked an eyebrow at her. "Why do you care?"

"Because I like her!" Felicity said hotly. "She's not like everyone else. Her mother was punished for making a love match, but why should that reflect on her?"

"Perhaps that explains her," Justin said. "Badly brought up." He would have added, 'ill-mannered baggage' if Miss Harwell hadn't already shown her support for the chit.

"We must help her!" Felicity said impulsively. She turned to Justin. "Not just show her the way to behave in society, but bring her into fashion. I'm sure she has little if any portion, so she needs our support if she's to make an advantageous match."

Justin stared at her. "If you're determined on this course, you've begun well," he said at last. "Here she is out walking with society's Incomparable, and engaged in debate with the Duke of Winton."

"And you'll help, won't you?" Felicity pleaded. "You're such a leader of fashion, if you approve her, others are sure to follow."

Justin couldn't help but be flattered by Felicity's assessment of his status in society, and touched by her crusading instincts. And it would certainly be a challenge. "If this is what you truly want," he said at last, "I'll do my best." The sparkling smile she gave him would be reward enough.

***

Cleo returned from her outing to find Peter in the parlor, being entertained by Miss Merrihew. "Peter!" she exclaimed. "Aren't you fine as five-pence?"

Peter stood and gave her an elegant bow. "I could say the same to you," he said. "Merry tells me you've been taking the air in the park, unexceptionable young lady that you are."

"Yes, indeed," said Cleo, taking a seat. "And Merry, you'll never guess! Remember the young man who carried the bird seed for me? Mister Ramsey?"

Merry nodded. "The helpful young lawyer."

"As it turns out, he is not a lawyer," Cleo told her. "Only think! He is the Duke of Winton!"

"A duke? Here? Extraordinary."

Peter frowned. "Be wary of Winton, Cleo."

"What? Now, don't tell me he is a scoundrel," Cleo protested, "or I will lose all faith in my own instincts. He seems such a harmless, good-natured man."

"Harmless and good-natured he may be," Peter told her. "But he's too discerning and observant for my liking. Do you know, he actually recognized me as the waiter at Almack's?"

"Peter!" Merry clasped her hands in distress. "Are we undone?"

"Not a bit," he reassured her cheerfully. "I thought on my feet, I did, and told him it was all a bet. It's not the most absurd bet these society gentlemen have made; he accepted my explanation without question."

"How clever you are!" Cleo approved.

"Still, I would advise you to avoid him as far as possible," he told her. "What business has a duke to be looking at a waiter? Such a level of observation bodes ill for us."

"I don't see how I can avoid him," Cleo said. "For he is courting Miss Harwell, who promises to be my great friend and an enormous help in my entry into society. I shall just have to be as clever as you."

Mrs. Mimms appeared at the door of the parlor, inquiring if Peter would be joining them at table. "Just a light luncheon," she said. "I've set a place for you, as I know you admire my jellied eel."

"I rather think so!" Peter replied, and the ladies rose to join him in the hall. Drumming footsteps overhead heralded Han, who thundered down the stairs with the unerring instinct of a boy knowing food is in the offing.

At the door to the dining room, Cleo stopped and called "Mrs. Mimms?"

The cook turned. "Yes, Miss?"

"There are only four place settings. You've no place to eat."

"Indeed I have, Miss Cleo. In the kitchen."

"Oh, but surely – "

"My mind's made up," the cook told her sternly, "and don't you go arguing with me. I tolerated Mister Miles' odd fancies because what did it matter then? An artist's residence in heathen parts. But this is London, and I might say I know London, better nor anyone here. And one thing you don't find in London, Miss, no, not as ever it was, is the cook sat down to dine at my lady's table!"

"But who would know?" Cleo asked.

"I would!" With that, Mrs. Mimms turned and disappeared into her kitchen fastness.

As the group took their seats, Cleo said, "It just seems so odd, the household residents eating in different locations."

"It's not odd at all," Miss Merryhew told her. "Mrs. Mimms is exactly right. She was in service in some of the best families before she married Sergeant Mimms. And a sensible course it is, too. Do you imagine that the household servants at these grand residences would even wish to eat at the master's table, on their best behavior at every meal? No, let them relax in the servants' hall, which is quite jolly in many establishments."

The butler was moving slowly around the table, ladling soup into the soup plates. Cleo appealed to him. "Does this strike you as the sensible arrangement, General?"

In a rusty, seldom-used voice, he replied softly, "I can't remember."

"Of course," said Cleo, abashed. She had grown up in a household where her parents considered the strays they collected along the way as part of the family. Mrs. Mimms cooked for them because she knew how. Everyone did their part. How odd, she thought, that Peter could stay with them but not dine with them as a footman, and dine with them but not stay with them as a gentleman. London was very strange.

She turned to Peter. "So tell me, how do you get on?"

"Famously!" he said. "I have a neat little set of rooms and am quite comfortable. And I must say, playing the role of London gentleman in real life is infinitely to be preferred to playing even a king on stage. The clothing is of much better quality, and the food is superb."

"How are you established?" Merry asked.

"I already have a circle of friends, and they couldn't be better fellows," Peter said proudly. "And they are without exception the silliest bunch of gudgeons you could imagine. Gaming mad, of course. In fact – " he produces a roll of banknotes from his pocket. "Let me make a contribution to our operating expenses."

Cleo's eyes widened at size of the roll. "Gracious!"

"And all from cards."

"I hope you haven't been cheating. It would be fatal for you to be caught out and banned from polite society before we even put our scheme into motion."

61

Peter scoffed at her concern. "I don't have to cheat," he assured her. "How these nodcocks can remain so fond of a pastime they are so terribly bad at is the mystery. I win in perfectly straight play, and I take pains to lose almost as much as I win. It's the losing that's the difficulty."

Han had been listening intently and now spoke up. "But cards have nothing to do with our scheme!"

"It's character development," Peter told him loftily. "If you studied the drama as I have, you would know about character development. I'm establishing myself as a young man of leisure and a sporting gentleman. But rest assured, I am also letting it be known that I consider myself a turf fancier and quite a knowing one. I've been several times to Tattersall's and placed some judicious bets. I even took care to place several sizable bets that I calculated quite accurately I would lose."

"Famous!" Han replied.

"Since you are so impertinent as to question your elders," Peter said, "perhaps you'd care to report how your part of the scheme progresses."

"I shall be ready at any time," Han said. "The General and I went to Newmarket just yesterday, and released the ladies at the agreed upon hour of two. Merry logged them in here; Athena made the trip in an hour and seven minutes, and Minerva was right behind her at one hour twelve."

"Extraordinary!" Peter marveled. "I do believe this will work."

"Of course it will work!" Han said dismissively. Turning to his sister, he added, "And you'll quite appreciate the wagon, Cleo. It looks like a decrepit old thing after the General and I finished chipping the paint and bashing it about, but it's quite sound and comfortable."

"We should test it out," Cleo said. "The full process, race, message, bet, everything. All that remains is to determine a suitable race."

Racing forms were fetched, and the little party spent the dessert course hotly debating odds and equine history.

62

The Countess of Dorwood, calling the next afternoon on her young protégé, was surprised to hear that the Coopers were out of town.

"An old family friend has been taken ill," Merry explained.

"I wasn't aware Cleo had friends in Town," Lucinda said.

"They're not really in Town," Merry said. "And not precisely *ton*, so you wouldn't know them. Friends of Miles Cooper. We met them in Italy, a respectable merchant family."

"Common!" sniffed Lady Silvia, who would come along.

Lucinda was nonplussed. "It rather oversets my plans. I'd been meaning to introduce Cleo to a few people at a private dinner. When do you expect her back?"

"Oh, it shouldn't be long," Merry said comfortably. "Han wanted to go along, they have boys about his age and he should keep them entertained and out from underfoot."

"And they went without you?" Silvia asked.

"Unfortunately, someone must remain here to tend Han's menagerie," Merry said. And that was true enough – try as he would, Peter had never gotten the knack of bird handling.

"Then it's just us for a nice coze," the Countess decided, taking a seat in the parlor. For thirty minutes, she quizzed her old governess on life with the Coopers. Merry was glad to discuss the adventurous life she had led since her dismissal from the Buffords, though with suitable edits to make it all sound more respectable. She wasn't sure she succeeded, judging by Lady Sylvia's frowning countenance, but reminded herself that Sylvia had always disapproved of most things as a matter of principle.

When the callers took their leave, Merry promised to have a message sent round when the travelers returned.

***

Meanwhile, on the road from London to Newmarket, a pair of disreputable gypsies rode a shabby old wagon toward the racing town.

"How is it," Cleo asked, "that the upper classes wear such uncomfortable footwear?" She stuck out a foot to admire the disgraceful leather contraptions on her feet.

She sat beside Han on the wagon's bench. "Even better," he replied, displaying his own foot that sported no footwear at all. His feet, along with the rest of his exposed skin, had been colored a dusky hue. Unbleached pants suitable for a field laborer barely covered his calves. A gaudy but faded vest covered his smock, and a bright scarf covered jet black hair.

Cleo's own skin was similarly darkened, and her dark chestnut hair had been tightly wrapped and topped by a wig of similar jet; Peter's theatrical connections had been instrumental in their outfitting. Her skirt was a virulent purple, her blouse a clashing red-orange, and a sash of grubby green clashed with both.

"It's baffling," Cleo mused. "If I were a very wealthy woman, I would contract with the shoemakers to make me shoes that were both attractive and yet comfortable, but when out shopping with Aunt Lucinda, I heard more than one lady of rank complain about her shoes. It's as if they believe that a shoe must pinch to be pretty."

"None of them have much sense," Han suggested. "Peter's reporting indicates that the men aren't much better."

"And well for us that it is so," Cleo said. "I'll warrant we could confound an intelligent man, but the stupid, incurious ones are much to be preferred." She looked around with a satisfied sigh. "And lovely to get out of the city for a while. The noise and the smells – how do they tolerate it?"

"I can't say I think much of London," Han told her. "I did some sight-seeing on my own, and do you know? The buildings they boast have such great antiquity are none of them more than eight hundred years old!"

Cleo laughed. "A mere eight hundred years? How paltry!"

It was a beautiful spring day. A recent rain had laid the dust, making it less of an annoyance when a gentleman's sporting curricle dashed past the gypsy wagon. This happened with regularity; much of the male population of the *ton* were off to the races.

Cleo pointed out neatish country estates they passed, properties that she speculated could supply a gentleman a comfortable competence. Han's only reply was an indifferent "how nice."

***

As they made their way toward the viewing stand at Newmarket, Justin and Arthur debated the merits of the horses running that day. Arthur held out for Wind Runner's merits over the favored Ladybird.

"Care to put a pony on it?" Justin asked, though he knew better.

"Of course not," Arthur said. "You know I never wager on races."

"I know it, I just don't understand it," Justin replied. "It's not as if it's cards."

"Wagering on horse races is actually less rational than betting on cards," Arthur told him. "In cards, the only factors you need to consider are your own skill and the skill and honesty of your opponent. And even then, how many practitioners overestimate their own abilities, to their detriment. In a horse race, the factors are so multiplicitous the calculations required are beyond human capacity. You must consider the condition of the track, the weather, the speed and physical condition of the horse, the skill and the honesty of both trainer and jockey, and the mood and behavior of the horse, and factor all that across up to a dozen horses, and many of these points would be unknown to the person placing the bet. It's a fool's errand."

"I'm sure you're right," Justin said. "No doubt winning is purely a matter of luck. Though it adds spice to the spectacle."

"A bitter spice indeed to the loser," Arthur pointed out.

As they approached the stands a young gentleman lifted his hat to Justin, who looked through him and turned away. Arthur tried to gain his friend's attention, but Justin had already moved on.

Mounting the steps, Arthur called, "Justin, that man…"

"That man is no acquaintance of mine, or any decent person," Justin said shortly. "That was the cut direct. I have no desire to know him. Earl or no, Salford will always be a commoner."

"Good heavens!" Arthur had never seen his friend so censorious. "What is wrong with him?"

"That's right, you weren't in Town last season." Justin said. "Salford is a scoundrel. He came into the title but lately at the death of a cousin and society thought to rehabilitate him, but he's bad through and through. Ruins women for sport. Miss Morrisey had to leave Town and hasn't been seen since, rusticating in the country. Never make a decent match now."

Arthur frowned. He hoped the Esquimaux had less cruel sports.

There were several races being run that day, and Justin had placed bets on all of them. Nothing he couldn't lose, just enough to make an interest. And also because, he had to admit privately, it was the established mode to do so.

While Justin eyed the stands, nodding to acquaintances, Arthur scanned the race track and the crowd come to watch the races from the ground. "I say," he said, coming to attention. "Isn't that Miss Cooper?"

"Miss Cooper? Where?"

Justin turned to eye the other side of the viewing stand.

"There." Arthur pointed downward, to the milling mass of merchants, laborers, young bloods, and others without the social standing to gain entrance to the stands.

"She wouldn't be down there," Justin said positively.

"Just there," Arthur insisted. "In the purple skirt."

Justin saw where he was pointing. "The gypsy?! My dear fellow, she's got hair black as pitch! Why on earth do you suppose that to be Miss Cooper?"

"I'm not sure," Arthur admitted. Then he said, "She moves like Miss Cooper."

Justin sniffed. "Miss Cooper needs to learn to move like a lady."

Arthur, still watching the crowd on the ground, stiffened. "Whoever she is," he said, "she appears to be in difficulty." He began to push his way toward the exit.

Justin looked at Arthur, then back to the ground. He saw that the gypsy in purple was surrounded by three young men, who appeared to be determined to make sport of her. "Arthur! I say, Arthur!" He pushed after his friend.

"My dear fellow," he said, catching up to him. "What is it to us?"

"Whoever that young woman is," Arthur told him austerely, "she did not appear to welcome their attentions."

"Oh, but – No, really, those chaps are undoubtedly drunk. Do you want to cause a scene?"

"If necessary."

Justin gave up the argument and followed Arthur silently. He hoped there wouldn't be too much of a rumpus. Under other circumstances, he might have found it amusing, but not now, not

66

when Arthur was courting Miss Harwell. Should it become known that the Duke of Winton had been involved in a drunken brawl over a gypsy wench (for that was surely how the *ton* would view it), the insult to Miss Harwell would be intolerable.

Struggling to keep the Duke in sight, he felt that the first objective was to keep any imbroglio out of the society papers. If it could be managed to not even make club whispers, that would be a great thing. He hoped the young men were not too disguised to be reached by a bear garden jaw, if they were of gentle birth. If they were of the lower orders, the best course would perhaps be a well-placed gratuity.

But when they reached the place where the gypsy had been, she was nowhere to be seen. The three young men were there. On closer view, they were obviously of the gentry. They were very young, either undergraduate or just down from university. One lay on the ground in a protective curl, cursing, while his companions bent over him quizzically. They were all three drunk as wheelbarrows.

"What happened here?" the Duke asked sternly.

The tow-headed young man in the virulently striped waistcoat looked at them and blinked. "Just a little fun and gig," he slurred. "Cholly here tried to get friendly with a gypsy wench, but she would have none of it."

His friend in puce nodded vigorously. "Very handy with her fives, she was," he said admiringly. "Not the sweet science, at least not as I understand it. But devilish effective, as you see."

"That last hit, though," said the tow-head with a frown, "not sporting. No, not sporting at all."

"Help me up, you clunches!" howled Cholly.

"Oh, you ready to get up now?" asked puce amiably, and gave Cholly a solicitous assist to his feet. The young man was not yet able to stand quite upright.

"I hope you've learned a lesson here," Justin said. "You had no call to be interfering with that young woman."

"I would have paid, and well," protested Cholly.

"Not every woman is willing to sell herself," the Duke said with a frown. "No, not even women of the lower orders. Do you treat your family's maidservants so?"

67

"Of course not!" Cholly said. "M'father would give me a rating that never ended if I tried to sport the servant wenches. But a gypsy at a race meet?"

"Women willing to make the transaction will approach you," the worldly Justin advised. "Making the approach yourself is unmannerly. Not to mention dangerous. Gypsy women tend to come equipped with large brothers or husbands, often with large knives."

"And that wench had a knife herself," said tow-head.

"Did not!" said Cholly.

"Did!" said puce. "Saw it in her sash. Wondered at you persisting when she sent you about your business."

"But she didn't need a knife to send you to grass!" chuckled tow-head.

Forgetting the presence of Justin and Arthur, the three wandered off, still arguing. The two men watched them go.

"Well!" said Justin with relief.

"What a remarkable woman," the Duke said admiringly.

"Remarkable?"

"Why, yes. Consider how often one hears a young lady described as 'accomplished' because she can paint a screen, or sing a ballad while accompanying herself on the pianoforte. How much more sensible to teach them a useful accomplishment, such as how to incapacitate an importunate rascal."

Justin snorted. "Well enough for a gypsy perhaps, but a young lady of rank and breeding would never be in a position to need such an accomplishment. She would not be abroad to be accosted without a brother, maid, or footman."

"But what if the footman were the rascal?" Arthur asked impishly.

Justin threw up his hands. "I should know better than to try to debate with you."

***

"Meat pie?"

Han turned from his seat in the wagon. "There you are! You've been an age. Any problems?"

Cleo scrambled up beside him and passed the greasy bag. "No problems. Just some silly boys in the way, too drunk to be sensible, but I sent them about their business." She settled herself comfortably and looked over the race course.

"Nothing like Il Palio," Han remarked.

"No indeed, much less raucous," Cleo agreed. Hearing coos from the bed of the wagon, she asked, "How are your ladies?"

"In fine fettle and anxious to spread their wings."

The two ate their al fresco repast and watched the races with interest, Cleo frequently referring to a scribbled sheet of figures.

***

Shielded from street view by the fronting parapet, two people sat on the roof of the townhouse on Upper Wimpole Street, but only one of them sat at ease. Peter lounged in a dainty bamboo chair, lightly swinging a quizzing glass, for he had such a glass now and no longer needed to make shift with sewing scissors. But Miss Merrihew scanned the sky with increasing anxiety.

"The races must have begun well over an hour ago," she said fretfully.

"That's of no consequence," Peter told her. "The first few races might well be won by the favorite, with odds that make it not worth sporting our blunt. Trust Cleo and Han to know what they are about."

"I suppose you're right," Merry said. But she still looked anxious.

"I see no cause for concern," Peter said. "The thing is simplicity itself. In fact, it sounds much like a similar rig the Coopers ran in Florence, or I'm very much mistaken."

"It is," Merry admitted. "And yet – "

"And yet? "

"This is England!" she burst out.

"So? I don't understand."

"It didn't matter in Florence!" Merry said. "Oh, it all went well, but if it hadn't, we could have just decamped in the night. We did that often enough, and found a new place to settle. But now that we're back in England, I find that I don't wish to leave."

Peter was surprised. "Did you miss it so much?"

"I didn't realize how much, not until we came back." Merry fluttered her hands. "Please don't take me wrong. I'm ever so grateful to the Coopers for taking me in, and heaven only knows what would have become of me if they hadn't. And I've enjoyed my life with them – or most of it. There were certainly some anxious moments I wouldn't care to relive. But now I keep thinking how

69

lovely it would be to be really settled. To know you'll be tomorrow in the same house you woke up in today. To make friends and keep them for years, not just a few, but a wide circle of friends. To no longer have to ask — what if we're caught?"

"Steady on, old girl," Peter advised her. "Isn't being settled the whole point of the scheme? That takes funds. A few runs with the birds, and we can be all set up."

"If only Cleo can be satisfied with a simple country estate and moderate income," Merry said with a frown.

"Let's not borrow trouble," Peter said. "Everything is going swimmingly so far. I might even decide to stay a gentleman when we've reached the end, now that I know how simple it is."

Merry might have followed this conversational gambit, but Peter pointed at the sky. "There! Isn't that one of ours?"

Merry turned to look where he indicated, and saw a pigeon flying strongly toward them. "Indeed it is! Which one, I can't tell. Only Han can tell them apart. But it's certainly one of his birds."

The bird landed with a flutter on the platform outside the pigeon coop. Merry competently gathered it up and tucked it under her arm, gently removing the message cylinder attached to its leg.

"You make that look so easy," Peter said admiringly.

"It is easy," Merry said in her stern governess voice. "You just need to apply yourself."

"Ah, but I mustn't crumple my attire," Peter said with an air. "I must go on the toddle as soon as you give me the word."

Unrolling the tiny paper scroll, Merry read, "Fourth race. Fancy Nancy."

"I've got it." Peter nodded to Merry, gave her an elegant bow, and went on his way.

Twenty minutes later, Peter Barton strolled into Watier's, yawning the yawn of a young town buck just rolled out of bed. He was full of effusive praise for a young opera dancer met the previous night, declaring her as complaisant as she was beautiful. In honor of his new inamorata, for Nancy was the fictional lightskirt's name, he whimsically bet a monkey on Fancy Nancy, racing that day at Newmarket.

Young Baron Hillard took the bet, telling Barton with a laugh that tomorrow when the race results posted, he will have wished that he'd spent his roll of soft on jewelry for his light-o-love, since the ill-omened Fancy Nancy was given very long odds indeed. But it was commonplace for gentlemen to make wagers for such frivolous causes, and no one thought the worse of him for it.

SEVEN

Seated in a gilt chair beside the wall at Lady Thistlethwaite's ball, the Countess of Dorwood could not suppress a complaisant smile. "So she has taken, you see," she remarked to Mrs. Harwell, seated beside her.

She was watching Cleo dance the quadrille with Lord Wainwright. Cleo's ball gown of deep rose satin under a net overlay was much admired, and she had heard Cleo herself warmly described as 'not just in the usual style'.

Mrs. Harwell nodded approval. She could afford to be magnanimous; her daughter was still the acknowledged Incomparable of the season, and dear Belle's sweet daughter would not affect that. "She's danced every dance but the waltzes," she agreed.

"And only sat those out because I told her to," Lucinda said. "And even then, she has always found a young man to bear her company when she abandons the dance floor. Yes, I think she will do well, and be quite a credit to me."

"Hmmph!" The wordless snort turned Lucinda's attention to her other side, where Lady Sylvia sat scowling at the dancers. "Have to remind you," Sylvia said sourly, "that her mother had quite a brilliant season too, before she brought disgrace to the family."

The Countess pressed her lips tightly together to prevent a hasty response. To her way of thinking, it was her brother William who brought true disgrace to the family, losing his fortune and the country seat that had been Bufford property for five generations, capping the sorry chain of events by putting a period to his own existence. But one didn't say such things to that gentleman's relict, however disagreeable she might be.

Mrs. Harwell gave Lucinda a sympathetic look but otherwise made no reply to Lady Sylvia. "Does dear Cleo waltz?" she asked.

Lucinda frowned. "I scarcely know. I wouldn't suppose that she does."

"Then she must attend Felicity's waltzing party," her friend urged. "An informal morning affair, just the young girls who are newly out, with a few young fellows dragooned into helping. It's more a lesson than a party, but the girls enjoy it. And Cleo will need to know the waltz. A pretty behaved girl, and with your sponsorship, I'm sure she'll receive vouchers to Almack's."

***

Cleo was enjoying herself. The plan was working, she thought smugly. She'd thought it all through. Han needed to be a gentleman. For that, he needed more than money. He needed acceptance by the *ton*, by what was known as 'polite society'.

Miles Cooper had explained it to her very clearly. Money was not enough. Papa's own father was a wealthy merchant, well able to buy the entirety of the Bufford estate and ten more like it. But he was unacceptable to the *ton*. One must have money, not work to gain money. The maker of a fortune was stigmatized as a 'Cit'. The children of that fortune, however well-educated, well-behaved, and gentlemanly, were described as 'smelling of the shop'. It was only by the time the third generation had inherited wealth that they had not had to toil for themselves that society would look upon them as gentry in their own right.

Therefore Cleo's plan had two main elements. First was money. They needed money, but must not be seen to be earning money. That was well on track. Second was social acceptance. For that, the Bufford connection via Aunt Dorwood would get their foot in the door, and Cleo's own wit and charm must do the rest.

Cleo had come to London determined to make a fortune and crash society at the same time. What she hadn't expected, though, was to find it so enjoyable. The season was nothing but a series of parties! Routs, drums, balls, card parties, theater outings and dinners. The Countess had pointed out to her that behind the glitter was a serious purpose. This was the way a young lady provided for herself. But Cleo, with secret other means of providing for herself, could afford to relax and simply enjoy herself.

Moving through the figures of the quadrille, Lord Wainwright asked, "How did you enjoy Mrs. Linster's Venetian breakfast?"

"A very great deal," Cleo said brightly. "Though I confess it puzzled me to determine what was Venetian about it."

Wainwright looked thoughtful. "You have me there. I've no notion. It's just what an afternoon party is called, don't you know?"

73

"I know that now," Cleo replied. "But I was expecting, oh, I don't know... I thought there would at least be boats involved."

The Baron laughed. Amesbury was right; Miss Cooper was an original.

Wainwright's opinion was shared by many young men in society. Talking to new debutantes was a chore; they were all so perfectly coached by their mamas that one could ask the same question to half a dozen of them and get the same answer. Oh, the breakfast was lovely, everyone was so amiable, the music was heavenly, they were so vastly amused. Miss Cooper never gave an expected answer to the usual questions, and her perspective on the social whirl was frequently entertaining.

Society's approval of Cleo was by no means universal. Some of the more censorious of the old ladies found her manner too self-assured and her remarks too unusual. "A pert miss," was the terse verdict of the Dowager Marchioness of Woolston.

"But that's only to be expected," Lady Jersey confided to Lady Dorwood, as she came to call with Cleo's vouchers to Almack's. "She says that of all the lively girls. Pay it no mind. In my opinion, your niece is a charming, unaffected girl, and I would hope to see some of these milk and water misses take heed of her example, before society becomes too insipid to be borne."

Among the young men, Cleo's popularity was more assured, though some of the shyer and slower-witted found her often alarming and always perplexing. But the general view was positive. She was pretty, she was amusing, she was sponsored by a Countess and seen frequently in the company of the season's Toast. She could sustain a conversation with the frivolous Lady Jersey as well as the serious Duke of Winton.

Some found other reasons to see in Cleo appropriate marriage material. One late evening at Boodle's, Viscount Fenwick, a young peer with a long horsy face, pale hair, and a pronounced air of amiable vacuity, announced over the third bottle of port that he was giving serious thought to making a push for Miss Cooper. The Duke, who had accepted Amesbury's invitation for a 'convivial evening with friends', had retreated some time ago to a table in the corner, where he occupied himself scratching numbers on paper, absorbed in planetary orbits. He looked up at this, and followed the conversation with interest.

Justin Amesbury smiled to himself at his success in advancing Miss Harwell's protégé, but said, "Indeed? I could have sworn you were trying to attach Miss Dumphreys."

"And so I was, old fellow," Fenwick replied. "Was on the point of offering, if you want the truth with no bark on it. A narrow escape."

"Escape?" asked Amesbury. He and Arthur had concluded that the pretty redhead was too silly for Arthur, but to his mind she seemed ideally suited for a genial young dunce like Fenwick.

"Fact," said Fenwick. "I discovered in the very nick that I'd been greatly deceived in Miss Dumphreys' character."

As far as Amesbury knew, Miss Dumphreys was the most conventional of debutantes. This was news indeed. "How so?" he prodded, passing the port bottle.

"It was like this," Fenwick replied. Others gathered around the table, hoping for an interesting scandal. "Was at Almack's, you know. Took my mother there, doing the pretty, danced with Miss Dumphreys and several other charming gals. Miss Dumphreys sat out to talk with my mother, and I went to fetch them some lemonade. Appalling lemonade, by the by, but that's beside the point."

He refreshed himself from his glass and continued. "So there I am, returning to the ladies, and they're facing the other direction, so I hear what they're talking about. And there's my mother, talking, in a general way, don't you know, about how she looks forward to my marriage and setting up my nursery, that sort of thing."

"Quite unexceptionable," Amesbury prodded.

"But then!" Fenwick said, aggrieved, "then she says that when that happy day arrives, she sees no need to remove to the dower house, but intends to remain fixed in the manor with me and my family! And there's Miss Dumphreys, smiling and nodding and saying that she quite agrees!"

He looked surprised and ruffled at the roar of laughter. "No, really, fellows!" he protested. "Now, I ask you! If your bride is unwilling or unable to shift your mama to the dower house, why, what's the point in getting married at all?"

Amesbury clapped him on the shoulder. "No point in the world," he agreed.

The Duke joined the conversation. "But you have no doubt of Miss Cooper's ability to effect the desired removal?"

Fenwick nodded vigorously. "That's the dandy. Very masterful sort of gal, ain't she? She'll have things all sorted out in a trice, I give you my word."

"You'll be living under the cat's paw, Fenwick," Baron Dorne said.

"I already do," Fenwick said gloomily. "You chaps all know my mother. Still," he added, brightening, "if I'm to live under the cat's paw, it might as well be a pretty paw, eh?"

He drained his glass and stood up. "It's my fate, I think," he concluded. "I'm a peaceable sort of gent, can't abide brangling and pulling caps." He bowed hazily to the company and wandered out the door.

"So he's looking for a bride willing to do the brangling for him," Amesbury concluded.

"Perhaps someone should warn Miss Cooper," the Duke suggested.

"Not at all, old man!" Amesbury told him. "Repeat club talk to the ladies? Don't even think of it. Besides, in the natural course of events Miss Cooper will meet Fenwick's mama and will certainly draw her own conclusions, if she's as clever as you think she is."

"Very true," the Duke agreed, and returned to his orbits.

***

Looking over the scene at Mrs. Harwell's waltzing party, Justin Amesbury felt like the veriest graybeard. The young ladies ranged from sixteen to eighteen years old, all newly out, all apparently shy to the point of paralysis. Well, perhaps not all. Miss Harwell carried herself well, with the assurance that only social success gives. The source of Miss Cooper's poise was less easy to determine; perhaps it was just her extra years that allowed her to consider publicly twirling about in the arms of a young man with tolerable equanimity.

He had to give Mrs. Harwell credit, though. The young men she had recruited as dancing partners were the least threatening specimens imaginable. No Corinthians, no splendidly eligible *partis*, no alarmingly witty men of fashion. Justin knew himself to be the most fashionable man present, but his obliging good nature could soothe the terrors of the mousiest of debutantes. And indeed, after listening to the instructions of the plump martinet of a dancing master, the young ladies gradually relaxed and were soon giggling as they twirled about the room.

Felicity and Justin danced first, since they both were quite competent waltzers, and the dancing master pointed out to the audience how they were doing the forms of the waltz, foot placement, hand placement, turning. Then Justin danced with some of the other young ladies.

After several waltzes were danced more or less successfully, Justin spoke up, addressing the dancing master and the room at large. "If I might make a suggestion? The beauty of the waltz is that the lady dances an entire dance with one gentleman, making it possible to have a conversation not interrupted by the changes and separations of other forms. Yet often for a good half of their first season, debutantes are unable to speak during the waltz, so concerned are they with how they are performing the dance steps. I suggest for the next and subsequent dances, the dancers should carry on a conversation with one another. Only when you can do this should you consider yourself competent at the waltz."

Several waltzes later, Justin was paired with Cleo. "What shall we talk about?" she asked him as they moved and twirled.

"Half a moment," he said. "I've already discussed Almack's, Vauxhall Gardens, the Queen's drawing rooms, Bath versus Brighton, and the theater. So... Ah, I have it!" He looked down at her and asked smoothly, "Do you ride, Miss Cooper?"

"Well," said Cleo doubtfully. "I have ridden. But not recently. We don't keep horses in Town."

"You should ride," he suggested. "Unless you prefer driving?"

"I suppose that depends," Cleo answered.

"Depends? On what?"

"On how fast I need to get somewhere, and whether or not I'm taking anything with me," she answered.

Justin blinked. "Get somewhere?"

"Yes. When you ride in London, where are you going?"

"Generally we hack in Rotton Row," Justin explained. "It's in Hyde Park and is the most popular place for riding and driving."

"But riding and driving to where?" Cleo persisted. Then she had a flash of comprehension. "Oh, I see. You're not riding to get somewhere, you're riding as a social pastime?"

"Exactly." Justin hadn't realized this would require so much explanation.

Cleo chuckled. "Now that I understand what we're talking about, you may proceed."

What a peculiar girl. Justin wondered if there was another debutante of the season who didn't know about leisure riding and Rotton Row. He talked easily about the Row, the carriages and the horses and the riding costumes, until the waltz ended.

Later, Cleo mentioned riding to Felicity and learned that she loved it above all things. Aunt Lucinda had insisted that Cleo have a riding habit, so Cleo was anxious to make the attempt. She believed that one could rent a horse from a livery stable?

"Ye-es," Felicity said doubtfully. "Livery horses are disparaged, but perhaps to start with, to see how you go on. The horses are quite manageable at least."

And so it was that two days later, Mister Amesbury breezed into Winton House, waved away Tolliver with a negligent, "Breakfast room? Thanks, I'll show myself in," and joined the Duke and his mother at the breakfast table.

"Ah, here's my favorite flirt!" the Duchess greeted him.

"Morning, Auntie," he said, kissing her on the cheek before going to the sideboard and helping himself to the breakfast offerings.

"I am not your aunt, and you only call me that to make me feel old," she complained.

Justin placed his hand on his heart. "I only claim the relationship to signify my deep regard for you, dear lady." He set his plate at the table and pulled up a chair. Turning to Arthur, he asked, "What are your plans for the morning?"

"The Buildings Committee for the British Museum is meeting to discuss – "

"Stop right there," Justin interrupted. "Let me rephrase. You are going riding this morning."

"I am?"

"You are. Miss Harwell has expressed an interest in riding; she will be riding in Hyde Park with Miss Cooper, and we are promised to join them."

"Oh, do, Arthur," the Duchess urged. "You look so elegant on a horse and you ride so well."

"A trivial accomplishment, surely," Arthur told her. "Anyone with significant acreage to cover quickly must ride, and sheer repetition would engender ease."

"Call it trivial if you wish," Justin argued. "But it's an accomplishment that society sets great store by."

Arthur seemed about to protest, but the Duchess said enigmatically, "The Esquimaux, dear."

"I suppose I must change then," Arthur said, pushing away from the table.

As the door closed behind him, Justin cocked a quizzical eyebrow at the Duchess. "Esquimaux?"

"Never mind, dear," she told him placidly. "Tell me about Miss Harwell."

"If you're asking about her suitability to serve as your successor, ma'am, I would say she was born to take that role."

"An encomium indeed!"

"Arthur has met many young ladies in the past several weeks, Aunt, and of them I consider Miss Harwell to be not merely the best of the lot, but entirely ideal."

"You reassure me," the Duchess said. But as Justin left the breakfast table, she admitted to herself a slight uneasiness. The cause of her unease she could not say.

As Pelton brought out the Duke's riding attire and assisted him in changing, the Duke apologized for the inconvenience.

"Think nothing of it, Your Grace," Pelton told him smoothly. "It is after all only my job."

Pelton was not only not offended, he was elated. As he said later in the butler's pantry, "Pantaloons not two hours ago, and then to change to riding dress? There's nothing like a young lady to make a young gentleman so changeable and indecisive. I give you my word, Mister Tolliver, Winton will have a Duchess before the snow flies."

"It is greatly to be wished," Tolliver agreed. "Not a word of this in the Hall, mind."

"As if I would!" Pelton told him. The Duke's personal life was not a topic for the lower servants in the servants' hall, but the exclusive property of the more elevated ranks. A footman who had speculated as Pelton had just done would receive a severe setdown from Tolliver, or Pelton himself.

The two gentlemen rode to the entrance of Hyde Park where they found the young ladies awaiting them, Miss Harwell on a dainty white mare that enhanced her fairy image, and Miss Cooper on a serviceable brown mare which, while not displaying obvious conformation errors, was a horse that would never be described as 'a fine bit of blood and bone'.

After exchanging greetings, the party rode gently down the path. "How do you like your mount, Miss Cooper?" Amesbury asked.

"She suits me admirably," Cleo replied. "She's a livery stable hire, you know."

"I guessed," he admitted.

"Her name is Princess, I'm told."

Justin had to laugh. "An ambitious name for such a... common beast."

"Don't disparage Princess," Cleo protested. "She is a perfectly fine mount for me."

"Perhaps you would outline her better points, because I confess that they escape me."

"Easily," said Cleo. "To begin with, she's just the right height."

"Height!"

"Yes, indeed. For with a donkey you must keep your feet raised lest they drag on the ground. Whereas with a camel you are so far off the ground that you ride in fear that a fall must be fatal."

"A camel!" said Justin faintly.

Cleo sniffed delicately. "Then too, Princess doesn't smell as horribly as a camel. Many people find the scent of horse to be agreeable, something that no one would say about camels. And when given the office to proceed, she does so without requiring a single curse, shout, or threat, showing much more willingness to obey than either camels or donkeys. So you see," Cleo concluded with a triumphant smile, "she is indeed a paragon among mounts."

Justin fell behind to ride beside Arthur for a ways, murmuring to his friend, "I confess that Miss Cooper baffles me."

"She seemed to me to raise valid points," Arthur said.

Justin gave him an exasperated look and continued, "I am never able to determine if she's being sincere or if she's quizzing me."

"Why does it matter?"

"If I'm to bring her into fashion, I would like to know whether to describe her as refreshingly natural or to praise her dry wit."

"Are you bringing her into fashion?" Arthur asked, surprised.

"Why, yes," Justin said, and hesitated. Somehow he didn't like to own that he was doing so at the request of the lady that Arthur was courting. "I've taken a fancy to the notion," he said at last.

80

The party closed ranks again and conversation became general. Arthur followed absent-mindedly, puzzling over his exchange with Justin. His friend said often enough that he had no thoughts of marriage just now, but Arthur could not remember a time when Justin had made the effort to actually bring a young woman into fashion. Arthur knew himself to be a novice on the subject of human relationships, but he wondered if Justin was forming an attachment for Miss Cooper all unaware.

And he wondered what he thought of the notion if it turned out to be true. On the whole, he rather thought he approved. Miss Cooper was such a sensible creature, after all. Justin had wasted his time gallanting much sillier women.

While the young ladies rode in the park, Mrs. Harwell hoped to catch up on her correspondence. Neither receiving nor making morning calls, she counted on a rare quiet morning at home. But it was not to be. She heard no knocker, but noises at the front of the house presaged an arrival. It was too soon for Felicity, surely?

The matter was resolved when the door to the drawing room opened to reveal Mrs. Harwell's lord and master.

"Mister Harwell!" she exclaimed. "Well, I call this nice. We weren't expecting you for weeks yet!"

Mister Harwell, a bluff, good-natured man, looked about the room assessingly. "You home to callers this morning?"

"No, and Felicity is riding with friends, so we may enjoy a comfortable coze."

"In that case, you'll excuse my dirt, I know," he said, saluting her with a kiss on the cheek and taking a seat in his riding clothes.

"What brings you to Town so early?" his helpmeet asked.

"Wanted to find out what you and my Filly were getting up to that has all the young men in such a pother," he replied.

"But dearest, you know! Felicity has come out! She is a brilliant success. Of course all the young men are in a pother. They are supposed to be."

"So much so that three of the silly gudgeons have posted down to Sussex to solicit my daughter's hand!" Mr. Harwell grumbled. "If a man ain't safe in his own greenhouses, might as well come to Town!"

"Indeed, did they so?" Mrs. Harwell preened. "Well! No doubt they're trying to steal a march on His Grace."

"His Grace, eh?" Mr. Harwell raised his eyebrows, but then frowned. "Oh, I say, Maria. Not gouty old Fanborne!"

"*Mister* Harwell! As if I would countenance such a match. No indeed. Our daughter has caught the eye of the young Duke of Winton. His attentions are becoming quite marked."

"Winton, eh? Pretty well to pass, I believe."

"Fabulously wealthy!" Mrs. Harwell exclaimed. "As well as young and handsome. And a genuinely nice young man."

"Indeed? Well done, ma'am!"

"I had nothing to do, it was all Felicity. Once he spotted her dancing at Almack's, that did the trick, I'm sure."

"Our little Filly, a duchess!"

"Let us not get ahead of ourselves, Mister Harwell. He has yet to offer, remember. And I hope you don't intend to use that absurd pet name in public."

Harwell gave a comfortable laugh. "I may not have much town bronze, m'dear, but I'll try not to embarrass you. Well, well, well. I see I must remain in Town. Wouldn't do to make a duke journey out to Sussex to offer for our little gal. Make it easy for him, eh?"

In Hyde Park, the riding party was joined by Viscount Fenwick. Riding a neat grey and precise to a shade, Fenwick tipped his hat to the ladies and proceeded to perform what he would call 'doing the pretty'. Arthur and Justin exchanged a speaking glance as Fenwick focused his gallantry on Miss Cooper. Felicity, however, heard the badinage with an increasing sense of indignation.

After Fenwick went on his way, she said, "I had thought Lord Fenwick to be a good sort of fellow. His understanding is not of the strongest, but his manner is pleasing and his instincts quite nice. But now I must confess I perceive in him a level of volatility that can only be deplored."

Cleo was surprised at her gentle friend's strictures. "I must say, I saw no such volatility."

"That's because you are unaware that he had been making up to Lillian Dumphreys these past two months. His attentions were quite marked. I believed him to be on the point of offering. But it seems he is just a heartless flirt."

The Duke looked as if he would speak, but Amesbury gave him a significant glance and a slight headshake. "Leave Fenwick to sort out his own reputation with the ladies," he told Arthur later.

"I doubt he means anything serious," Cleo said with composure. "I've no fortune and I'm sure many are calling my birth unsuitable. I'm persuaded that Lord Fenwick has no serious intentions towards me." She hoped so, certainly, as she had no intention of marrying.

EIGHT

The Almack's assembly some days later gave society much food for thought. In an environment where an unsaid thought was a waste of brain activity, gossip found fertile ground.

The first wonder was the arrival of the Duke of Winton. His presence in the rooms had become a commonplace, not to be wondered at. But on his arm was the Duchess of Winton. Since Her Grace was well-known to prefer the society of her roses to the society of the *ton*, her appearance this evening must mean something. Observers thought they knew quite well what it meant, and those few who still doubted that His Grace was in the market for a bride were silenced at last.

The Duchess, charming in lavender silk, scanned the assembly and declared, "Isn't this nice? I vow I could do this several times a year." She greeted the patronesses with an airy wave, not at all intimidated by their status as society's gatekeepers. "Drummond-Burrell, dreadful woman," she murmured to Justin, who had come with them. "Oh, but there's Countess Lieven. I must have a word with her, and then you must point out to me all the girls Arthur has been dancing with."

"I won't point, Aunt Phyllida. You must follow the subtle inclinations of my head," Justin chided her with a grin.

"That's what I meant, you silly boy."

They were joined by Countess Lieven, with two young ladies in tow. The young men must perforce dance, and the Countess engaged the Duchess in conversation and found her a comfortable chair.

The Duchess was kept tolerably well amused while her escorts danced; many old friends stopped by to greet her and catch her up on the *on dits* of the season. They also tried subtly to extract information from her regarding her own family's potential expansion, but not so subtly that she was unaware of it. Well able to defend herself against impertinent curiosity, the Duchess enjoyed the exchanges hugely.

Amesbury joined her after several dances, indicating to her the various debutantes of the season and Arthur's reaction to them. "And Miss Harwell?" the Duchess asked.

"Mrs. and Miss Harwell are not here yet," Justin informed her. "You'll know it when they arrive by the swarm of young men converging on the entryway."

"I look forward to it," she said. "Oh, and there's Lavinia Cholmondeley-Jones," she added, spotting a crony across the room. "Do fetch her for me and then you can go about your own business, since we'll be talking gardening, which I know you young men find tedious."

This office performed, Justin went back to his preferred pursuits, dancing with several of the young ladies of the season, chatting with them and their swains, and seeing that Arthur spent more time on the dance floor than in the corner with his notebook.

And then the Harwells arrived. As Amesbury had predicted, a swarm of young men moved toward the party at the doorway. Amesbury, with the Duke at the punch bowl, murmured, "Damnation!"

Because Mrs. and Miss Harwell were not alone. Accompanying them was a hearty squire who looked sheepish in knee-breeches. Miss Harwell was quickly swept into the dance, while Mister and Mrs. Harwell chatted with Lady Sefton.

The Duke gave his friend a quizzical look. "What confounds you so?"

"Harwell is with them!" he said.

"I'm unfamiliar with the man. What is wrong with him?"

"Nothing, to be sure! But he's here!" Seeing Arthur's incomprehension, Justin continued. "His distaste for London society is as well known as your mother's. And yet, here he is. And here she is. It looks, it must look, like prearrangement. Old friend, expectations are being raised. You must prevent your mother –"

Across the room at the chaperons' chairs, the stir at the door was noticed. "Ah, there's Harwell," exclaimed Mrs. Cholmondeley-Jones to the Duchess. "You must speak with him. He's very sound on succession houses." She waved at the Harwells and called in a penetrating, fluting voice, "Yoo-hoo! Henry! Come over here, man."

At the punch bowl, Arthur awaited the completion of Justin's sentence. Finally, he prompted, "Prevent my mother…?"

Justin sighed as the Harwells joined the Duchess and Mrs. Cholmondeley-Jones. "Never mind."

Cleo was enjoying herself. The gypsy wagon had made two more trips to Newmarket, and the Coopers' fund was growing respectable. Cleo could almost picture the country seat with tenant farms that was the ultimate goal. Something rather like the Buffords' Grange, she thought. Rents and funds in the Consols. It was coming closer every day.

Now permitted to waltz, Cleo had waltzed several times, as well as taking part in a cotillion and a country dance. Thanks to Mister Amesbury's tutelage, she was well able to dance and converse simultaneously, and thanks to her indifference to matrimony, she was able to maintain an ease of manner that the marriage-minded young debutantes could only dream of matching.

Her progress around the rooms, on the dance floor and in sociable conversation, was under observation.

George Deaver, rising star of the Tories, watched Cleo dance gracefully with a dashing young officer in regimentals, laughingly deflect the heavy-handed gallantry of a superannuated earl, and chat easily with Lady Castlereagh and Mrs. Drummond-Burrell, the most daunting of the Almack's patronesses, and knew that he had found his political hostess at last.

Accordingly, he sought out a patroness to assist him, and Cleo soon found herself hailed by Countess Lieven. The Russian Ambassador's wife had in her train a young man of sober countenance and pleasant demeanor. "Miss Cooper!" the Countess began, "you must allow me to make known to you Mister George Deaver. He is something in the government, a Tory if that matters to you, and Mister Canning describes him as a very useful man. He also dances well, making him equally useful here."

Mister Deaver bowed and solicited a dance. The dance thus gained was the supper dance, allowing him to take Cleo down to supper and engage her in conversation. The experience exceeded his expectations, and he went home that night well satisfied with his progress, for Miss Cooper was both intelligent and amiable.

Deaver was not a stupid man; he was quite aware that subjects he found fascinating were less so to his peers in society, especially among the fashionable fribbles to be found at Almack's. He was seldom able to speak for more than five minutes about the topics of greatest interest to himself before the subject was changed to something less substantial. The gowns on display, the connections being made, who was in pursuit of whom. He was used to such treatment by now.

But Miss Cooper listened with apparently unflagging interest. Corn laws and enclosure acts alike kept her interest and drew from her salient questions. Deaver was quite impressed with her ability to maintain the appearance of interest in his conversation, a skill that would prove invaluable in his future plans for her. And that she took the effort to display such a skill indicated to him that she was not averse to his suit.

Viscount Fenwick was less satisfied with the evening. He had hoped to further his acquaintance with Miss Cooper, but had succeeded in obtaining only one dance and that a quadrille. He'd had hopes of gaining the supper dance, but that meddlesome Countess interfered with the notion, pairing Miss Cooper off with that prosy bore Deaver. "As if a lively gal like Miss Cooper would care a rap for such a fellow," he complained to Wainwright. "Look at those paltry shirt points!"

"And yet, there is a solidity about him," Wainwright said, "that might appeal to some. Don't sell him short, by any means. Never know what appeals to the ladies."

To add to Fenwick's discomfort, Miss Dumphreys was present, and several times he caught her looking at him with an expression of bewilderment and hurt. Dash it, she was such a pretty little thing; he wished she'd stop looking at him like that. Made a chap feel like the greatest beast in nature.

In the carriage returning to Winton House, Justin asked the Duchess, "So how did you find Miss Harwell?"

"She seemed a very sweet girl," she replied hazily.

"Did you have much conversation with her?" he persisted.

"Very well, you have found me out!" she said. "I am the worst mother who ever lived, and I allowed myself to be distracted by Miss Harwell's papa." She turned to the Duke and clutched his sleeve. "Oh, but Arthur, *do* say I might have a pinery! Mister Harwell assures me that it is not at all complicated."

"You know you have free rein in the gardens, Mama," he told her.

She bounced slightly in her seat. "And so I shall, then. The vicar's wife has become so puffed up with conceit about those orchids of hers." She waved a hand graciously. " 'Do try some fresh pineapple, Mrs. Tooting. We grow them here at the Court, don't you know?' "

Arthur smiled. "I hope you can bear Mrs. Tooting patiently, since I believe it takes several years for pineapple to come to fruit."

"Once I know her comeuppance is well in train, I can bear anything," she promised. "And I didn't entirely neglect my maternal duties. I had some conversation with Miss Harwell, and found her charming. Some girls would become unbearable if they'd attained the social success she has done, but she remains quite unspoiled by it."

***

Cleo came down to breakfast the next morning to find two floral offerings awaiting her. "Oh!" she exclaimed. She took the cards from the arrangements and took a seat at the table.

Miss Merryhew and Han, not having had a late night dancing, had preceded her to the table and were finishing their breakfasts. "You sound surprised," Merry said.

"I suppose I am," Cleo admitted. "I am seeking social acceptance, not a husband. But I know of no way to make that plain."

"Nor should you," Merry said. "If any gentlemen come up to scratch, you have only to refuse them, after all. But tactfully, of course."

Cleo examined her cards and relaxed slightly. "I don't think I need to be concerned," she said. "This one is from Viscount Fenwick, and I am led to understand that he is a here-and-thereian. His attention will soon turn to some other young female. And this is from Mister Deaver."

"Deaver?"

"Oh, what a useful man!" Cleo said. "He knows all about English agriculture and industry. Anything we need to know to establish ourselves as landed gentry, he will be able to assist us."

"Sending flowers is not the sign of a useful man, but of an interested man," Merry cautioned her.

The Coopers were home to callers that morning, with Aunt Lucy in attendance for countenance and advice. Judging by the overcrowding in the small parlor, the event was quite a success. That useful, interested man was there, chatting easily with Miss Merrihew about his office and his patron and his plans for the future. Across the room, Viscount Fenwick scowled at Deaver and attempted to flirt with Miss Cooper under the satiric eye of her younger brother. And a new addition, the Honorable Mister Wilbur Morton, broke in frequently urging Miss Cooper to describe her travels.

Morton was a young man, not yet twenty, whose undeniably well-made clothes were worn with an air of dishevelment. In place of a cravat, he sported an enormous neckerchief worn in a floppy bow, and his long fair hair continually fell over his eyes.

The arrival of the Duke of Winton, the Honorable Mister Amesbury, and the Incomparable Miss Harwell broke up this grouping, with the gentlemen already in attendance being brought to the awareness that they were in danger of overstaying the correct thirty minutes for a morning call.

Cleo's three suitors (if suitor was indeed what Mister Morton was) took their leave and the reformed group settled in for a comfortable coze. Mister Amesbury, lips twitching with amusement, said, "I see you've acquired Mister Morton, Miss Cooper."

"What an extraordinary young man!" she exclaimed. "I don't recall being introduced to him before he showed up here today, and I have no notion why he came!"

"He came to borrow your travels," Justin explained to her. At her puzzled look, he elaborated. "Wilbur Morton, fourth son of the Earl of Meriton, and a young man until recently at a total loss for what to do with himself. Lately, however, he has decided to set himself up in rivalry to Lord Byron. He is hampered in this endeavor not only by a lack of poetic ability, but also by the fact that he's never been anywhere. I believe his latest grand opus is to be called *Tales Of The Levant.*"

Cleo laughed heartily. "How absurd to write about things you have no experience with. Why, one might tell him anything!"

Han's eyes grew wide. "Why, so one could. I say, what sport!" He sat back in his seat, deep in fantasy.

The Duke, who had been brought to the pursuit of science by an insatiable curiosity, could never leave a puzzle unaddressed. He said, "Miss Cooper, if you don't mind telling, why do you call your butler 'General'?"

The Countess of Dorwood, who never noticed what people called their butlers, asked, "Do they so?"

"Yes," Arthur told her. "I'd heard it before, and again today."

The guests turned questioning eyes on Cleo. She said, "Well, you see, we must call him something and we don't know what his name is."

"Don't know his name!" Aunt Lucy exclaimed. "How did you come to hire a man who wouldn't tell you his name?"

"We didn't hire him so much as we collected him," Cleo said. "And he couldn't tell us his name because he doesn't know it himself. We found him on a battlefield, you see."

Felicity gasped and put her hand to her throat. "A battlefield!"

"Oh, the battle was long over," Cleo told her cheerfully, "so there was no danger."

Fascinated, Justin asked, "Where did this battle take place, Miss Cooper, and why were you there?"

"It was on the Peninsula," Cleo said. "It was several years ago, and I'm not perfectly certain if we were in Spain or Portugal. But we were traveling, and you know there's a war there."

"We know," Arthur said faintly.

"What were your parents thinking, taking you there?" Aunt Lucy expostulated.

"Dear Mrs. Cooper was several years dead by then," Merry said.

"Yes, and Papa always said that a small mobile group might easily avoid an army, which is a monstrous great thing that moves very slowly," Cleo said with a smile. "And so it proved, because we never found ourselves in an actual battle."

"How fortunate," said Justin. "So. The battle was long over?"

"Indeed it was. Long enough that the looters had already been there and gone. I don't suppose that you are aware, but after a battle, the local residents move through the site and collect any useful items they find. One can scarcely blame them, considering what has become of their own property when a war passes over it." Cleo's smile was gone. She was staring into the distance, remembering the sights of that battlefield. "It's… rather terrible to see."

There was silence for a moment.

"But I heard a sound!" Han exclaimed.

"Indeed you did," Cleo said brightly. "It was Han who first noticed that one of the bodies was actually still alive."

"And that was the General?" Arthur asked.

"So it was," Cleo said. "He'd sustained a head wound and was near death. We couldn't just leave him there, so we took him with us."

"Good Samaritans, in fact," Justin said.

"What else could we do?" Cleo asked. "However, looters loot the bodies as well, so our wounded man had no uniform nor anything to tell us who he was. Papa joked that he was surely an important general and we would be well-rewarded for his care, though of course I suspect that even the most disastrously defeated army would keep track of their generals, and no doubt he was a common soldier. But we started calling him the General. Then when he recovered, we learned that he had lost his memory and had no notion who he was."

"Is he at least an Englishman?" Aunt Lucy asked.

"He speaks English," Cleo assured her.

"As well as French, Spanish, Portuguese, and Italian," Han reminded her.

"He could be French?!" Felicity squeaked in alarm.

"Frenchmen are much like Englishmen," Cleo told her. "They are not all ogres simply because we are at war with them."

"A broad minded viewpoint," Justin said.

"Inarguable, rather," Arthur replied.

At this point, the General entered with a tea tray and conversation turned to other matters. The guests watched the Coopers' butler from the corners of their eyes, but there was nothing in his appearance to denote any particular nationality.

In the ducal town coach after the visit, Felicity exclaimed, "What an intrepid woman! I should have been terrified every day to live as she has done!"

"And what an odd, scrambling upbringing those children must have had," Justin agreed. "What could Miles Cooper have been thinking, taking them across the Peninsula? 'An army is easily avoided', indeed. Such a man should not have had children in his care."

"You think so?" the Duke asked. "For myself, I was struck by the instinctive generosity he must have instilled in them. A family of foreigners crossing a war-torn land, and take in a wounded stranger?

91

'What else could we have done?' Miss Cooper asked. Surely that is to be admired."

"Perhaps," his friend replied doubtfully. "But they should never have been there in the first place."

"And yet, I try to put myself in his position. I'm standing on the shore of a land at war, and I'm confident in my ability to cross the country without encountering an army. Could I do so?" Arthur wondered.

"I hope you would not be so foolhardy," Justin countered.

Felicity placed a hand on Arthur's sleeve. "I hope not, also," she said timidly.

Arthur shook his head and laughed. "What absurdity we are talking!" he said with a laugh. The conversation turned to upcoming social events. Arthur joined in the talk and tried to ignore the growing feeling of admiration and envy for a man whose impetuosity had caused his ouster from polite society.

***

The following day, the Coopers entertained a distinguished guest. Dukes, lords and honorables Cleo could receive with aplomb, but she was thrown into a ferment when the General approached her and murmured, "Mister Thomas Lawrence has called, Miss. He is in the morning room."

"Gracious! Mister Lawrence!" Cleo whipped off her apron, for she had been inventorying the stillroom, and patted at her hair. "I'll be right there. Fetch Han, for he'll wish to meet Mister Lawrence. He's on the roof, I believe. I mean Han is on the roof, for of course Mister Lawrence is in the morning room."

She hurried to the morning room to find her guest facing the wall, studying the painting of Mama as Athena. Mister Lawrence, premier portraitist of the age, heard the door and turned, saying, "This is excel - !" and stopped as he saw her.

Cleo sketched a curtsey. "Mister Lawrence? How do you do, sir? I am Cleo Cooper."

"You needn't tell me that, nor anyone else who ever met your father," Lawrence told her.

Cleo gestured to the chairs and they sat. "You know I knew your father?" the painter continued.

"Indeed I do!" Cleo assured him warmly. "We got English periodicals overseas, often very late, but whenever your name

92

appeared, Papa would say, 'My old friend Lawrence is making news again', and read us the piece."

"And now the periodicals have brought me here," Lawrence told her. "I saw in the Society column that Miss Cleo Cooper, daughter of Miles and Belinda Cooper, was being sponsored by the Countess of Dorwood. And just last week, my old friend Kendall returned from abroad raving about the Miles Cooper frescoes he'd seen in Venice." He gestured at the paintings on the wall. "Your father was a good painter when I knew him, and I see he grew to be a great one."

"I think he was," Cleo agreed, "and only wish more people had thought so while he was alive."

"I would like to see your father's work exhibited at the Royal Academy," Lawrence said. "I wish it could have happened sooner, but this work deserves recognition. If you'd be willing to loan some of his paintings?"

"We only have five!" This from Han, who had just entered.

Cleo hastily performed introductions. "Mister Lawrence, this is my brother Han."

"Only five!" Lawrence exclaimed. "The rest I suppose were sold in Europe? Perhaps collectors might find them now that this infernal war is winding down – "

"Well over eighty of them vanished with that scoundrel Marcuse," Han grumbled.

Lawrence looked an inquiry at Cleo. "Oh, it was the shabbiest thing!" she told him. "It was just as Papa was finishing those frescoes you spoke of. We'd met an Englishman in Venice who called himself Baron Marcuse. He seemed quite a nice gentleman and presented himself as a patron of the arts. Papa planned to move household to Sicily for a time, and Baron Marcuse offered his services and the services of his own ship. All our goods were packed into the ship, which sailed off and was never seen again. We had gone on ahead, Marcuse claimed business was detaining him, but the ship never arrived at Sicily nor anywhere else that we could determine."

"Did the ship sink, perhaps?" Lawrence asked in dismay. Eighty Miles Cooper paintings on the bottom of the Mediterranean.

"I almost wish it had," Cleo said. "There's a reason Han calls Marcuse a scoundrel. Marcuse, we later learned, was not his real name. And from friends in Venice we heard of various other swindles he had been involved in. Our shipment included Papa's payments from works he had performed in Venice, in gold. No, Mister Lawrence, we were taken in, and our property was stolen."

"I'm sorry to hear that," Lawrence said sincerely. "For your own sake and the sake of the world of art."

NINE

As the season progressed, Cleo was now well-established among the *ton*. She was more popular with the young gentlemen than with the young ladies, and was sensible enough to realize that not all the young men eager to speak with her were actually courting. Many of them simply wanted to hear about her travels.

"After all," said Duddy Wainwright at Mrs. Portier's rout, "Our fathers were allowed the Grand Tour to travel about and see something of other lands. These days if a fellow wants to travel, he must purchase a set of colors. And that comes with the requirement to thrash about in the muck and the dust and kill people, even. Not to be thought of."

"With the Emperor presiding over Elba now, your way to the Continent is open," Cleo suggested.

"Oh, so I suppose," Duddy said doubtfully. "But one is out of the way of it now. There's getting there, you see, and no way to do so other than by boat, which are such chancy things. And then, once there, I greatly fear that the lands have been much knocked about, the war lasting so long. Better to let things settle first. The more intrepid will be the first to go and they will report back on the best routes, I daresay."

"I should set myself up as a tour leader, perhaps," Cleo suggested jokingly.

Wainwright was much struck by this. "I say, what an excellent notion!"

Peter's arrival rescued Cleo from this absurd conversation. They were established as friendly acquaintances by now. Peter explained privately to Cleo that he would make up one of her court, but that he dared not appear to be seriously courting her or any other young lady, lest older relatives feel compelled to inquire into his family background. "I can't claim 'good blood' on even one side of the family tree," he pointed out. "Actors and performers begetting actors and performers, back no doubt to the days of Lionheart. Utterly ineligible."

"I don't need any more suitors," Cleo told him loftily. "I already have two and very fine they are."

"Deaver will make something of himself," Peter said, since he knew very well of whom she spoke. "But Fenwick? He'll never be other than a fool. Why Miss Dumphreys is still wearing the willow for that addlepate is the mystery."

For indeed, Miss Dumphreys was taking her loss of Fenwick's affections to heart. So altered was her demeanor that even the Duke noticed. Lillian Dumphreys was one of the first young ladies Arthur had danced with, and well he recalled how silly he'd found her. But he also recalled the bright cheerfulness she had displayed early in the season. Now she was listless and unsmiling. She seemed less foolish now, perhaps because she rarely opened her lips to say anything.

What he found surprising, though, was the realization that visible sadness made a young lady subject to the mockery and scorn of society. Some of the remarks Arthur heard, delivered as jokes, shocked him with their careless brutality. He doubted the original Esquimaux could be any less gentle to a weak member of their tribe.

And she didn't even know why she had been rejected! That seemed to Arthur the unfairest thing of all. He thought of discussing the matter with Miss Harwell, but that avenue too would be purveying club gossip to a lady, and thus one of those things which are not done. Could nothing be done? One evening at Almack's, he thought he saw a way.

Miss Dumphreys was there, dragged unwilling by her mama. And Fenwick was there too, in fruitless pursuit of Miss Cooper. Arthur saw Miss Dumphreys flinch several times and knew that she must be overhearing some of those mocking remarks, knew too that she was probably meant to overhear them.

That gave him a notion. He had waltzed with Miss Harwell, and then surrendered her to another member of her court. Miss Dumphreys, he saw, left the dance floor to the ladies' retiring room, perhaps to pin a torn flounce, but more likely to escape the comments that bedeviled her.

He wandered to the edge of the dance floor, motioning Amesbury to follow him. A flash of red hair and blue silk from the corner of his eye informed him that Miss Dumphreys was about to return. "Tell me, Justin," he said clearly, "is Miss Dumphreys truly as easy to browbeat as Fenwick believes?"

Justin gave him a puzzled look. "Difficult to say," he said slowly. "She did agree with the Viscountess about the benefit of them all living under one roof."

"But perhaps she was merely being polite to an older woman," Arthur argued, "and would actually dislike the scheme as much as Fenwick himself did."

"Perhaps," Justin said. "I suppose we'll never know."

A young lady strode past him then, head high, eyes flashing. It took a moment for him to realize that the Amazon in blue silk was Miss Dumphreys. He turned to his friend. "Arthur! You did that on purpose!"

"Did what?" Arthur asked, the picture of innocence.

Some time later, the Viscount Fenwick was seen to be waltzing with Miss Dumphreys. The young lady was doing all the talking, while Fenwick simply nodded, a foolish smile on his face.

"She's looking rather masterful this evening, don't you think?" Arthur asked Justin.

Justin just shook his head. "I'm seeing unexpected depths in you," he replied.

Several days later, a notice appeared in the Gazette, announcing the engagement of Charles, Viscount Fenwick and Miss Lillian Dumphreys.

Walking in the park with Felicity, Cleo expressed relief at the news. "I couldn't seem to hint the silly fellow away. I was afraid I was going to have to become cruel, but somehow it's all worked out. I wonder what caused the rift between them in the first place?"

Felicity chuckled. "Oh, Lillian told me about it. It's so droll. She happened to overhear gentlemen gossiping about the matter – and gentlemen do gossip, don't let them tell you otherwise. And as it happens, weeks ago she had been talking with Fenwick's mama at Almack's and the Viscountess spoke as if she intended to remain in the manor when her son marries. Lillian nodded and agreed as anyone would, and Fenwick overheard the exchange and took that to mean that Lillian really did agree with the old harridan. And of course he wants his mama shifted to the dower house, anyone would."

Cleo laughed heartily to hear this. "Whatever did he expect? That a young lady would get into a fractious debate with an older woman? At Almack's? And that older woman the mother of the man she hoped to receive an offer from?"

"We must remember," Felicity said generously, "that he really isn't particularly clever. Neither is Lillian, for that matter, but she's well enough to be able to take good care of him. They will suit very well, in fact. But you have lost a suitor."

"Lost and pray never to find again," Cleo said.

While the young ladies strolled in the park, Miss Merrihew sat in the Countess' parlor. The topic was the same. Young ladies and their suitors.

"There's Fenwick gone," said Lucinda with a sigh. "And I know Cleo could have had him if she would, for he was making quite a play for her."

"It's for the best," Merry insisted. "He never could have made her happy, and the whole business with Miss Dumphreys appears to have been some sort of lovers' quarrel anyway."

"Does she mean to accept Deaver?" Lucy prodded.

"I don't know," Merry said mendaciously. "Though I suspect not."

"But what is she about then?" Lucy asked. "The season will soon be over and nothing achieved for her establishment."

Merry knew quite well that marriage was not in Cleo's mind at all, but also knew better than to say so. In this society, a young woman's claim to be uninterested in marriage would not be believed, and were it to be believed, would label her a complete zany. "Oh, there's no rush," she said vaguely. "Cleo wants to get her footing in society before she thinks of establishing herself. Mister Deaver is a well enough man in his way, but I doubt they would suit. His interest in politics is obsessive, and Cleo has little interest in the matter herself."

"No couples have perfect matches of temperament and interests," Lucy said. "I hope she's not setting her standards impossibly high."

"I don't think so," Merry said. "And if she loved Deaver, she would tolerate his politics. You must remember, dear, that Cleo grew up in a home where her model was a true love match. It would be difficult for her to accept anything less."

Lady Sylvia, who had been knitting furiously and scowling silently, exclaimed, "Folly! If that chit is taking her mother as an example of how to establish herself, the sooner you rid her of that notion, the better!"

Merry bristled. "I know that Belle's marriage might be considered imprudent by worldly standards, but I know this as well. Since I've been here and gone about in society, I've seen no woman, however brilliantly matched, who is as happy as she was."

Lucinda hastened to calm the discussion. "I'm glad to hear you say so," she said, "and it relieves me to know that my sister was happy with the life she chose. But do consider, Merry! Cleo is two and twenty! If she's not to be on the shelf entirely, time is of the essence. Is there no young man she seems to prefer?"

"None that I can see her accepting before the season's end," Merry said bluntly.

"How provoking!" the Countess said, and fell into deep thought. Then she smiled. "I have it!" she exclaimed. "You must all come with us to Bath this summer."

"Bath?"

"Yes, indeed. It's not so fashionable as Brighton these days, but it's also less rackety. A smaller society, with a delightful casualness of manner. I think Bath might be just the answer."

"I don't know," Miss Merrihew said doubtfully. "I believe that Cleo plans to spend the summer traveling around the country, looking for an establishment to purchase for Han."

"Oh, no!" the Countess cried. "My niece and nephew to dwindle to cottagers? I can't bear the notion."

"No such thing," Merry replied. "A small gentleman's estate, with a few farms and a bit of woods and gardens."

"Oh, indeed. That doesn't sound too dreadful."

Merry smiled and said nothing. She and the Coopers had deliberately not stated a specific amount for their legacy from their father, so that it might be subtly boosted as their scheme progressed. Now it was described vaguely as a 'competence'. Should they continue to have success, they would start to describe is as an 'easy competence'. As for a 'small gentleman's estate', that was open to a great deal of interpretation.

***

Arthur was finding his entry into society surprisingly enjoyable. Oh, it wasn't serious, and it didn't stretch a man's mind to engage in the endless round of socializing, but as an occasional break from more intellectual pursuits, it made a nice change. He thought he was doing rather well, in fact.

At least that's what he thought until the afternoon when Amesbury came by to talk. He found Arthur in his book room, which was usual. The two friends discussed past and upcoming social activities, which was also usual. But Justin had something on his mind. Finally, standing and striding back and forth, he asked, "Arthur, are you going to offer for Miss Harwell?"

There was a long silence.

"Well?"

"I'm not sure," Arthur admitted.

"If you're not going to offer for her, hedge off now," Justin said.

"I don't understand," Arthur said.

"Stop paying so much attention to her."

"I enjoy her company. She's a friend."

Justin threw up her hands in exasperation. "She's not in Town seeking a friend. She's here to establish herself. I know Harwell has already refused at least five offers for her."

"Five!" Arthur was astonished.

"Oh, some of them were obviously ineligible," Justin admitted. "Gazetted fortune hunters and foolish young men intoxicated by her beauty. But in the eyes of society, you have been paying court to her. If you don't mean to offer for her, you must make that clear. Spend more time in the company of other young women and less time with Miss Harwell."

"I don't know if I'm going to offer for her or not!" Arthur exclaimed. "You said if I did as you directed I would find myself preferring one young lady and form an attachment."

"And have you not?" Justin said, looking closely at his friend.

"I certainly prefer Miss Harwell to the other young ladies of the season," Arthur said. "But an attachment? What does that feel like?"

Justin stopped. "I can't say," he said at last. "I suppose it is different for everyone. But the season progresses. You must make up your mind."

"I hadn't realized there was a deadline," Arthur grumbled.

"There isn't, not really," Justin said. "Look at me, I've been on the town for years and still unattached. And even men who are actively seeking a bride don't always find one in a season."

"So what's the problem then?" Arthur was deeply perplexed.

Justin sighed. "If you're not going to offer for her, you should hedge off now to avoid insulting Miss Harwell. Once bets start being laid in the betting books at the club, then if you decide not to marry her, she will be deemed to have failed, making her a figure of fun."

"Oh. I hadn't realized."

"Which is why I'm explaining it to you."

Arthur nodded. "You've given me something to think about, certainly. I forget sometimes how cruel society can be."

The Duke was abstracted at dinner that evening. He and his mother dined alone. The Ramseys of Winton had never adopted the modern scrambling manners of some aristocratic families, who would blithely discuss the most personal of matters in the presence of servants, so conversation was general and desultory.

But as the Duchess rose to leave the table, she asked, "You're not really interested in the port tonight, are you?"

"Not at all," said the Duke promptly. "Filthy stuff."

Tolliver bore without a flinch this slur on the fine vintage port laid down by His Grace's father over thirty years ago, because he realized instinctively that great things were in motion.

"Then come talk to me," the Duchess said, and she and her son left the dining room together.

As the door closed behind them, the first footman said, "Now there's a queer start! What to make of it, eh?"

Tolliver said repressively, "It is no concern of yours, James." The Family would be allowed privacy in their own home until time for the tea tray, and this latest intriguing clue could be debated in the butler's pantry with Pelton and perhaps Mrs. Quinn the housekeeper.

In the drawing room, the Duchess took her usual chair by the fire and turned to her son. "Something is on your mind, dear. Please say it's not a planet or an equation."

Arthur smiled slightly and took a seat in the other chair. "It's neither of those things. It's just that Justin came by today and asked me if I was going to offer for Miss Harwell."

"What did you tell him?" the Duchess asked, quite interested.

"That I didn't know."

"Oh."

Arthur leaned forward and clasped his hands. "Mama, what do you think?"

"I?! It's not my decision."

101

"But what do you think of Miss Harwell?"

The Duchess was torn. She could see a life for her son with Miss Harwell without a sense of dread or horror, but with just the faintest niggling bit of unease. "She's a beautiful girl, of course," she said, buying for time. "And with a very sweet nature. She's not at all stupid and would make any man a nice wife. How do you feel about her?"

"I like her," Arthur admitted. "I like her quite a bit."

"That's more than many could say, even on their wedding day," the Duchess said.

"When you married my father – ?" the Duke asked. He didn't know how to finish the question.

"I barely knew him," his mother told him. "Things were very different in those days and it was quite the usual thing for a young lady's husband to be chosen for her."

"Did you want to marry him?" Arthur asked. He felt a sense of surprise to realize he'd never thought to ask these questions before.

"I wanted to marry, of course," the Duchess said. "And your father was a brilliant match. I didn't dislike the notion, don't think that for a moment. I just really...didn't know what I felt about it, other than that it was my duty."

"Did you come to like him? Eventually, I mean."

"Arthur! Of course I did!"

"I thought as much. You were quite distraught when he died."

"I was most fond of your father! One comes to be fond of a person, you know, when you're partners in all things, when you have children together."

"Not every wife cares for her husband," Arthur said darkly. "This I have seen. Some of them despise their mates, and some are simply indifferent."

"I'm afraid you are right," the Duchess admitted. "But some of the worst marriages I know of began with the pair wildly in love, so there's just no knowing, is there?"

Arthur sighed. "There's no science to it at all. It seems a total gamble."

"And I know how you dislike gambling," his mother said sympathetically. She leaned over and squeezed his clasped hands. "But my dear Arthur, you know you must marry."

"I know," said Arthur. He knew he had a lot to think about. He was still thinking the next evening, when the decision was made for him.

It was after dinner when Arthur went to White's. He had a vague notion that he would find Justin there and they could continue their discussion on the pluses and minuses of Arthur offering for Miss Harwell.

As he entered the club, a wave of hearty laughter washed over him. A number of club regulars, he saw, were standing in a convivial group, glasses in hand, obviously enjoying their conversation. When he arrived, however, the laughter died and the group broke up, some to the card room, some murmuring about a late supper. The departure of the chattering crowd revealed that they had been grouped around White's betting book.

With a sense of foreboding, the Duke approached the book and flipped it open.

And there it was. Lord Alvanley bet Mister Quillon that the Incomparable Miss Harwell would bring the Duke Of Winton up to scratch.

How vulgar! Staring at the book, Arthur felt a sudden wave of an unfamiliar emotion. It took him a moment to recognize it as pure rage.

Struggling to maintain his composure, the Duke remained at the book, idly flipping the pages. He noted in passing that Peter Barton of the Almack's waiter bet had been betting lately on horse races. If his memory was correct, these horses succeeded against long odds. Mister Barton must have an encyclopedic knowledge of horse flesh.

Feeling that his facial expression was under control, the Duke turned from the book, ordered a brandy and took a comfortable chair in front of the fire. He sat lost in thought and was given a wide berth. Members of the laughing group were too self-conscious to approach him, and other members were used to the Duke's abstractions; it usually portended a scientific puzzle. But this evening's puzzle was a personal one.

Hedge off before society was betting on the matter, Justin had advised. It was now too late for that. To fail to offer now would expose Miss Harwell to some very ill-natured gossip. Of course, Miss Harwell was not Miss Dumphreys. She was the Toast of the Season and would always have hopeful suitors. But Arthur knew

103

enough about society now to know that there would be many who would glory in seeing a young lady so beautiful, so popular, and so successful taken down a peg. It would be deuced unpleasant for her.

Very well, then. Arthur reminded himself he had entered society with the intent to gain a wife. He had begun the endeavor with a list of qualities he was looking for, and Miss Harwell met all the criteria on the list. To hedge off now would not be the act of a gentleman, and would expose a genuinely nice young lady to unmerited derision. Seeing the betting book tonight was a signal, he concluded. It was time for him stop dithering and make a decision. It was time for him to offer for Miss Harwell.

Decision made, he stood. "Amesbury not in tonight?" he asked the room in general.

"There's a mill tomorrow in Hungerford," someone called out. "He's off to that."

"Ah. Thank you," said the Duke and took his leave. He would see Mister Harwell tomorrow.

TEN

Tolliver handed the Duke his hat and cane, and bowed him out the front door. As soon as the door closed, Pelton appeared mysteriously at his elbow.

"It's today, Mister Tolliver," Pelton said softly and significantly.

"Ah, indeed?"

"Depend upon it. Three coat changes before he finally settled on the Bath superfine. A young man in great turmoil of mind, I give you my word."

Tolliver eyed the ceiling with fervor. "May you be correct, Mister Pelton."

"I suppose John Coachman will confirm where His Grace went?" Pelton asked hopefully.

"Now, you should know better than that. His Grace walked, of course."

Pelton sighed. "Perhaps a duchess will break him of that common habit."

Tolliver frowned. "A proper duchess would not so presume," he said repressively. "If His Grace does it, it cannot be common."

"To be sure, Mister Tolliver." Pelton made a noiseless departure.

At the Harwell townhouse, the butler favored the Duke of Winton with a slight smile that said he was recognized as a friend of the family. "The ladies are in the morning room, Your Grace." He made a move to lead the way.

"Ah, but..." the Duke stammered. The butler turned and raised an inquiring brow. "Actually, I'm here to see Mister Harwell."

"Oh, indeed! This way, if you please." The Duke was led to a ground floor apartment, which was identified as "the library, Your Grace." In fact, it was a comfortable sitting room with several shelves of modern novels and horticultural journals. "I will inform Mister Harwell you are here. May I get you a drink, sir?"

"No. Thank you, no." As the door closed silently, the Duke paced the room quickly several times, then took a seat on the very

105

edge of an overstuffed chair. He soon heard footsteps clattering down the stairs and Harwell breezed into the library.

"Ah, Winton!" Harwell greeted him. "You bring those cuttings your mother promised?"

Arthur sprang to his feet. "No! Was I supposed to – I'm sorry, I haven't spoken to my mother yet today."

Harwell laughed heartily and waved Arthur back to his seat. "Pardon me, Duke. I was joking. Unfair of me, I know you must be nervous as a cat in a windmill. No, I know you're not here about your mama's cuttings. Have a pretty fair idea of what you are here about, eh?" He gave Arthur a significant look.

"I suppose you must," Arthur said, fighting the urge to stammer. "The fact is…" He took a deep breath and continued in a rush, "Iamheretoaskyourpermissiontopaymyaddressestoyourdaughter!"

"There!" said Harwell encouragingly. "Wasn't so hard, was it?"

Arthur sat back with a sigh. "I've never done this before, you see."

"I guessed as much," Harwell said. He took a seat across from Arthur. "And you certainly have my permission to speak with Felicity. I can't speak for her, the decision is up to her. I think I've a fair notion what she's going to say, but will leave it to her to say it. But you have my blessing for what it's worth. And Mrs. Harwell's, of course."

"Thank you."

Harwell slapped his thighs and stood up. "I'll just send Filly along to speak with you, shall I?"

"If you would be so kind."

Harwell breezed out of the room and Arthur was once again left alone to regain his nerve. Halfway there, he reminded himself.

Upstairs in the morning room, Felicity and her mother sat decorously, at home to callers. Felicity had a piece of fancy sewing in her hands, but it was purely for show; she hadn't set a stitch in days. They were having a comfortable coze when the door opened and Mister Harwell peered around the edge.

"No old tabbies underfoot?" he asked.

Mrs. Harwell frowned reprovingly. "No, we have no callers at the moment."

"That's good." Harwell advanced into the room. "It's good because I've got Winton downstairs, come to offer for Filly!" he said triumphantly.

"Oh!" Felicity exclaimed faintly. "Oh, Papa!"

Harwell stared at her curiously. "You don't dislike it, do you, pet?"

"Oh, no, of course not," Felicity assured him. "It's just…"

"It's just that you're eaten up with nerves," her papa said sympathetically. "And it might help you to know that so is Winton. So why don't you go down there and get it over with? Put the poor fellow out of his misery, eh?"

Mrs. Harwell jumped up. "Wait!" she commanded. She scanned her daughter anxiously. "Should you change, dear? Neaten your hair?"

Felicity looked from one parent to the other. Her father took command. "You are being foolish beyond permission, ma'am," he advised his wife sternly. "Your daughter is dressed for callers, and her hair is perfectly neat. What d'ye think, that Winton would change his mind if her dress ain't grand enough? We should leave the poor fellow pacing the library while you and your silly dresser gild the lily? I'm bound it would take three quarters of an hour once you started."

He turned to Felicity. "You just run along to the library, pet," he advised her in a kind voice. Felicity took her leave then, her thoughts and emotions in a whirl.

The Duke was indeed pacing when Felicity entered the library. He turned at the sound of her entry. Seeing her sidle cautiously into the room, he exclaimed involuntarily, "Ah, don't be frightened!"

She was startled into a giggle, and they both relaxed slightly. With a slight curtsey, she answered, "I'm not frightened, Your Grace."

"Let's be comfortable with one another," he suggested. "People do this every day."

"But we don't do it every day," she said. "It might become more easy with practice."

"Did your papa tell you why I'm here?"

"Oh, yes," she said, and suddenly felt shy again.

He strode to her and took her hand. "Miss Harwell – Felicity! Do you dislike the notion?"

Eyes downcast, she murmured, "Dislike? Oh, no."

Arthur took a deep breath and spoke strongly. "Felicity? Will you do me the honor of becoming my wife?" There! He'd said it.

She looked up now. "Yes, Your Grace."

He smiled with relief and suggested, "I believe you could call me Arthur now."

"Arthur," she said.

Arthur racked his brain, wondering if he was forgetting anything. Oh, yes! He fumbled in a pocket. "I remembered a ring," he said proudly. "I hope you like sapphires; this was my grandmother's. It can be altered if the size is wrong." He produced the ring, which boasted a large, fine sapphire, and slipped it onto Felicity's finger.

"It fits perfectly," she said.

"And perhaps..." he suggested, "a kiss?"

"Oh! Oh, of course."

Their lips met briefly.

Heavy footsteps and loud throat clearing in the hall warned them they were about to be interrupted. They had moved apart when Mister Harwell entered. "Got the business done, eh?"

"Yes, Papa," Felicity said with a blush.

"Capital, capital! This calls for champagne!" He rang the bell, which in startlingly short order produced the butler. "Ask Mrs. Harwell to join us, Wandle, and bring champagne."

The celebration that followed was stilted and unnatural. Mrs. Harwell was brimming over with good will and celebratory spirits, but constrained by breeding and awe of her future son-in-law from making the exclamations that came readily to mind. One could scarcely congratulate a man to his face on his rank and wealth.

After a few moments the Duke excused himself, telling the Harwells that he must inform his mother and that he would see to the announcements. Mrs. Harwell made a dithering comment about a public announcement, some sort of celebration before the end of the season, and he agreed that such a party would be appropriate.

After he left, Mrs. Harwell embraced her daughter and burst into tears. "Oh, my dear! Duchess of Winton! I don't know if I'm on my head or my heels!"

Felicity followed her exclaiming mama back to the morning room, feeling a strange sense of unreality. She had done what she set out to do. She had made the brilliant match. Why then was she wondering 'what comes next?' She knew that, surely. The brilliant match would be followed by the brilliant wedding, and a lifetime of luxury and every good thing as the Duchess of Winton.

It didn't seem real, somehow.

***

The Duchess was still at the breakfast table when her son returned home. He sat down across from her and smiled. "I've done it, Mama."

She noted the suppressed air of excitement and thought she knew the cause. "Oh, that orbit that was troubling you? I knew you'd work it out."

Arthur laughed. "No, not an orbit. I've offered for Miss Harwell. And she's accepted."

His mother screamed, "Arthur!" and dropped her teacup. Then she scurried around the table to hug him from behind.

He laughed and patted her hand. "Are you pleased?"

"Indeed I am. My baby is all grown up!"

"I gave her Grandmama's sapphire ring," Arthur said. "And said that I would see to the announcements. I'm going to need help with that."

"Easily done," the Duchess assured him. "Oh, but there is so much to be done!"

"I suppose there is," Arthur said thoughtfully. "I had thought I had merely to propose and the deed was done, but there's much more involved, isn't there?"

"Indeed there is!" his mother said with a chuckle. "We must decide on a date, and host parties. And dear Felicity has never even seen Winton Court!"

***

"What on earth are you doing?"

Han turned from his sketch pad at the dining table to see his sister leaning over his shoulder. "I'm drawing scenes from our travels for Mister Morton," he said.

"*That* is from our travels?" Cleo said skeptically.

"Oh, indeed," Han said loftily. "I just the other day told Mister Morton about how we followed the apes of Gibraltar to their hidden lair and witnessed the Parliament of Apes. When he calls again, I'll tell him about the wise and noble legislation they enacted while we crouched behind rocks and witnessed the marvel."

Cleo held up the sketch pad. The Parliament of Apes was marvelously rendered. You could almost see from their facial expressions which apes were in opposition, and the noble apes were easily told from the corrupt and venal apes. Awed, she asked, "He can't possibly believe this, can he?"

Han crowed with laughter. "So far, he's believed every bit of nonsense I've spun. I keep thinking, this story will finally be the one that makes him realize it's all a hum. But we haven't reached that point yet. He's talking to publishers!"

Cleo flipped back through the sketch pad.

"Those are the snake-pigs of Crete," Han told her. "One of them almost killed you, but I saved you."

"Thank you for that, at least."

"I'm amazingly intrepid," Han said. "I believe in Mister Morton's verses, his hero, who is really himself, will be the doer of the great deeds."

"These are quite good," Cleo said. "Papa would have liked them." She handed the pad back to her brother. "But Han, you must tell Mister Morton that these are fantasies. And soon, if he's meeting publishers."

Han looked mutinous. Cleo sat beside him and gave him a serious look. "You really must. A private joke is one thing, but do you really want to make that young man a figure of fun to all of society? Would you really be that unkind?"

"I suppose not," Han sighed.

The door to the dining room opened and the General made a stately and soft-footed entrance. "Miss Harwell has called, Miss," he said. "She is in the morning room."

"I'll be right there," Cleo said. On her way out, she turned back and shook a finger at her brother. "Tell him," she said.

In the morning room, Felicity turned from the window as Cleo entered. She smiled tremulously and exclaimed in a rush, "Oh, Cleo, I'm going to be a duchess!"

"How wonderful!" Cleo gave Felicity a hug.

"Isn't it?" Felicity said, almost doubtfully.

"Of course it is! Why, you've attached quite the nicest man in London."

110

Felicity was much struck by this. "Thank you for that!" she said. "You know, Mama has been exclaiming and blessing herself so much over the grand estates and manors and the coronet and all those things that I was beginning to become frightened of my own future magnificence."

"You will no doubt be quite magnificent," Cleo said. "But you'll have plenty of help managing it all."

***

Amesbury was just back to his rooms and looking through invitations when the Duke was ushered in. "Arthur!" Amesbury said. "You didn't miss anything by staying in Town. I know you don't like mills anyway, and this one was a sorry excuse for an exhibition. The challenger had no business being in that ring. A worthless spectacle altogether. What have you been doing? I hope you found more amusement than I."

"Well, my morning has been quite interesting," Arthur said with pardonable pride.

"Oh?"

"I've offered for Miss Harwell. And she accepted."

The news seemed to paralyze Justin for a long moment. Finally, he said, "Arthur, are you funning?"

"Not at all," Arthur replied, nettled. "I went to the Harwell townhouse, spoke with Harwell and then with Miss Harwell, and gave her my grandmother's sapphire."

Justin sank into his favorite chair, trying to absorb this news.

"Wasn't this the whole point of my social activities these past few months?" Arthur asked. "To find and select a bride?"

Justin shook his head in wonder. "Of course," he said weakly. "I'm just… surprised, I suppose. I'd been certain that I'd need to be nipping at your heels like a herd dog before you could be brought to make an offer."

"But as you see, I could manage the business on my own," Arthur said. He took a seat and chuckled. "To be honest, I was quite proud of myself that I remembered about a ring. Without even being instructed!"

"Well!" said Justin. "This is… splendid! Yes, it's splendid! And you are to be congratulated. You've certainly borne off the catch of this or any other season."

"I have, haven't I?" Arthur said complacently.

111

Justin thought for a moment. Then he said, "Not to meddle, but have you thought about the announcement?"

"Mother was deep in composition when I left her not an hour ago."

"Well," Justin said, and could think of nothing to say but to repeat, "Splendid!"

***

Returning to Winton House, the Duke found his mother in the drawing room, pleasantly involved in wedding planning. "You just missed Mrs. Harwell," the Duchess said.

"That's a relie... I mean, what a shame," her son replied.

"Do be serious, dear. Now. The Harwells are having a ball in just two days; it's their end of the season affair. We thought the engagement could be announced there. We'll have the newspaper announcements placed to appear the next day."

Arthur nodded. "That sounds sensible."

"And I had a notion," the Duchess went on. "Since Felicity has never been to Winton Court, what about a house party?"

"A house party! It's been years since we've entertained so."

"Then it's about time we got back in the habit," his mother said. "Several weeks at the end of the season. We can invite the Harwells and Henry can give me advice on my pinery and the new succession house. And perhaps some young people, Felicity's friends, to make her feel more comfortable. Otherwise, with all the neighboring families wanting to meet her, she'd be pitchforked into a society of strangers, which can be very unnerving."

"You're full of excellent notions today," Arthur told her.

Two days then until society was informed that the Duke of Winton was off the market. The servants, of course, were already well aware.

112

ELEVEN

In a season crammed with incident (the *ton* was still discussing the visit of the Duchess of Oldenburgh and the presentation of Princess Charlotte), the Harwells' ball stood out as the fitting crown of the social whirl.

For the *ton's* most noble and eligible bachelor announced his engagement to the season's most brilliant Toast, and the hopes of many an aspiring suitor and many a doting mama of daughters were dashed at last.

As the ball began, several of Felicity's swains were searching for reasons to travel to Sussex in the summer, and several of the hopeful mamas were conning lists of who they knew in Hampshire in the vicinity of Winton Court whose hospitality they could solicit. These travel plans were smothered in the cradle just before the late supper, when Mister Harwell mounted the musicians' stand and called for attention to an announcement. When he called the Duke of Winton to the stand, the assembled crowd knew the substance of the announcement without having to hear the words.

Which was fortunate, since few not in the forefront of the crowd could hear the words. The Duke, easily able to speak with force and persuasion about planetary orbits in the lecture hall at the Royal Society, was daunted to be speaking to a milling mass of nobility and gentry who would not stop murmuring. He made his way through a set announcement that he'd been practicing all day, and Felicity stepping up to join him made the matter plain.

The Duchess, scanning the crowd, saw Justin watching the happy couple with an expression of such regret and dismay that she gasped.

She was immediately surrounded by a group of congratulating well-wishers and had to leave Justin to his misery for the time being. Moving easily through the crowd, she found the Countess of Dorwood and invited her and her niece to the house party at Winton Court. Later in the supper room, she found Miss Dumphreys, Viscount Fenwick, Baron Wainwright and Marianne Keene, and her guest list was complete.

The Duchess and her son ate supper with the Harwells, the house party was discussed at length, and the Duchess rewarded herself for all her efforts by having a good discussion with Henry Harwell about the siting of succession houses and the growing of grapes.

After supper the assembly returned to the dance floor, and the Duchess found time to seek out Justin. She found him chatting with a group of young people. "I must borrow Mister Amesbury from you," she said easily, and bore him off to a side alcove.

"What do you need, Auntie?" Justin asked.

"I need to know what you are about, and what you were thinking," the Duchess told him. "What was the idea of encouraging my son who is your best friend to offer for the girl you were in love with?"

Justin gave a groan and sagged against the wall. "I didn't know! I didn't realize... And then it was too late."

"Much too late," she told him severely. "So what are you going to do about it, eh?"

"I don't know," he admitted. "I suppose... I suppose I must avoid her in the future."

"Avoid her? She is to be Arthur's wife! You cannot avoid her. Not without avoiding Arthur as well."

"Then perhaps I must avoid Arthur," Justin said reluctantly.

"You will do no such thing!" the Duchess said. "How would that appear?"

Justin looked at her, puzzled. "I don't understand."

"Look at it as an outsider would," she advised. "What if you knew of a man who'd recently gotten married, and since getting married he was no longer seen in the company of another man who'd been his best friend all his life. How would you interpret that?"

Justin winced and nodded. "I would suppose the two had quarreled over the woman," he admitted.

She nodded. "Either that or the wife was a managing kind of female who dictated who her husband might be friends with. Those are the only two explanations I can think of, society would choose one or the other, if not both, and neither of them is at all flattering to the woman in the middle of it. How could you treat Felicity so?"

He didn't answer. She went on, fiercely, "And I will not have the world saying the Duchess of Winton is a heartless flirt, nor that

114

the Duke of Winton lives under the cat's paw. Do you hear me, I won't have it!"

"What would you have me do?" he asked tonelessly.

Her face softened. "Oh, dear boy, I don't know. You must just get over this somehow. I can't tell you how, but you see that you must."

He took a deep breath and squared his shoulders. "I must, indeed."

***

"A house party?" asked Miss Merrihew over the breakfast teacups.

"A house party," Cleo confirmed. "And Aunt Lucinda has already accepted for us. I don't know what to think about it. Will you mind staying in London with Han?"

"Not at all, dear. I think it's a wonderful idea. It certainly establishes you in society, which was after all your goal. And perhaps you can learn something about how country estates are managed, though of course you'll be seeing it on a much grander scale."

"It's not for a week yet," Cleo said. "I think we can manage one more trip to the races."

"Oh, dear," Merry said. "We have enough now, surely."

"Just once more, Merry," Cleo said coaxingly. "And then we're done. I promise." She looked at her brother, who was carefully eating toast with his left hand while sketching another of his fantastic scenes with his right. "Will you miss it?" she asked him.

Han looked up. "Miss what?"

"The gypsy life."

"Oh, that. It's well enough, I suppose," he said indifferently. "It's become a bit of a mail coach run by now, covering the same territory."

***

"So you told him?"

The battered gypsy wagon was once again on the road to Newmarket.

"Told him?" Han asked. "Oh, Morton! Yes. Well, what I said was that it made the whole gag better if he never admitted the stories were anything other than the truth."

"And he understood what you meant?" Cleo persisted.

"He certainly did," Han assured her. "His eyes got quite big for a moment, and then he laughed rather sheepishly and said 'to be sure, to be sure'. Got rather red-faced, but I didn't let on that I knew he'd been taken in, so we're playing it that he was in on the jest all along."

"Excellent. Save the poor man's pride."

"And do you know? I think he's really going to find a publisher! He tells me he's getting a lot of interest from the completed cantos. He took some of my drawings with him and hopes to get illustrated editions out of it. 'With illustrations by Hannibal Cooper', that's what the frontispiece will say!"

"Han! How splendid for you!"

"So I shall have plenty to do while you're gadding amongst the nobility," Han informed her loftily.

"I see that you will." Cleo looked about her. It was a beautiful day in early summer, not too warm. She gave a contented sigh. "Are you sure you won't miss this?"

"What, traveling about? We've traveled about our entire lives. There's no novelty to it anymore. I think you're the one who will be missing it."

"Perhaps you're right," Cleo admitted. "In society, young ladies' movements and activities are so restricted. It's hard to become accustomed to it."

Han hesitated, and then said, "But you know something that I think might be a bit of a lark? I've talked to some of the other fellows my age in the park..."

"Yes?" Cleo prompted.

Han took a deep breath and blurted, "What about me going to school?"

"School!"

"Yes, all the other fellows go to school. Some speak of Eton, others of Harrow. One is with a bunch of chaps one's own age, which is something I've never experienced in my life, and there are classes of course, but sports and activities and all manner of fun and gig. And then, don't you see, then they have all these fellows they know. I thought it sounded prime."

Cleo blinked. "Now, why didn't I think of that? Of course, the very thing. I must do some research on the matter, fees and entry requirements and so on. But it would certainly establish you, which is our goal, after all."

***

Arthur settled into the viewing stand at Newmarket with a sigh of satisfaction. He was in a state of great restlessness and hoped the races would prove a diversion.

First he had been driven from his home by a mother who appeared to have gone mad. She kept appealing to him with nonsensical questions about the house party, whether the guests would prefer a picnic or an excursion to nearby ruins, whether the guests would consider the local assemblies a nice diversion or too rustic, who they should invite to dinner, who they should invite to tea. As if he knew! That was her job, and would soon be Miss Harwell's job.

He had tried his clubs, but found everyone there wanted to congratulate him and stand him drinks; a fellow would be in a constant state of inebriation if he weren't careful. Even the Royal Society, usually a haven, proved to be full of gentlemen paying more attention to his matrimonial plans than to his scientific theories.

So the races it must be. He'd invited Justin, who turned out have other engagements, so here he was, off to the races with only his groom and valet in attendance.

Arthur looked about, knowing himself to be the most serene spectator at the race track. To Arthur, horse racing was a performance, a spectacle to enjoy much like theater or opera. Not wagering on the races allowed him to appreciate the entirety of the scene, rather than concentrating on the specific animals which would justify or blast the hopes of a gambler. A horse race was a beautiful and graceful performance, cheapened by the gambling fever that surrounded it.

Society, of course, was gambling-mad. Arthur could observe at the end of each race which spectators had lost and which had won. Such folly. Nor was it just the rich who were infected with gambling fever. Arthur saw the same exaltation, the same despair, among the laboring class down on the ground. He wondered if children would go to sleep hungry tonight due to their fathers' losses at the race track.

And just there, a flash of tawdry purple. Arthur leaned forward. Indeed, it was the gypsy again. She stood against the fence watching

117

the horses flash by. Arthur wondered whimsically if she had been reading the cards or gazing into a crystal to learn which horses to back. The race ended with a roar from the crowd as a rank outsider romped across the finish line. The gypsy turned from the fence and began to make her way through the crowd.

Arthur was once again struck by the resemblance to Miss Cooper. What was it? The way of moving was not, as Justin had meanly suggested, a sign of commonness. There was something else, a fluidity and graceful strength, not seen in either the dawdling women of the gentry nor the prosaic plodding of the commoners. On impulse, Arthur moved out of his seat and made his way down the stands. He wanted to get closer to the woman and see if the resemblance held on nearer view.

She was moving through the wagons now, and Arthur saw her approach a battered gypsy wagon. A gypsy boy was waiting for her, about the age, Arthur thought, of Han Cooper. And of all things, the boy was holding a bird. The woman was screwing something small together as she approached, and then the small item was attached to the bird's leg. The boy stood back and lifted the bird, releasing it to the sky.

It was a pigeon! It attained the sky and flew off, wings beating strongly.

Arthur stopped and stared at the bird as it disappeared into the distance. He knew of carrier pigeons. The military used them, and financiers, to send messages quickly over long distances. Something nefarious was afoot here.

He began to move again toward the wagon. But the gypsy couple whisked onto the seat of the wagon and rattled away before he could gain a closer look.

Arthur spent a troubled night. He dined in a private parlor in the best inn in Newmarket, accompanied only by his own thoughts. Planets swung along their age-old orbits unconsidered by the Duke of Winton, as the problem of the gypsies was mulled and chewed over.

Could it be the Coopers? Was that possible? Were they sending advance word of race results to a confederate? That conclusion was inescapable, for what other information gleaned at Newmarket merited rapid and private transmission?

118

Why would they do such a thing? Oh, it couldn't be the Coopers! That sensible, gently-bred young lady involved in such a dishonorable business? Surely he'd been misled by a chance resemblance. There was the boy, though. It wasn't merely that the gypsy woman moved like Cleo Cooper, but also that she associated with a young boy who bore a striking resemblance to Cleo's brother Han. With a sinking heart, Arthur remembered his first encounter with Miss Cooper, as she struggled down the street with a large bundle of bird seed. For her brother the bird fancier, he recalled. At the time, he'd assumed that her brother kept parrots or perhaps fed wild birds, but now the incident was open to a more sinister explanation.

Arthur wished he'd remained in the stands and hadn't followed the gypsy to the wagon. Perhaps he should just continue as if he hadn't seen what he'd seen. But upon reflection, that was a coward's option. The damnable thing was that Miss Cooper was close friends with Miss Harwell. Should this outrageous business become public, the scandal would be sure to redound on her as well. Arthur couldn't allow that.

When he finally retired to his restless bed, Arthur knew he would have to investigate further. He couldn't allow the matter to rest; the consequences could be too dire.

According, shortly after his return to Town, the Duke of Winton made his way to White's and consulted the betting book. To his dismay, he found confirmation of his worst suspicions. Yesterday, Peter Barton had placed a sizable bet on the fortunes of Cabin Boy, the very horse whose long-odds victory was cheered the moment before the gypsy woman left the fence and returned to the gypsy wagon.

The Duke reminded himself that while he'd proved to his own satisfaction that Peter Barton was in league with the Newmarket gypsies, he was not entirely certain that the gypsies were the Coopers.

Early the next morning, the Duke set out on his morning walk. Clad in the despised brown jacket, he made his way to Hans Town. But this time, rather than striding down the main streets, he made his way along the alleys behind the townhouses, along the stables that served those houses. At the stable behind the Coopers' townhouse, the Duke cautiously looked around. Seeing himself unobserved, he slipped inside.

In the dim, dusty light, he moved deeper into the stable, and found what he was seeking and hoping not to find. There was the gypsy wagon. Confirmation.

The Duke's shoulders slumped. He crept back to the alley and made his way home, lost in thought.

Arthur spent the day in great turmoil of mind. The situation he found himself in was unprecedented in his experience. What was the proper course of action when one becomes aware of nefarious dealings, not among the criminal class, but among members of society? People that one knew? Knew, and indeed liked? At least, he'd thought he liked the Coopers, but now he wondered if he'd been misled by a sham.

He wondered if he should take counsel with his mother, or with Justin. But to do that would risk the secret becoming public. Not that he distrusted their discretion, but their behavior toward the miscreants would certainly change. Then there were servants, who were everywhere in one's life and seemed to know everything. No, he couldn't tell this story to either of his usual confidants. It never even occurred to Arthur to wonder if he should consult with Miss Harwell.

Finally, Arthur came to the inescapable conclusion that he must confront Miss Cooper. Undoubtedly, it would be unpleasant, but it had to be done.

TWELVE

It was just after breakfast and Cleo sat in the morning room, going over figures. She was pleased with her findings. She subtracted fees for school for Han, put aside amounts for annuities for the General, Mrs. Mimms, and Merry, and there was still quite enough for a nice gentleman's estate, with money left over for the Funds. In the original plan, Peter was to have a cut, but now he was insisting that setting him up as a man of fashion was quite enough; he considered himself well-compensated for his efforts.

Cleo was feeling proud of herself. She'd analyzed the problem, formulated a plan of attack, marshaled her forces, and carried the campaign through to success.

The door opened and the General announced, "His Grace the Duke of Winton, Miss Cleo."

Cleo looked up in surprise as the Duke advanced into the room. It was early for calling. "Your Grace!" she said, gathering her papers into a pile and shoving them back into the desk. She rose to greet him. "We weren't expecting callers. Merry is at the market, and I believe Han is in the park."

She thought the Duke was looking uncommonly grave. "That's perhaps just as well, Miss Cooper, because I particularly desired to speak with you alone."

"You do?" Flustered, Cleo gestured to a chair. "Won't you sit? Is all well with Felicity?"

The Duke sat. "This has nothing to do with Miss Harwell," he said, and then stopped. He seemed to be in a quandary.

Cleo sat across from him and composed herself to listen. "Yes?"

Finally Arthur blurted, "I saw you at Newmarket."

Cleo's eyes widened. "Newmarket?"

"And I saw the bird. The wagon is in your stables. I saw the wager in the betting book at White's." Then he started forward in concern, for Miss Cooper had turned so white he feared she would faint.

121

She waved him back and took a deep breath. "It seems you know all," she said faintly. "What shall you do? Have you notified the authorities? Will we be transported?"

Startled into profanity, Arthur exclaimed, "Transported?! Good God, ma'am!"

"Well? Have you reported us?" Cleo asked impatiently.

"No, I have not." Arthur replied.

"Will you?"

"Of course not! Great stars above, the scandal!"

Cleo relaxed slightly. At least they wouldn't have to take flight on the instant. "What then shall you do?" she asked. "What do you expect of us?"

"I scarcely know," Arthur admitted. "This is something entirely outside my experience. You cannot be allowed to continue, of course. I hope to be able to stop you and also to prevent these events from becoming public."

"Very well then," Cleo said, folding her hands primly. "I am as reluctant as you for this information to become public, and we will stop. I promise you that."

Arthur looked at her skeptically. "How much is your promise to be relied on?" he asked.

She flushed now. "I keep my promises," she said, "though you don't know me well enough to know that. And as it happens, you observed us on our last trip to Newmarket. We will stop because we had already determined to stop."

It seemed Arthur had succeeded in his task. And yet he was unsatisfied. "Why did you do it?" he asked. "Was it some sort of lark?"

"Why did we do it?" Cleo asked, astonished. "Why, for the money, of course."

This was worse that Arthur supposed. "You're... professional criminals, in fact?"

Her eyes flashed and she didn't speak for a moment. Then she said defiantly, "Since we live off our ill-gotten gains, perhaps that is accurate."

A criminal! In the heart of society! And best of friends with his fiancée! Arthur stood and paced the room in agitation. But then he said, "Ah, I can't believe it. You've not been a criminal all your life. What brought you to this?"

"What brought me to this was a lack of other options," Cleo said frankly. "After my father died, once we'd sold virtually all our possessions, what was left was enough to buy passage to England and rent this house for a season. And what then?"

"There are honorable occupations, even for ladies," Arthur reminded her.

"Indeed there are," Cleo said disdainfully. "Governess! Companion! Poorly paid, browbeaten and downtrodden, and without the ability to support a family. I suppose I could have found a position with some ill-tempered old woman, and then what of Han? Perhaps I should have sent him to the workhouse? Is that your honorable solution? And Merry, and the General and Mrs. Mimms? Throw them out onto the street?"

Arthur was surprised. "Your aunt would surely take you in," he suggested.

"But did I know that? When we returned to England, all we knew of my mother's relations were that they'd cast her off without a penny when she married my father. Should I have looked to her for assistance?"

"But now you surely know that the Countess is an excellent woman who would never let you go without."

Cleo gave him a look of contempt. "Yes, we could become the Poor Relations, dependent on another for every bite of food and every stitch of clothing."

He wondered at her vehemence, because such poor relations were a standard feature of society.

She threw up her hands. "Oh, could *you* live so?"

"We're not talking about me," he told her austerely.

"Well then, perhaps we should! You, who've never spent a day of your life without a roof over your head or without food in the pantry! What do you know of the shifts that must be taken by those without?"

Arthur sighed. "I still believe there were honorable options open to you."

"I assure you I researched the matter carefully," Cleo told him. "And the only occupation open to women that would pay enough to sustain a family would be as a gentleman's particular." Arthur flushed at such an indelicate subject mentioned by a single young lady. Cleo continued, "And what does it say about your society that a man's mistress is paid so much more handsomely than the woman he employs to tend and educate his children?"

"I am not society's defender, ma'am," he told her, rising to his feet. "You have suitors now. Will you marry? That is how women provide for themselves."

She lifted her chin defiantly. "Marry to provide for myself? I am too much my mother's daughter to marry without love. No, I'll not marry, and I've provided for my family without needing to do so."

"Very well." He turned toward the door, but thought of another question and turned back. "Peter Barton," he said. "Your confederate. Is he your lover?"

She slapped him.

Hand to his cheek, he said, "I take that to be a no?"

"I'm a thief, sir, not a whore!"

"Very well. I will bid you good day."

As he walked toward the door, Cleo said, "I'll find an excuse to make to Aunt Lucinda for missing your house party."

He stopped. He'd forgotten all about the house party. "Better not," he said. "It would occasion comment, as you have already accepted."

"Comment?" Cleo said with a snort. "What of that?"

Arthur frowned. "I have learned that social gossip can be devastating. The society pages have already published the house party guest list. If you failed to show, the gossips would create a reason, one that would undoubtedly be detrimental to your reputation."

"Why do you care?" Cleo asked defiantly.

Why indeed, Arthur wondered. While he would not expose Miss Cooper and her scheme, her social ruin ought to be no concern of his. And yet, he found that he couldn't contribute to such an outcome.

At last, he said, "Your friendship with my fiancée is well known. Gossip involving you would reflect poorly on her. And it would hurt Miss Harwell. I can't permit that." So he said, but he realized uneasily that there was more here than just that.

"Very well," Cleo said. "I'll attend your wretched house party. After the house party, I intend to find a country estate to purchase for my brother. We will be in very different social circles then, so I think you need not fear to meet us."

Arthur felt a strange combination of relief and regret. But he arched a brow at one detail. "A country estate? Your... enterprise must have been lucrative indeed."

"I have succeeded in providing independence and security for my family, something I will never apologize for," she told him tartly. "Now good day, Your Grace."

The Duke bowed wordlessly and left the room. He accepted his hat and cane from General, the nameless amnesiac, and went on his way.

As he made his way down the streets of Hans Town, it occurred to him to wonder why he felt such relief to learn that Miss Cooper was not Barton's mistress.

***

The door had barely closed behind the Duke when Cleo leaped to her feet and began to stride hastily around the room. "Insufferable man!" she exclaimed aloud. " 'There are honorable occupations, even for ladies'," she mimicked bitterly. "Odious, *odious*, top-lofty, judgmental..." She ran out of breath and stopped on a strangled sob, sinking into a chair.

She tried to regain her composure, reminding herself that the situation could be much worse. They could be under arrest right now. Or exposed to society as gambling cheats, which many in this world considered worse than common criminals. She had lost nothing after all, and would still be able to establish her family comfortably. Lost nothing, that is, other than the good opinion of the Duke of Winton.

And what did that matter, she asked herself sternly. He was not the man she took him to be. She had thought him to be someone who analyzed a matter clearly, unimpeded by the biases of society, but she was obviously mistaken. Dishonorable, he'd called her. A woman of no virtue, whose word was not to be trusted.

The unfairness of the judgment scalded her. In her position, what would he have done? She had people who depended on her, she couldn't abandon them. Perhaps a 'proper' society damsel would have simply swooned on a divan until they were all out on the street.

Cleo tried to regain her earlier sense of triumph. It was a triumph, she reminded herself. Starting from almost nothing, in a matter of months she'd reestablished her family's fortune. She'd

125

done it with no real harm to anyone, since Peter had been under strict instructions to only place bets with those well able to stand the loss.

And who else in this society made those distinctions? When her Uncle William was gambling away his fortune and home, that was considered foolhardy, but who called it dishonorable? And what of the men who took the wagers they must have known were leading to his ruin? Who censured them?

Of course, no true lady in this world would dream of donning a gypsy disguise and mingling with the dregs of society at the race track. But Cleo could scarcely have gone to the races as herself, with brother and pigeons in train; it needed to be done. Perhaps she would have been more the lady if she'd gone shrinking and dragging her feet, woebegone at this distasteful necessity. Very well then, she'd enjoyed it. She'd enjoyed the freedom, the escape from the strictures of an unnaturally strict and hidebound society.

Perhaps she was no true lady after all. But that didn't make her dishonorable!

The sound of the front door heralded Merry's return. From the morning room, Cleo heard the old governess chatting amiably with the General as she made her way back to the kitchen. That gave Cleo a few moments to decide on a new problem – should she tell Merry that they had been discovered?

After some thought, Cleo decided to keep this from Miss Merrihew. Just this morning at breakfast, Merry had been almost giddy with relief that the pigeon scheme was over and they hadn't been caught out. "Now I may be comfortable at last!" she'd said. No, it would be cruel to tell Merry that someone outside their circle knew of the scheme. Cruel and pointless, because what could Merry do with the information? It would fret her to no purpose.

So when Merry sailed into the morning room, full of advice for Cleo's trip to the ducal house party, Cleo arranged her face into a smile and tried to sound enthusiastic.

***

Arthur walked home in great perturbation of mind. Obviously, he had been mistaken in Miss Cooper's character. She seemed like such a level-headed, self-assured, and sensible sort of woman! But there must be some defect of character that brought her to a scheme that any person of honor could see was quite beyond the pale.

126

He hoped that time would wean Felicity of her preference for Miss Cooper's company, because he could not consider her a good influence, not at all.

At dinner, the Duchess chatted happily about the house party, while the sound washed over her son unheard. Finally she said, "Arthur!" He blinked and looked at her. "There you are!" she said.

"Sorry. What were you saying?"

"Nothing of importance, I suppose," she said. "But do tell me, Arthur. Are you content with this engagement? Did I pressure you to make a step that you are reluctant to take?"

"Not at all!" he said hastily. "Don't run away with that notion. You know I must marry, and I am well content with my choice."

After they left the table and adjourned to the morning room, the Duke suddenly asked his mother, "How much did we pay Miss Godwin?"

The Duchess laughed merrily. "My dear Arthur, I see you are eager to establish your nursery, but there are years yet before you need to consider governesses! Nannies and nursery maids will be adequate for a number of years."

Arthur flushed. "I wasn't thinking of my personal situation, just... I had a bit of a debate today with someone about occupations for women. There are so few of them for gentlewomen, and I have no idea how well they are compensated."

"Miss Godwin was a most superior woman," his mother told him. "She managed Clara quite nicely, and was paid fifty pounds a year."

"So little! Why, I just paid four hundred for a horse, and it wasn't the dearest on offer."

"Fifty pounds is quite ample for a governess," the Duchess said. "I'm not a nip-farthing, dear, and neither was your father."

"And yet, how does one live on such a sum?"

"Consider that they also receive room and board," his mother reminded him. "So they needn't pay for their food or housing. That's quite a savings."

"And if they had dependents? Say, a widow with a young son?"

"Then they wouldn't be governesses," the Duchess said. "That is a position for a single lady."

"So what would the widow do, then?" Arthur wondered.

"I have no notion. I suppose some of these benevolent societies would have some sort of scheme. And of course the widow would have relatives to assist her. Or there is sewing to take in, any number of possibilities. Really, Arthur, have you been letting the reformers trouble your peace? Don't. We can't cure all the world's ills, after all."

THIRTEEN

The Dorwood traveling coach bowled briskly down the lanes of Hampshire, as Cleo looked eagerly out the window. After months in Town, she felt her spirits lift to be on the road and seeing new places again. She had mixed feelings about this trip. While she was not looking forward to meeting the Duke of Winton again and seeing the condemnation in his eyes, she had to confess to a great curiosity about Winton Court.

Her aunt was in good humor. "Perhaps it is ill-natured of me to say it," she said, "but what a relief to be away from Sylvia for a time!"

"I would imagine so, ma'am," Cleo said with polite understatement.

"And this could be just the thing for you," the Countess went on. "The neighbors will surely call, so you will meet the prominent Hampshire families. There could be some man there who would suit you. Are you sure you won't have Deaver?"

For indeed, Deaver had made his offer in form, which had been politely declined. So politely, in fact, that he refused to be disheartened and generously told Cleo that he'd give her more time to consider his offer. She thanked him for that, and parted from him with no intent to ever see the man again.

"Oh, dear Aunt, I just couldn't!" she said now. "I'm sure he's quite a... worthy gentleman. But... I just couldn't."

"Very well then," her aunt said smoothly. "Far be it from me to urge the making of a distasteful match. There are plenty of fish in the sea."

Cleo giggled. "I can't see myself reeling in a husband."

"Silly child. It's a shame, almost, that you are so clever. You see right through these men and their poses and follies, which makes it difficult for them to attach you."

"They attach me!" Cleo exclaimed. "Now who is the fisher and who is the fish?"

"That depends," the Countess said composedly. "Dear Harold, now, pursued me with great diligence until I caught him."

Justin was dreading the house party. He'd tried to cry off, but the Duchess would not allow it.

"Just for now, Auntie," he'd pleaded privately. "Just while the engagement is being celebrated. I'll come about presently, but..."

"Dear boy, I insist," she'd told him firmly. "I understand these things, probably better than you. If you take yourself off, avoiding Felicity, what will happen is that you'll brood and exaggerate, seeing every imaginable perfection in the poor girl. Then when you encounter her again, as you surely will, you will be bound to expose yourself by making your feelings plain in an unseemly scene. We would be forced to cut the connection, and only think how uncomfortable for your mother."

"But to live under the same roof! For two weeks! I don't think I can."

"You can and you must. It will become easier with time. Trust me on this."

And so Justin relented, with a great sense of foreboding. He drove his curricle to Hampshire, caught up in plans to keep himself busy and make himself scarce. Perhaps he'd find a flirt to serve as a distraction and a disguise.

***

Cleo found Hampshire very beautiful, but was alarmed to read in a guidebook she'd brought with her that Winton Court was ten miles around. She read aloud to her aunt about the grand Palladian front of the new manor, built a century ago by the current duke's great-grandfather, and the former Tudor manor that now served as the Dower House.

"Even the Dower House sounds grander than what I hope to find for Han," she said with a slight frown.

"Oh, Cleo!" her aunt said. "Just for a few days, can you leave off managing for your family and simply enjoy yourself?'

Cleo was puzzled. "I always enjoy myself," she said.

They were turning in a drive and through a massive gate now. "Ah, here's the gatehouse," the Countess said with satisfaction. "At last. I want my tea."

From the gatehouse, the drive covered three miles of gently tamed parkland. The manor sat amid manicured gardens tended by

130

an army of gardeners, and at the carriage's arrival, a team of footmen raced from the house to deal with the baggage.

Cleo and her aunt entered the grand hall, a vast expanse of marble, adorned with suits of armor and tapestries. It would have been oppressively intimidating if not for their hostess. The Duchess greeted them with a twinkle in her eye. Gesturing vaguely around her, she said, "I know, isn't it absurd? But we shall make you comfortable."

She herself showed her guests to their rooms, urging them to cast off their bonnets and freshen themselves and join the company in the drawing room, where tea was expected momentarily.

"Tea!" said the Countess in a deep voice, as one who hears the trumpets sound the charge. "With all my heart!"

The party awaiting them in the drawing room faced the coming days with a variety of attitudes. The Duke himself was resolved to be as pleasantly sociable as the stupidest man alive. His intended found herself soothed by his demeanor and hopeful that his alarmingly scientific front was a Town affectation.

Mister Harwell was well pleased with his situation. Winton Court, however grand, was country, not Town, and from his bedroom window he saw gardens and greenhouses that would take him at least a week to explore sufficiently. The grandeur of the house pleased him because it thrilled his wife to speechlessness.

Baron Wainwright responded to the conversation with a beatific smile, half asleep. He looked forward to an excellent tea, a still more excellent dinner, and perhaps billiards or whist to follow. A country house party seemed to him a foretaste of heaven, because what pleasure could equal that of eating well at another's expense?

Viscount Fenwick and Miss Dumphreys didn't see the grandeur surrounding them, being wholly involved with appreciating one another. Their past estrangement seemed now to be an excellent thing; it had blossomed in their imaginations into an epic of tragedy and comedy and would make an excellent story, they were sure, for the children.

Mister Amesbury chatted with Miss Keene and her mother, distracting himself from the sight of his beloved sitting beside his friend as his acknowledged duchess-to-be. Miss Keene plumed herself on his attention, which served as a balm to her feelings, because Marianne Keene was a disappointed woman.

A reigning Toast in Warwickshire, she had descended on London certain of reigning there, and in any other season she might well have done so. But she had the misfortune to come out in the same season as her dear friend Felicity, who quite cast her in the shade. Beside Felicity's golden locks, her own blonde hair resembled straw, and her blue eyes faded to an uninteresting grey beside the cornflower sparkle of Felicity's.

She had had her suitors, but found fault with them all. The wealthy lacked titles and the titled lacked wealth. She had ample offers, if few compared to Felicity, but had refused them all, always hoping for better, and now faced the prospect of returning home unpromised and facing the scorn of two younger sisters who had suffered under her queening for too long. In these circumstances, and after a stern talk from her mama, she was wondering if perhaps she ought to lower her standards.

Mister Amesbury was but the younger son of an earl, and as such would have been dismissed out of hand earlier in the season when the future seemed limitless, but now she reminded herself that his fortune was handsome, his address was polished, and his position in society was of the highest. She eyed him speculatively and considered the possibilities.

Fortunately, she was one of only two unwed and unpromised young ladies at the house party, and the other one was that quite old creature with the odd background who had thrust herself into the *ton* to compete with her betters. But Miss Cooper, oddly enough, had taken and was not to be dismissed as negligible.

So when the Duchess returned to the drawing room with the news that Lady Dorwood and Miss Cooper had just arrived, Miss Keene narrowed her eyes in affected puzzlement and said, "Miss Cooper? Ah, yes, the drawing master's daughter."

Amesbury had all but settled on Miss Keene as his house party flirt, but at this calculated gaucherie he blinked in surprise and decided to reconsider.

Her remark went unanswered, as the Countess and her protégé entered the drawing room.

"Did someone mention tea?" the Countess asked.

"We were just waiting for you," the Duchess told her.

"Then wait no longer!" the Countess urged. "Summon the reviving pot!"

"Ah, another addict," the Duchess said happily, and rang the bell.

Tea was a dawdling affair, and Cleo was surprised to learn she was expected to be too exhausted from travel to do anything other than lie down until dinner. All that jouncing in a carriage, was the general opinion. The Countess fell in with the plan, but Cleo, used to traveling over much worse roads in much worse vehicles, had found the trip in the well-sprung traveling coach to be perfectly comfortable, and chose to roam the shrubbery with Felicity.

Felicity was pleased to see her friend; Miss Dumphreys was too wrapped up in her own romance to be a good listener, and Miss Keene was too eaten up with her own jealousy and spite. Cleo listened patiently to the elaborate arrangements being made for the nuptials, agreeing that it was all very grand, and nodding without comment at Felicity's assumption that Cleo would of course be a wedding attendant. She wondered if the Duke would have objections to the notion, but left the matter for the time being.

The friends parted to dress for dinner, and Cleo changed into a bronze evening dress that she thought very well of.

The dining room at the Court was a long apartment, brilliant lit with hundreds of candles. Cleo opened her eyes at the number of footmen deemed necessary to serve a ducal dinner. The dinner was excellent and very long. Oysters, a green goose, salmon, and collops of veal starred in the first course, with innumerable vegetable surrounds, and the second course featured partridges, a boiled turkey, lamb cutlets, and a roast of beef. The Duke and his mother partook more of the fresh vegetables than the meat dishes in heavy sauces.

Conversation centered on plans for the house party. Riding horses were on offer for all the guests, as well as carriages for expeditions into the surrounding countryside. "But alas," Amesbury told Cleo, "we have no camels for you."

"Just as well," she replied. "Ill-natured beasts, I have no fondness for them and have resorted to them when no other transportation was available."

"Camels!" exclaimed the Duchess. "Where did you have to resort to camels?"

133

"In Egypt, ma'am," Cleo told her. "There is much of interest to see there, but travelers must either take the river or sway about on camels."

"Well! We must have a good talk later," the Duchess promised.

Arthur pressed his lips together and said nothing. He hoped Miss Cooper wouldn't worm her way into his mother's regard.

Plans for a picnic were discussed, and trips to the village and to sites of interest in the neighborhood. Miss Keene leaned forward and offered a suggestion. "We might have a sketching party," she said, "and Miss Cooper could advise us on how to go on. I'm sure she would excel at that."

The reference to Cleo's plebian background was unmistakable, an insult that was instantly recognized by everyone in the room but the intended target. Cleo, who had never been taught to despise her origins, took the suggestion at face value and shook her head with a laugh. "No, I'm afraid I'd be no help in that. Papa always said that he'd always believed that anyone could learn to draw, until he tried to teach me and learned that at least some of us are unteachable. My brother seems to have inherited all the artistic ability in the family."

It never occurred to her class-conscious audience that the insult wasn't apparent to Cleo, so they were quite impressed by what they saw as her ability to feign indifference to it. "Oh, well done!" the Duchess murmured to the Countess.

When the ladies left the gentlemen to their port and withdrew to the drawing room, Marianne made her way to the piano, well pleased to be able to display an accomplishment that she knew Cleo lacked. She was sure she made quite a pretty picture, tinkling away at an etude as the gentlemen finally joined them. But rather than attending her at the piano, Mister Amesbury made his way to Cleo's side.

Upon entering the room, Justin felt his steps instinctively turn toward Felicity, but overrode instinct and made his way to Miss Cooper, joining her on the settle. Casting about for a conversational topic, he suggested, "Tell us about Egypt, Miss Cooper."

"Oh, do!" the Duchess suggested.

"Egypt is a strange country," Cleo said. "Rather eerie, I found. Huge monuments half buried in sand, and entire cities that are nothing but giant tombs."

Miss Dumphreys, happily seated beside her Viscount, gave a delicious shudder and squeaked, "Tombs!"

"They're all empty now," Cleo said, "but we were told that they were once stuffed full of treasure, gold and precious gems and many wondrous things."

"I visited a house recently that I was assured was decorated in Egyptian style," the Duchess said idly. "I thought it all looked most peculiar. Lionesses on the chair arms and crocodile legs holding up tables. Quite an unnecessary abundance of wild animals, I thought."

"The present day Egyptians have a plainer style," Cleo said. "They are lovely people, quite generous and with a happy nature. But they won't have their images taken. Papa was able to draw and paint the monuments to his heart's content, but if he wanted to paint a dragoman or a boatman, they simply wouldn't permit it. He said it was good for him, though. He would walk about storing up images in his mind, and then later he would render them in private. He said it was a great way of training his memory, and trained Han in it as well."

"Han?" asked the Duchess.

"My younger brother, ma'am." Cleo smiled, lost in memory. "They would return from a walk and both take out their sketch pads, having selected the scene to be rendered on the way. Then they would compare sketches and Papa would point out to Han where he'd gone astray."

"Did you enjoy it there?" Justin asked, curious.

"I've found something to enjoy everywhere I've been," Cleo said. "But don't be misled. Egypt isn't particularly comfortable. It is a poor country for the most part, and hot and very dry. Mama and Papa loved it, though. They had been there years before, before I was born, and found it most romantic."

"That explains the name, perhaps," her aunt suggested.

"Certainly," Cleo said. Seeing the rest of the company looking puzzled, she explained, "Cleopatra – that is my full name."

"Unusual," was the Duke's comment.

"Unusual indeed," said Miss Keene with a titter, abandoning the piano and joining the conversational group. "Named after a famous courtesan, how droll!" Marianne actually knew very little about history, and Egyptian history least of all. She only knew that *Antony and Cleopatra* was not on the approved list at Miss Frobish's Select Academy, being considered too warm for young ladies.

"Named after a famous *queen*," Cleo corrected gently. "Absolute monarch and in fact a goddess to her people. And wouldn't that be lovely? To be able to just chop the heads off of those who provoked you? I'm not saying," she added conscientiously, "that I would necessarily do so, but how nice to have that option!"

Arthur stared at her for a moment and then said, "I see. You're joking."

"Oh, well done, Arthur!" said his mother, adding in an aside to the Countess, "He never used to be able to tell when people were joking. I assure you this season has improved him past all recognition."

Conversation returned to more local concerns, and the company soon retired to their beds. Felicity left the drawing room with a strange sense of abandonment. How odd it had been to see Mister Amesbury seek another woman's company. He had joined her court as her season commenced, and insensibly she had come to expect his presence. She had found his conversation amusing and flattering and she relied on his advice and support.

Felicity reminded herself that with familiarity, she would soon come to rely on the Duke for advice and support – and then further reminded herself that she simply must start to think of the man as 'Arthur'.

Arthur too had noticed Justin's attentions to Miss Cooper. He was perplexed as to what to do about it. Should he tell Justin the truth about Miss Cooper? Or warn her to keep her distance? He certainly could not allow his friend to be taken in by a woman who was not as she seemed. He had to confess it would be easy to be taken in, because even knowing what he knew, he found himself unwillingly liking her, finding her refreshing and uncomplicated and enjoying her company. The sooner she took herself and her brother off to a country estate, preferably on the farthest reaches of the isle, the better.

As for the subjects of this scrutiny, Amesbury took himself off to bed well satisfied with his diversionary tactics, while Cleo had seen nothing but a pleasant evening among friends.

The next day was devoted to touring on the estate. The first tour was devoted to the manor itself. While very grand, the manor possessed a sameness that Cleo soon found tedious. She was not alone. The Duchess flung open a door to a bedroom in the east wing and waved them inside. Her company looked around, with murmurs of 'very nice'. As they regained the corridor, the Duchess came to a decision. "Well, this is all very dull, isn't it? The other rooms on this wing are just the same; do we need to view them all? Let's go look at the Dower House."

The suggestion was met with acclaim, and the ladies hurried to don their bonnets and pelisses to outfit themselves for the arduous trek across the lawn on a mild summer day.

As they walked, the Duchess told them, "The Dower House was the original manor. It's most inconvenient in some ways, but quite cozy and comfortable. The family should have stayed where they were, if you ask me, rather than build that enormous barn." A disparaging wave over her shoulder toward the manor indicated the barn in question.

"I blame Marlborough," she went on. "Once Blenheim was built, the aristocracy of his day found themselves quite dissatisfied unless they too had an edifice built for giants." She smiled at Felicity. "I quite look forward to taking possession of the Dower House and I swear you will come to envy me."

Miss Keene and her Viscount exchanged a secret smile.

The Dower House was a hit with the tourists. They rushed from room to room, exclaiming over the strange woodwork and odd little steps that connected one part with another. The faded tapestries were closely inspected to tease out their images, and the priest's hole was greatly admired by the novel readers.

There was, alas, no dungeon.

Following the Dower House tour was a mild introduction to the grounds, which were too extensive for a full tour. The ladies exclaimed over the roses and the mannered shrubbery, but Cleo was most impressed by the vegetable gardens. "You could feed an army!" she said.

"That's what the staff seems like at times," the Duchess replied.

After dinner that evening, the guests got up an impromptu dance. It was only a few couples in the drawing room, accompanied by the Countess on the piano. But the Harwells took a turn about the floor, and the younger folk enjoyed it immensely. Arthur danced first with Felicity, and then took the opportunity during a dance with Cleo to issue a warning.

"I should warn you not to accept an offer from Amesbury," he said in an undertone.

Cleo gave him an astonished look. "I have no expectation of any such thing!"

She could see he didn't believe her. "He is paying you such marked attention," the Duke said. "And I won't have my friends imposed on. If he does offer for you, refuse him, or I will be forced to expose you."

Eyes flashing, Cleo replied, "Rest assured, Your Grace, that I will not accept an offer from any man so unfortunate as to claim your friendship."

With that, he had to be content.

Cleo, now that her attention had been drawn to the matter, realized that Amesbury was indeed often in her company. At first she thought he was avoiding the lures of Marianne, but she noticed now how often his eyes turned to Felicity. It didn't take long for her to grasp the true nature of Amesbury's affections. Since he was endeavoring to hide them, she began to work on his behalf to help him hide his unrequited passion from both its object and her fiancé. To Arthur, her preference for Amesbury's company began to look like defiance.

FOURTEEN

For several days, the group indulged in common house party pursuits. The men fished while the ladies played with battledore and shuttlecock. There were rides across the countryside and carriage rides down shady lanes. Evenings were spent in dancing, billiards, and card playing.

At breakfast one morning, the Duke asked his guests if there were any activities they would desire for the day. Amesbury spoke up. "A trip to the village might be in order."

His suggestion was greeted with acclaim by the younger members of the party.

"The village?" asked the Duke, puzzled. "What is there to do there?"

Miss Dumphreys clasped her hands and said with glee, "Shopping!"

"Shopping!" said the Duke. "When you've just left London?"

"Shopping," said the knowledgeable Mister Amesbury. "Consider that it is now almost a week since we left Town. It is obviously past time to purchase overpriced ribbon, admire provincial bonnets, and eat an indifferent nuncheon in a smoky parlor of the public house."

Felicity admitted diffidently that she had just been thinking that her favorite chip straw needed new ribbons, since the ones it currently bore had become sadly limp and faded.

"There you have it," Amesbury said. "Faded ribbons; that will never do. And while we're in the village, old fellow, you must step into the church to give thanks to the Lord for sending you a woman who will refurbish an old bonnet rather than clamor for a new one."

"It's quite my favorite," Felicity said. "So comfortable and shaped just right. A new chip straw is never the same."

Miss Keene cried shame on the notion that a new bonnet could be in any way inferior to an old one, and the debate soon took the gentlemen well out of their depths.

The older members of the party were less enthusiastic about the proposed expedition. Mister Harwell spoke for them when he grumbled, "All this chopping and changing and dashing about you young people do, most fatiguing. Get where you want to be and stay there, says I."

Fortunately, the Countess of Dorwood admitted that she could always be brought to a scheme that involved examining a new assortment of lace and the elders thankfully deputized her to chaperone the group.

It remained only to set a time and arrange transportation. "We're agreed on eleven o'clock?" Arthur asked the table. At the nods of agreement, he turned to the butler and said, "Have the barouche and the landau brought round at eleven."

"And the phaeton," Justin said.

Arthur was puzzled. "The phaeton as well? Surely, with nine of us, the barouche and landau ought to suffice."

"Not in comfort," Justin argued. "This is a pleasure jaunt! The trip to the village might be merely uncomfortable in the two carriages, but if there are purchases – and trust me, there will be – the trip home would be insupportable."

"Mister Amesbury understands women far too well," the Countess said idly. "I think it is most shocking."

"The phaeton as well, then," Arthur instructed the butler.

"Very good, sir." Tolliver bowed and departed to pass on the instructions.

Promptly at eleven, the four gentlemen were in the front hall and the carriages were in the drive. The ladies were not yet in evidence.

"A pony says we're not departed at 11:30," Wainwright said to Fenwick.

"Done," said the Viscount.

Arthur looked out the door and sighed. "We'll be quite a cavalcade."

"And how the villagers will enjoy that!" Justin said with a smile. "Consider too that the local people know that you've chosen a duchess. How unfair for them if you show up in the village with four young ladies and no way for them to determine which is the chosen bride. You must take Miss Harwell in the phaeton and that will make everything plain."

"You have a point," Arthur admitted. He looked back up the stairs. "What could possibly be keeping them?"

"Only consider," Justin said. "They must locate their bonnets and their parasols and their reticules. Then perhaps someone's coin purse is not in her reticule and she must return to her room to fetch it. And perhaps someone else will call another's bonnet ugly, and she must go and change it, only to find that the other one clashes with her parasol and then change back to the original bonnet which she will decide is not so ugly after all."

Cleo joined them in time to hear this last. "Aunt Lucinda is right," she said to Amesbury. "You do know too much about women. In some countries, I think you would be burned at the stake. But never fear, Aunt Lucinda is taking charge, and we will be assembled momentarily."

Just then the other young ladies descended the staircase, with the Countess of Dorwood behind, herding them like a diligent sheepdog.

The party distributed themselves among the vehicles. Amesbury assisted Miss Keene into the landau across from Fenwick and Miss Dumphreys. She turned to the door to begin a spritely flirtation, but Amesbury had turned away, saying to Wainwright, "In you go, old man," and moved himself to the barouche.

The phaeton with the Duke and Miss Harwell took the lead, the barouche followed with Amesbury, Cleo and the Countess, and the landau followed. Viscount Fenwick pulled out his pocket watch as the landau lurched into motion and said smugly to Wainwright, "Eleven twenty-five."

Driving toward the village at a sedate trot, the Duke felt quite pleased with himself. Felicity, wearing something lettuce-colored with pink ribbons and rosettes, looked like a fairy princess. Laborers working in the fields stopped their tasks and stared until the phaeton passed out of sight. The Duke pointed out the sights as they drove, the mill, the dairy farm, the tenant farms, naming the families at each. She would help him here, and the people would love her.

Felicity too was feeling pleased. The Duke was acting for all the world like a sensible man who'd never thought of an equation in his life. She thought she could deal quite well with this man. She called him 'Arthur' three times on the way to the village; she'd been practicing.

Once the group arrived at the village, there was a few moments of argument about what to visit first. At last it was proposed that people follow their own fancy and meet at the Shield and Plow at two. The Duke tried to point the various places of interest in Winton-on-Test, but as soon as he pointed out the millinery, the ladies immediately darted off in that direction.

"Let it go, Arthur," Justin said, so the Duke availed himself of a bench on the green. Justin joined him on the bench and gave a contented sigh. "Ah, village life."

The two men sat in companionable silence for fifteen minutes. Arthur took out his small notebook and pencil and began some numerical tinkering. Then Miss Cooper left the milliner's alone and came over to join them on the bench. Wary of her motives, Arthur stowed his writing materials and resolved to keep watch.

Cleo sat with a sigh. "I fear I have exposed my essential unwomanliness," she said sadly. "Because I couldn't maintain interest in shades of ribbon for an instant longer. The other ladies are still going strong. I had no notion there were that many shades of pink in the world!"

Justin chuckled. "I knew this expedition would be a hit with the ladies."

Arthur looked about. "Where have Wainwright and Fenwick got to?"

"They eyed the duck pond for a few minutes and then went on in to the Shield and Plow," Justin told him.

Cleo was admiring the prosperous scene. "What a bustling village, to be sure!"

Arthur frowned. "It seems more bustling than I recall," he said at last. "I wonder what might be going on?"

Indeed, the scene was busy, housewives with baskets on their arms, maids sweeping doorsteps, errand boys hurrying about. Justin laughed indulgently. "They're here because of us," he said.

"Seriously?" Cleo asked.

"But of course. A ducal party comes to the village, that's fodder for news, especially with a young duke newly engaged to be married. Of course the village folk will find some task that takes them out of doors and able to look about. I assure you, a good three-quarters of these people would not be out and about otherwise."

Cleo looked about uneasily. "Suddenly I feel as if I were on stage. And I don't know my lines."

"Tell you what," Justin said decisively, "let us go admire the church. I understand that the vicar and his wife are to dine with us tonight, so someone of our party should have something to say about the church."

"Excellent notion," Cleo agreed, and they stood up and began to make their way across the green. Arthur joined them. Cleo, well aware that he was chaperoning his friend, turned from Justin and toward Arthur, sticking out her tongue and crossing her eyes, before taking Justin's arm in a proprietary manner.

Following Justin and Cleo into the dim recesses of the church, Arthur pondered that extraordinary gesture. What did she mean by it? Could she really be intending to attach Justin? Surely not, for the Duke had promised to expose her if she did so, and exposure would mean her ruin. Finally, after a moment's reflection, Arthur realized with shock – 'she was teasing me!'

No female, he now realized, had teased him since his sister had transformed almost overnight from what their mother stigmatized as a 'sad romp of a girl' into an overpoweringly dignified young lady at her come out. A younger Arthur had been exasperated by his sister's teasing, but now he found that he missed it. His lips curled up in an involuntary smile as he joined the others standing in the center of the nave.

Turning, Cleo said to the Duke, "Tell us what we are to admire. And please don't say the frescoes, because they are horrid."

Arthur racked his memory. "The church is considered an excellent example of Late Perpendicular."

"Perpendicular," Cleo said with an encouraging nod.

"The roof is often spoke of highly," he went on. "with the hammerbeam construction and the decorative carving."

Cleo peered upward. "Very well, I can admire the carving."

"Much is also made of the wooden chancel screen."

The trio duly admired the wooden chancel screen.

They were then joined by the verger, who had hastily thrown on his gown and scurried to meet them, almost overpowered by the honor of their visit but willing to tell them in exhaustive detail the church's history and fine points. By the time the three thanked the verger and left for their nuncheon, they would have been able to pass the most stringent examination on the subject.

The rest of the party was found to have preceded them to the Shield and Plow, the ladies surrounded by their parcels. Wainwright and Fenwick had been there for some time, and the excellent ale had made them amiable, sleepy, and slightly stupid. A cold collation of meat, cheese and fruit already awaited them.

Miss Keene narrowed her eyes to see Cleo enter with two handsome gentlemen. She had wondered where Amesbury had gotten to and had been trying her wiles on Wainwright, as a second string to her bow. But Wainwright was apparently too thick-headed to recognize a flirtatious remark, so the project had died an unmourned death.

"There you are!" the Countess called to them. "Come sit before this ham is gone. The beef is also excellent. Didn't you buy anything?"

"We toured the church," Cleo told her, taking a seat. "And there was nothing to buy there. Though I left a few coins in the poor box."

"How saintly," murmured Marianne under her breath.

The reunited party addressed the cold collation with a will until there was nothing left on the table but orange rinds.

"Well!" said the Countess. "This was quite a lovely expedition."

"Demmed fine meal," the Viscount agreed with a fatuous smile. "Demmed fine day, demmed fine drive, demmed fine ale."

"Oh, hush," said Miss Dumphreys, but tolerantly.

"Of course, m'dear," he said, patting her hand. Arthur and Justin exchanged a look and a smile. Justin mouthed the words 'the cat's paw', and Arthur coughed to disguise a laugh.

"Since this expedition was so successful," the Duke said to the group at large, "I am open to more suggestions."

Cleo raised her hand. "Oh, please!" she said. "I would like to see the new planet!"

Felicity felt a twinge of vexation, more at herself than at Cleo. Why hadn't she thought of that? "Oh, yes," she agreed. "What a marvelous idea. Arthur, you must show us the new planet."

"Newly discovered planet," Arthur corrected automatically. "For of course it's been there all along."

"Could it be done?" the Countess asked.

"I suppose it could," Arthur said doubtfully. "It would mean quite a late night of it, though. Would an activity taking place after midnight be objectionable, do you think?"

Lady Dorwood thought about it. "Of course, in Town one is often out and about well past midnight, almost to dawn sometimes. Late hours are less common in the country, but I don't think it would be seen as improper, precisely. Because there is a reason, after all. Viewing planets could scarcely be a daytime activity."

Amesbury warmly endorsed the notion and so did the other men, once they could be brought to understand the nature of the scheme. Arthur could not delude himself that their interest in the project was strictly scientific.

"I say," Baron Wainwright said, "what a tale for the club! Whatever the others have done this summer, I doubt they can claim to have seen the planets. Will we be able to see other planets, Winton?"

"I'll have to have Jenkins, my librarian-astronomer, make us some sky charts and find the best time to see the various planets," Arthur said.

"Librarian-astronomer?" Lady Dorwood asked.

"Yes, the library of Winton Court is extensive enough to need a librarian," Arthur explained. "And I found one who is also an astronomer, to assist me with the observatory. He's done some splendid work on the moons of Jupiter this season, while I've been otherwise occupied." He smiled at Felicity to denote his other occupation.

"Jupiter, by Jupiter!" said Wainwright with a foolish laugh. "What a facer for the fellows who went to Brighton. Oh, surely, perhaps they went to dine with Prinny, but really, who hasn't these days? And that great gaudy barn of a Pavilion, I'm out of patience with it."

"You're in the right of it," said Fenwick, much struck. "And whatever new geegaw he has to display, you must praise, praise, praise the thing or he pouts like a giant baby. It's frightfully fatiguing. Frightfully."

***

That evening, the ducal dining table was graced by the presence of Reverend and Mrs. Tooting, and also Mister Jenkins, ducal librarian-astronomer. Arthur tried to keep track of the various conversations, and found something to amuse himself wherever he turned.

His mother, he noted, listened with serene sympathy to the vicar's wife discoursing at quite unnecessary length about her beloved orchids. "It sounds frightfully difficult!" the Duchess murmured admiringly. "My dear, how do you do it?"

Miss Cooper, meanwhile, kept the vicar entertained with questions about the history and construction of the village church, questions to which she already knew the answers, thanks to the comprehensive education they'd been given by the verger just that afternoon.

And Jenkins, the poor fellow! He was talking of planets. Wainwright and Fenwick pestered him with their questions, questions that made it obvious that the two amiable peers had never so much as thought about planets in their lives.

Ah, well, the Duke thought, it's good training for the young man. Science was so much a matter of patronage these days, and Jenkins needed to learn how to talk about his projects with the profoundly ignorant.

The vicar and his wife left soon after dinner, and Jenkins scurried back to his lair in the library. The house party gathered in the drawing room for their usual evening of conversation, music, and various flirtations.

"What are our plans for tomorrow?" Amesbury asked idly.

"I'll leave you all to your own devices tomorrow," the Duke told him. "I will be walking to the home farm."

Felicity heard that and saw a way to enter into her fiancé's interests. She'd been trumped by Cleo on the planet suggestion, but here was a chance to make up for it. "Oh, could I come along?" she asked.

Arthur hesitated. "Certainly, you may come," he said at last. "But perhaps we should ride."

"It was your intent to walk, wasn't it?" Felicity asked. At his nod, she said, "Then we should walk."

"How far is it to the home farm from here?" Justin asked gently.

"No more than four miles," Arthur replied.

"I doubt that Miss Harwell would want to walk that far," Justin said.

His reward was a glare from his beloved. "Of course I want to walk," she said. "Consider that in Town Arthur must walk as we do. Here at his home, shouldn't we walk as he does?"

146

Wainwright was dozing in an armchair after the excellent dinner and the port that followed, but now his head nodded and he awoke with a start. "Eh?" he said. "Where are we walking?"

"To the home farm," Felicity said patiently.

"A walk to the home farm," he said. "Splendid thing, a home farm. There are pigs to look at, sometimes kittens in the hay loft. What an excellent notion. When are we going?"

Arthur looked around and saw a circle of expectant faces. It seemed his solitary walk had become a general expedition. Resigning himself to the inevitable, he said, "I intend to leave after breakfast. There will certainly be pigs, but I can't guarantee kittens."

Cleo said, "The working part of a country estate is exactly what I hope to see."

As the company retired for the night, Felicity went to her bed well satisfied with her notion. Here at last was an activity of Arthur's that she could participate in. Sometimes she would open the Newton book, hoping that this time it would seem less bewildering, but it remained obscure to her. But any fool could walk.

FIFTEEN

At breakfast the next morning, it seemed that all the younger members of the party were to join in the walking scheme, and none of their elders. Lady Dorwood felt that a party of well-behaved young people walking country lanes and not leaving the estate could be trusted to manage without a chaperon. She had never seen the attraction in a country ramble, even in her salad days.

At breakfast, Justin, who was skeptical about the whole project, demanded to see everyone's footwear, and sent Miss Dumphreys, Miss Keene, and Viscount Fenwick back to their rooms to don sturdier shoes. Finally, with appropriate shoes and the ladies equipped with parasols, the expedition set off.

The day was warm but not hot, and the shady lane made for a comfortable walk. After a few minutes of walking and allowing Arthur to set the pace, Felicity noticed that their numbers were diminished. "We seem to have lost Lillian and Lord Fenwick," she said.

"They dropped out before we left the ornamental plantings at the end of the gardens," Justin informed her. "I saw them slip into the shrubbery."

"You didn't say anything," she said.

"I didn't expect them to go much further, to be honest," he told her.

As the smaller party tramped down the lane, Arthur pointed out the grain fields, the hay fields and the new tree plantations. The Duke instinctively set a pace more rapid than his fellows were accustomed to. Baron Wainwright mopped his face with a handkerchief. "I say, getting a bit sultry, ain't it?" he remarked.

"Arthur," said Justin warningly. Arthur turned, realized he was exhausting his party, and moderated his pace. Felicity glared a message at Justin. "What?" he asked in an undertone.

"We are to walk at Arthur's pace," she reminded him.

Now that Arthur had been reminded that his company wasn't used to rapid, long-distance walking, he did try to slow down, but would insensibly speed up without realizing it. Justin, prohibited

148

from mentioning the pace by Felicity's warning glance, tried various ruses to alleviate the rigors of the march, from pointing out a lovely stand of wildflowers that brought the group to an admiring halt for a few moments, to asking Arthur questions about the crops.

Cleo listened with bright-eyed interest, taking mental notes of the various income possibilities of the landed estate. Felicity soldiered on grimly, feeling a trickle of sweat down her spine, a most disconcerting sensation.

Finally Wainwright came to a halt in the middle of the lane. "I say, chaps," he said, "think I'll turn back. M'father's home farm isn't such a monstrous long way from the manor, I don't think."

"I'll join you," Miss Keene said thankfully. "I would like to write some letters and practice the pianoforte."

"Perhaps we should go back," Justin suggested.

"We're going on," Felicity said.

And then they were four. Cleo strode along easily, peppering the Duke with interested questions about home farm management, where did one find a manager, how many workers he had, who decided what to grow.

Felicity's feet were throbbing and her legs were burning. "What well-tended fields!" she panted. Then she decided not to waste any more breath on words, and trudged onward in silence. Bitterly, she remembered her insouciant certainty of the previous night that 'any fool can walk', and silently repeated the phrase to herself over and over as the nightmare trek continued.

Then she stumbled and would have fallen if Amesbury hadn't caught her. He called sharply, "Arthur!" as he half-led, half-carried her to a stile in the fence beside the road. She sat down and took deep breaths. She knew she couldn't continue and bit her lip to keep from crying. The rest of the quartet gathered around her.

"This is enough," Justin said with decision. "Miss Harwell, you should not try to go on."

She nodded. "I know. I am exceedingly vexed with myself, but I find that I am unable to continue."

"We should go back," Justin said to Arthur.

"You're right," Arthur said, frowning slightly.

"No!" said Felicity sharply. There was a tinge of hysteria in her voice. Arthur raised his brows. Felicity continued, "If I am unable to keep up with you, the least I can do is not hold you back. You have business at the farm. Cleo wants to see the farm. There is no reason for us all to turn back. I insist you continue as planned."

Arthur was in a quandary. He wanted now to return, deeply regretting the expedition. But it seemed that abandoning his plan would upset his fiancée even more. He gave Justin a perplexed look.

Justin saw his duty and accepted it, though it would place him exactly where he most feared to be, alone with Felicity on a beautiful summer day in the country. "You and Miss Cooper continue on, and I will escort Miss Harwell back once she's rested a bit," he suggested.

"I'd prefer to return with you," Cleo told Felicity.

"And I'd prefer that you continue," Felicity said. "You'll only make me regret my weakness even more if you abandon your outing on my behalf. Cleo, please!"

Cleo thought that if the debate continued Felicity would certainly begin to cry, which would mortify her even more. "If that's what you want," she said at last.

Felicity patted her hand and gave her a tremulous smile. "It is. And I'm sorry to find that I'm such a weakling."

"You are no such thing!" Cleo said warmly. "You are merely unused to the exercise, and that is no wonder, as little it is practiced among the ladies of the *ton*. I assure you that if you build up to it, you would find yourself walking distances that surprise you."

"Perhaps I will indeed," Felicity said with a little laugh. "But not today."

"I am reluctant to leave you," Arthur said with concern.

"Please indulge me in this," she told him with a pretty smile.

"You needn't be concerned," Justin told him. "I noted several places on the way that would make good points to stop and rest on the way back. We'll return to the manor by easy stages."

With that, the group split for the last time, with Arthur and Cleo continuing down the road, and Justin and Felicity watching them go.

"The grass here in the shade is cool," Justin suggested. "Why don't you remove your shoes and cool your feet? I will turn away and promise not to look."

Felicity blushed, but the promise of cool grass was too tempting, so she sternly admonished Mister Amesbury to mind that he kept his word, and slipped off her shoes and stockings. Ah, it was heavenly!

"Do you suppose Cleo is right?" she wondered, paddling her feet gently through the grass.

"Right about what?" Justin asked.

"About my being able to build up my walking endurance," Felicity explained.

"Why, certainly you might do so, if that is something you care to do."

"But of course I do!"

"You do? Why?" Justin felt this back to back conversation unnatural and had to remind himself not to turn around.

"Why, it's something I could do with Arthur," Felicity said. "For if not walking, what? Would you recommend I take up the study of mathematics?"

Justin chuckled. "Perhaps not. I see your point."

"I think it's important for a married couple to share some interests in common," Felicity continued. "Don't you? My parents both enjoy my father's gardening pursuits, though mother is less ardent on the matter than he. But it gives them something to share."

"Perhaps," Justin said doubtfully. "I can't say my parents have much in common, other than the estate and the family. They tend to rub along tolerably well. I think you'll find that your duties as a duchess and eventually as a mother will give you a great deal to share."

Felicity put on her stockings and shoes. "I suppose you're right," she said. "And yet I intend to make the effort to be a better walker. You may turn around now."

Justin turned and smiled at her. "I doubt you'll be making the effort tomorrow or the next day. I think you'll find that today's exertions will leave you with lingering aches that make you averse to hiking for several days at least. Are you ready to start back?" He pointed back the way they had come. "We will walk to the stile by that field and take another rest there."

Felicity took a resolute breath and stood. "Ready," she told him. He crooked his elbow and she took her arm, and the two set off at a much more moderate rate that the outward trip.

As she strolled at Justin's side, Felicity couldn't help entertaining the guilty wish that Arthur could be more like Justin.

The Duke and Cleo continued on the way toward the home farm in silence for several minutes. Then Cleo said, "I am quite confident that Felicity will soon be able to accompany you on your walks if you wish her to. You've seen the way the young ladies walk in Hyde Park; it is unsurprising that she would lack the ability without working up to it. It's not an accomplishment that society prizes."

Arthur realized with some surprise that he'd been walking at his usual rate and yet Miss Cooper had no difficulty keeping pace with him. "You seem to have no problem maintaining this pace," he observed.

"No, for I've often lived in places where long walks were necessary," she told him. "When we first moved to Sicily, I found the walk from our villa to the village to be quite strenuous, but in time it became a commonplace. The walk had to be taken for the shopping, so I did it regularly."

"I see."

They walked for a while in silence. Finally, Arthur said with some hesitancy, "I have been inquiring into the wage rates for gentlewomen's employment, and it seems that you are correct in that they are not such that one could support a family on such sums."

Cleo arched an eyebrow at him. "Is this an apology, Your Grace?"

"I don't know," Arthur said in honest puzzlement. "I don't think so. I still persist in the belief that there must have been other options available to you, but I can quite see how you might have seen the course you took as your only alternative."

"Then thank you for that at least," Cleo said.

"Once we reach the farm, I will ask Mrs. Stokes to show you around and answer your questions, while I deal with the farm's business with Stokes," Arthur said. "Then we may return home in the farm gig."

Cleo chuckled. "His Grace the Duke of Winton riding in a gig! Fancy that!" She looked about her with a smile of satisfaction. "How well such an estate as this would do for Han! Though on a much smaller scale, of course."

"This has all been to establish your brother?" the Duke asked.

"Of course," Cleo said. "Whatever else?"

"I believe it is more commonly considered that women need to be established, and men are able to make their own way," Arthur explained.

"Perhaps in the normal run of things," Cleo said. "But I know my brother well. He is like Mama in appearance but in all else he is just like Papa, and Papa, dear though he was, was quite impractical. Whereas I look like Papa but resemble Mama otherwise, and Mama was the most sensible woman I've ever known."

There was a pause as the Duke absorbed this extraordinary comment. Then he said, "I'm certain that your mother had many excellent qualities and I've no doubt that you loved her dearly, but I'm not sure that the choices she made in her life would be considered by most to be sensible."

Unoffended, Cleo laughed aloud. "But surely, Your Grace, it has occurred to you before this that society operates under a very faulty definition of sensible?"

"In fact, it has," he admitted. "And I am willing to be persuaded that society was wrong in your mother's case."

"Consider," Cleo told him, "that if Mama had married a man of wealth and family, she would have been praised as sensible even if she had been thoroughly miserable her entire life."

"That is certainly true."

"Instead, she spent her life with the man she wanted to be with, living the life she wished to live, and she was quite happy. How is that not sensible?"

"Perhaps it is," the Duke said. "And yet, was your life and hers not often uncomfortable? You speak of walking great distances, of riding camels, and I believe money was often scarce."

"All of that is true," Cleo admitted. "But here is something that very few people seem to grasp. It is not always necessary to be comfortable to be happy."

"Indeed!" Arthur said, surprised. "An astronomical observatory in the winter is an uncomfortable place, but how many happy hours have I spent there. The viewing conditions are best in the winter, you see. And even Amesbury calls me mad for it."

"You see! And yet if you were just as cold galloping about after a fox or tramping after pheasant, that would be considered quite sensible, would it not? Because those too are winter pursuits."

"I think we've concluded that we should not be bound by the general society's opinion on what is sensible," Arthur said. "But tell me this. You have spent a season in Town. During that time, did none of the young men you met seem to you to be what you would consider a sensible match?"

Cleo shook her head. "No, but I believe my standards might be impossibly high. You see, I ask myself if I would be glad to be with them during a storm at sea in a small boat."

"A strange criterion."

"It dates back to when Mama was still alive," Cleo said, "and our trip to Dalmatia. Han was but a baby. Papa wanted to see some sights in Dalmatia that he had been told were quite extraordinary. The views might have been inspiring, but we were set upon by brigands and robbed of all our money. We wound up stranded in a fishing village in Dalmatia, unable to convince anyone to take us home on promise of future payment. Perhaps, as Papa said, they didn't understand us. Or perhaps, as Mama believed, they were in league with the brigands. But there we were. There were no authorities to appeal to, no embassy officials, we were on our own. What would you have done?"

Fascinated, Arthur shook his head. "I can't imagine. Perhaps if I had longer to consider the problem, but for the moment, I confess to being baffled. What did your parents decide to do?"

"We stole a boat," Cleo said.

"You stole a boat."

"Well, Mama would insist that we borrowed the boat, because of course we had no intention of keeping it permanently."

"Of course."

"But, as she said, what other option did we have? We were stranded among an unhelpful if not outright hostile population and we needed to travel back to our home, which at that time was in Venice. So when the inhabitants had all gone off to some sort of celebration (from the costuming we believe it was a wedding), we borrowed a fishing boat and sailed away."

"How... intrepid."

"It was lovely until the storm came up."

"I can see how that would impair the loveliness of the event."

"I was terrified," said Cleo frankly. "I was in the middle of the boat, huddled into a cloak with Han well wrapped – you know how babies hate to be wet. I was sure we were to be capsized at any moment. Papa was bringing down the sails and Mama was at the

154

tiller. I was crying, I'm not ashamed to say, but then I heard a laugh."

"A laugh! Who could laugh in such circumstances?"

"It was Mama," Cleo said, with a remembering smile. "And she called out over the noise of the storm, 'Miles! This is *living*!'"

"Extraordinary."

"So when I would dance with Mister This or walk with Lord That, and I tried to imagine them in that fishing boat, well, I just couldn't quite picture it."

"That would indeed be a high bar to cross."

"But I needn't marry at all," said Cleo brightly. They were entering the farm yard now, and she exclaimed, "Why, how charming!"

Hearing voices, a stout woman emerged from the dairy. "Why, Your Grace!" She curtseyed hastily and called toward the barn, "Joshua! Here's His Grace crept up on us again!"

As her husband emerged from the barn, the woman gave Cleo a bright smile and a curtsey, saying, "And this must be…"

Too late, Arthur realized the inevitable construction that his farm manager's wife would place on his appearance with a young lady, since the entire county was aware that the Duke was in residence at Winton Court with his bride-to-be. Hastily he said, "This is Miss Cooper, a guest at the Court who is interested in farm management. Miss Cooper, Mister and Mrs. Stokes."

Cleo smiled warmly at the two and said, "Miss Harwell so wanted to come, but you know with a house full of company how hard it is to get away. This evening she will be sure to quiz me on all I see today, and she will manage to make it out here when things have calmed down at the Court."

"Miss Cooper has spent her life abroad," the Duke added, "and now intends to invest her father's legacy in a country estate for her brother. If Mrs. Stokes wouldn't mind showing her around, while Stokes and I discuss farm business?"

"Of course!" Mrs. Stokes was delighted. "Buying a farm? There's nothing better. Come along with me, Miss."

Cleo had a splendid time and learned a very great deal about the making of butter and cheese, and eventually joined the Duke at the gig in great good humor.

Back at the manor, they found the rest of the walking party partaking of a substantial nuncheon. Wainwright, eating large slabs of cold roast beef, waved expansively, genially inviting the Duke to sit at his own table. "Sit down, dear fellow! Nothing like a strenuous exercise to give a chap an appetite."

Miss Dumphreys was struck with an inexplicable fit of giggles. Fenwick shushed her and handed her a peach.

Arthur sat down beside Felicity. "How are you feeling?" he asked with concern. "I hope the return trip was not too difficult."

"I am quite recovered," she said, "and have vowed to start a walking regimen very soon." She turned to Cleo. "How did you find the home farm? I so wish I could have managed to continue."

"It was fascinating!" Cleo said, "and Mrs. Stokes so helpful and informative. I feel as if I could make cheese myself with no further guidance, so clearly did she explain the process."

"By Jove!" said Wainwright. "A young lady who could make cheese! Now that would be an accomplishment of note, far more than all this painting and needlework the young ladies seem to do."

"I must say," the Duchess said, "that the list of accomplishments young ladies are credited with is quite a limited assortment, is it not?"

Sounds from the great hall reached the group at the table. "Were we expecting anyone?" the Duke asked his mother.

"No, I'm sure we weren't," she said, cocking her head toward the door. Then she stood up, hand to her throat.

"Mama?"

But the Duchess threw down her napkin and raced out of the room. The hubbub in the great hall increased.

Arthur raised his eyebrows. "I, for one, am curious," he said mildly, and followed his mother out of the room. The rest of the company trailed behind him.

They found the Duchess in the arms of a tall laughing young man in regimentals. He had lifted her off her feet and was twirling her in circles.

The Duke smiled. "Welcome home, Charley."

SIXTEEN

Lord Charles Ramsey, a larger version of the Duke, with skin darkened and hair lightened by prolonged exposure to the Iberian sun, set his mother down and strode over to Arthur, pulling him into a bear hug. Then he stood back and held Arthur at arm's length. "Let me look at you. Still solving the mysteries of the universe?"

"Trying to," Arthur said. "You have leave?"

"I've sold out, big brother. The war is over, time to come home and enjoy the peace." He looked around. "And I see you've assembled a house party to enjoy it with me."

Arthur opened his mouth, but Charley was ahead of him. "No need to explain, Artie, I was fully briefed at Horse Guards; I know you've carried off the belle of the season. The general staff could talk of nothing else and cursed your name most soundly. In fact, they described your young lady so well that I may easily discern that this is she." He turned to Felicity with a broad smile. "Well met, sister!"

The other members of the house party were clustered at the door to the breakfast room, watching as if at a play, until Cleo said, "Perhaps we should give the family some privacy at this moment. I know I owe Han and Merry a letter."

The others started guiltily at her suggestion and discovered overdue projects that took them to various corners of the estate.

They gathered again in the drawing room before dinner, to find Lord Charles changed out of his regimentals and lamenting the wardrobe he had found waiting for him. "Fit for nothing but the rag bag! Nothing for it but to get all new. I've Weston working on some coats, and he promised to run them up speedily and dispatch them here."

Dinner that night was livened by the introduction of new blood. Miss Keene set out to fascinate the Duke's brother, and everyone wanted war stories.

Lord Charles, however, disappointed them. "I've no wish to relive the past years," he said without compunction. "But if it's war tales you want, just be patient. If all the old buffers who promised memoirs follow through with their intentions, you'll soon be reading all the war you can stomach. Some of the stories might even be true."

"As for me, I joined the army to see the world and now I've seen it. It's dusty, hot, and devilish poor, the insects grow to enormous size and the food is dashed peculiar. Nothing beats England, after all."

"So what are your plans, now that you've sold out?" Amesbury asked.

"I plan to rusticate on my acres in Dorset," Charley said. "Watch the fields. Raise dogs and children. Maybe some horses."

"That sounds most unadventurous," said Miss Keene, dissatisfied.

Charley grinned at her. "I know. Ain't it grand? But what are we doing? An English country house party! I want to be the life and soul of the party. What are our plans for tomorrow? Do we ride? Fish? Charades, perhaps?"

"Tomorrow we will rest and take naps," Arthur told him with a grin.

"Arthur! No, now really!"

"Really," Felicity said. "But that's because of the planet party, which starts at midnight."

Charley was impressed. "A planet party! Is that a new fashion? Much has changed since I went away."

"Perhaps not a fashion yet," said Arthur modestly.

"Oh, but wait till we return to Town!" said Wainwright. "Planet parties will be absolutely all the crack. Give you my word."

Once the ladies had retired to the drawing room and the port began to circulate among the gentlemen at the board, the Duke returned to a comment his brother made earlier. "You said you intended to raise dogs and children," he said. "You'll need a collaborator for that, especially for the children."

"Yes, indeed," Charley told him. "I'm inspired by your example and intend to find a wife and settle down. You must tell me how you did it."

"If you intend to follow my example, you can't do better than to seek the advice and assistance of Amesbury here. I was lost in the salons of London but he saw me through."

Amesbury hoped his smile didn't look as sickly as he felt.

***

158

On a promontory overlooking the River Test, the highest point in the estate and one that previous dukes had embellished with summerhouses and follies, stood the building that the current Duke called the observatory and that his mother privately called 'the monstrosity'.

Strolling at the end of the rose gardens, she pointed it out to Felicity, who walked with her in early afternoon, and said, "When Arthur first showed me the plans, I was so dismayed that I blurted out, 'couldn't it be placed back in the woods, where it wouldn't show?' Well, my dear, he gave me *such* a look! As soon as I spoke, I realized how foolish that would be, when the purpose of the building is to observe the sky after all. But Arthur has always been so patient with me, and simply said, 'what could I see from there?'"

Felicity looked doubtfully at the ungainly building with the fat telescope protruding from the top like a cannon. "It seems so flimsy," she said at last.

"It must turn, you see," the Duchess explained. "I've long become accustomed to it. Mister Jenkins calls it the finest private observatory in the nation, though Arthur continues to complain that Mister Herschel's is larger. But we've had scholarly gentlemen down from Oxford, and they were quite pleased with it. So I suppose we must be proud of it."

"I suppose," Felicity said.

The two women turned back toward the manor. "And whenever I see it, I remind myself that Arthur could be spending his money like too many of my friends' sons do, on cock fights and low company, and the sort of women (for of course I can't call them ladies) that you are I are far too well-bred to know anything about."

"Oh, of course."

"And now, we must drive our guests upstairs for a good lie-down and rest, so you will all be alert later tonight."

As the young ladies went up the stairs for their rest, Marianne wondered aloud, "What does one wear to a planet party?"

Cleo had no notion, but said positively, "Walking dress." She suspected that there was as yet no dress established for astronomical viewing, but if she allowed this bubble-head to set the precedent, young ladies would be walking about out of doors and into observatories in evening dress; delicate fabrics, tiny sleeves, thin shoes, perhaps even a spangled shawl. "Sturdy shoes," she elaborated, "sturdy gowns, and a comfortable pelisse."

Accordingly, the young ladies who descended the staircase at eleven that night were all so practically dressed that the Duke was moved to congratulate them on their good sense. The viewing party gathered in the breakfast room for a cold collation before repairing out of doors to the observatory.

All the young people were committed to the adventure. Among their elders, the Duchess and Lady Dorwood attended, as well as the Harwells, who felt a proprietary interest in the Duke's avocation.

The Duke gave the assembly a talk about telescopes. Perhaps it would have been comprehensible to another audience, such as the Royal Society, but to members of Polite Society the narrative was a jumble of names and terms mostly unfamiliar. Everyone had heard of Newton, of course, and Galileo, but Kepler? Cassegrain? Newton invented the reflector telescope, which was an improvement over refracting telescopes in some manner the listeners were unable to determine.

Felicity wondered if the book she hadn't managed to read would make any of this clearer to her.

The Duke then referred them to a brass contraption set up on a small table. It looked like a complicated version of a garden ornament, and the Duke called it an armillary sphere. The circles apparently represented planets orbiting the sun. Felicity wondered who decided such courses and why and what difference it made.

Cleo stared at the armillary sphere with a thoughtful frown. It wasn't a subject she had ever considered before, but she could see how a person of education and scientific bent would find it intriguing. "The other planets," she said, "they were named by the ancient people, correct? That is why they have classical names?"

"That's right," Arthur said.

"And these ancient people knew that the planets were not stars?" Cleo went on. "How could they possibly know that without telescopes? To the unaided eye, they look like stars."

Arthur was stunned for a moment. He was used to his social group humoring his astronomical pursuits, but here was something entirely unexpected – an intelligent question!

After a pause, he said, "They knew, you see, because the planets move."

"But so do the stars move," argued Cleo.

"Yes, but the stars move together."

Seeing her look of incomprehension, he elaborated. "The stars are so far away that when they move across the night sky, or more accurately, when the earth's rotation makes them appear to move, they move as one, all in a piece. Like... well, like a fabric pattern. The piece of fabric moves, but the small figures on the fabric maintain their position and distance from one another."

"Oh!" Cleo got it. "So you might have a piece of fabric with a pattern of violets. And if you put a violet on the fabric and blew on it, it would move while the fabric violets maintained their places. And you could tell which was the flower and which the fabric pattern."

"Exactly!" Arthur was ridiculously proud of himself.

"'strodinary," said Wainwright, stifling a yawn.

"Shall we proceed out to the observatory?" Arthur invited.

The path through the gardens had been well lit with lamps, and Arthur went at the front of the group carrying a shaded lamp. But when they reached the edge of the garden, they found only shaded lamps along the path up to the observatory. The lamps illuminated the path and left the surrounding area in darkness.

Outside the observatory was a large table, equipped with chairs and another shaded lamp.

"Arthur!" the Duchess said. "Send the servants back for brighter lamps, this will never do."

"No," Arthur corrected her. "We want as little light as possible. Only the shaded lamps and I advice you not to look directly at them. We don't want to ruin our night vision; that would impair the viewing.

"Oh." The Duchess leaned over and murmured to Lady Dorwood, "I didn't realize it would be so dark out here. Maybe we were wrong to endorse this."

The Countess shook her head. "It's not as if it's the Dark Walk at Vauxhall," she argued. "We're a private party, all known to one another, and all the young men are of good character. I don't think we need be concerned."

The Duke stood at the head of the table and addressed the group. "To point and focus the telescope, which is a twenty-inch reflector, is a fairly involved process, so Jenkins and I will adjust the telescope and then you can all file through to see the planet, and then we will move on to the next observation and repeat the process. The observatory is small and can only take several persons at a time, so we will move through one at a time for each observation."

"What will we be seeing?" Felicity asked.

"First we will see the new planet, which I prefer to call Uranus. Then we will examine Saturn, which has a system of rings that is quite remarkable to behold. Then we might view Neptune, which is rather featureless, and by that time the moon should be high enough to make some observations if there is interest."

He turned toward the odd-looking building and called, "Jenkins, are we ready?"

A head popped out of the door. "Ready, Your Grace. And what a beautiful clear night for viewing we have, indeed."

"Shall we?" invited the Duke. "Miss Harwell?"

Felicity was first into the observatory. It was an odd experience, moving up the steps into the small room in almost total darkness to peer through an eyepiece. She saw the fuzzy blue dot, and tried to think of something to say.

"Do you see it?" Arthur asked.

"Yes, indeed!" said Felicity brightly. "There it is. Certainly. Most interesting."

Cleo was next to view. "Why, it's blue!"

"Very blue," the Duke agreed.

"Does that mean it's covered with water?" Cleo asked. "That there's no land, but just an ocean?"

"No one knows," Arthur said regretfully. "It might be water, but at that distance from the sun, it would be very cold. So more likely it would be ice, or perhaps a permanent cloud cover."

"No one knows," Cleo said in an awed voice.

The rest of the viewing party took their turns in the observatory, all with comments similar to Wainwright's. "By Jove," said the Baron, "so that's the new planet, eh?"

Then the party sat at the table chatting while the telescope was turned and focused for Saturn. "We're ready," the Duke called from the door. "It's a spectacular sight tonight."

"You go first," Felicity told Cleo. "You're so interested in this." She hoped to eavesdrop on Cleo's comments for help in devising something interesting to say.

Cleo clambered into the observatory chamber and applied her eye to the eyepiece. "Gracious! What is that?!"

"Those are the rings of Saturn," Arthur told her, as proud as if he'd built them himself.

"They're lovely," Cleo said, "but what on earth are they? Although, of course, they aren't on earth at all. What on Saturn are they?"

"There are a number of theories," Arthur said. "The general feeling is that they are composed of dust and small debris, locked in orbit around the planet, like our moon orbits the earth."

"'The rings of Saturn'" Cleo said. "Why don't we have rings? They would cover the night sky! A Vauxhall illumination would be nothing to it."

"Oh, let me see!" said Felicity from the ground outside the door. Cleo gave place to Felicity, who viewed the planet and exclaimed over its beauty.

The party once again filed through the observatory to see this marvel.

After Saturn, Neptune was voted a great disappointment. "A paltry thing," said Wainwright, "and so I shall tell them at the club. Saturn, yes, worth the viewing, but Neptune, no."

Then the viewing turned to the moon. Arthur tried to explain why only half the moon's disk was currently visible, but soon gave it up, saying, "I'll have to show you on the armillary sphere; it's actually quite simple, really."

The party diminished at this point. The Harwells were yawning hugely, and Fenwick and Miss Dumphreys were frankly bored. The Duchess escorted the deserters back to the house, murmuring to Lady Dorwood, "I'll leave these silly children to you, my dear; I'm too old for these late nights."

The moon was much admired, though its aspect, seen through the telescope, was bleak and harsh. But it was large enough to show an actual geography, and have place names assigned to features on its surface.

"It looks so much less romantic seen up close," Felicity said ruefully.

Once they'd had their fill of the moon, the party sat at the table contemplating the return to the manor. "Must say, I'm devilish sharp-set," complained the Baron.

163

"You'll have to wait until breakfast," said the Duke austerely. "I certainly won't wake up Cook at —" he consulted his pocket watch, "at three in the morning."

Cleo chuckled. "How helpless you men are!"

"What do you mean?" asked Amesbury with a frown.

"You can't even assemble a snack for yourself? Food must be arranged and brought to you by a servant? You have all manner of edible food available to you, for we certainly didn't finish off that ham, and there is always bread. All you would have to do is find it."

"I say," said Lord Charles from the dimness at the far end of the table, "where does Cook keep the ham? Some cheese, a bit of bread."

Cleo laughed out loud. "I always thought my papa was the most helpless man on earth in domestic matters, but even he could make a simple egg dish. And you fine gentlemen need a map or a guide to find the ham!"

Arthur surged to his feet. "We will find the ham," he said decisively. "And the bread and the cheese."

"Huzzah," jeered Charley faintly.

"What's more," Arthur said recklessly, "I'll warrant I could make a 'simple egg dish', too." After a pause, he added more modestly, "with a bit of guidance, of course."

The party came to their feet and followed their leader toward the manor. Charley brought up the rear, providing a running commentary of the storming of the kitchen by the bold forces of the noble Duke of Winton.

Once the Duke's raiding party had entered the dim cavernous depths of the kitchen, however, they realized that before they could find the ham, they must first find the tinderbox and candles. The party fanned out, groping surfaces for these familiar items. Giggling was heard from various quarters. A snap and a waver of light indicated that the Countess had found the tinderbox and lit the small candle affixed to it. With its help, more candles were discovered and soon the room was adequately lit.

The kitchen-raiding party met in conference around the large, battered old table. "So," the Duke said. "What are we looking for?"

"The ham," said the Countess, from her seat at the head of the table.

"Don't forget the bread and cheese," added Lord Charles.

164

"Brandy?" suggested the Baron hopefully.

"Remember the simple egg dish," said Cleo. "You'll need to find the ingredients for that."

"Which are what?" Arthur asked her. "Eggs, of course."

"And milk," Cleo told him. "And whatever else you might fancy in your eggs. It's a good dish for using up leftovers."

"Very well." The Duke scanned the kitchen.

"You should look for the cold larder," Felicity suggested.

"Hush!" Cleo said.

Felicity turned to her, puzzled.

"We're giving the gentlemen the opportunity to demonstrate that they are not helpless in the arena of food preparation," Cleo reminded her. "Now, sit."

Felicity took a seat at the table. Marianne joined them, and Cleo sat as well. The men ranged about the kitchen, opening doors and cabinets, calling out findings to one another.

"Just pickles here," reported Charley.

"Pickles!" said Wainwright. "Fetch them out, man. Nothing goes better with cold ham than pickles."

"My word, but this is amusing," the Countess said.

The next discovery was Wainwright's, who appeared in triumph bearing several loaves of bread.

"A-HA!" The Duke appeared through a doorway and announced triumphantly, "I found the ham, and the eggs! Plus the milk and cheese. You fellows, come help me bring these out."

"The trove, by Jupiter!" his brother said gleefully.

The plunder was brought to the table and assembled. Wainwright had also discovered a large knife and went busily to work slicing slabs of ham and bread and cheese. "How the deuce do they slice these things so thinly?" he wondered. "Ah well, this will do."

Justin appeared from a door in the back, bearing ale. He was greeted as a hero.

Arthur looked at the eggs and milk, and then looked at Cleo. "Miss Cooper? You are committed to guide me through this simple egg dish."

"You need a large bowl and a skillet," Cleo told him, " and then of course, something to cook on." She looked at the large range

165

holding pride of place along one wall and gasped. "Gracious! What is that?"

"It's the latest in cooking apparatus," the Duke told her proudly. "A Rumford range. Mother said that Cook insisted on it."

"I'm afraid I'll only be able to give you general guidance, then," Cleo said. "I've never cooked nor observed cooking on so advanced a device. I presume, though, that the box holds the fire and has been banked for the night? Building up the fire ought surely to be the first step."

Between the two of them, they managed to get the fire burning brightly again. By the time they had achieved this, Cleo had a sooty smudge on her nose. Arthur laughed and wiped it off with a thumb before jerking back his hand and looking away in confusion.

**

Daisy the scullery maid slept on a pallet in the back of the scullery. She knew she owed this position, deliciously warm and quiet, to her secondary assignment. During the day, she was ever at Cook's beck and call, keeping the pots and pans and dishes cleaned. But during the night, her task was to prevent sneak thieving servants from pilfering in the kitchen.

So when she heard noises in the kitchen hours before dawn, Daisy knew she had to investigate. She crept out from the blankets, threw a shawl around her thin shoulders, and crept silently toward the door of the kitchen.

What action she would take would depend on who she found in the kitchen. If it was Jamie, the good-natured new footman, she would give him a stern talking to. (He really was a handsome lad.) But if it was Dirk, the cheeky boot boy, or that pinching lout Harry from the stables, she would scream the house down, that she would.

Cautiously, Daisy peeked around the corner of the door, and quickly she pulled her head back, hand over her mouth. Lawsamercy! It was the Quality! A whole crowd of them, all dressed fine as fivepence, laughing and eating and making free with Mrs. Osbourne's skillet which no one but herself and Daisy were even permitted to touch.

Daisy turned and quietly fled by back ways to rouse the cook.

SEVENTEEN

As the ducal house party reveled in the kitchen, an avenging angel in a flannel robe and braided hair was stumping down the servants' stair. Mrs. Osbourne was a formidable woman. Quality or no, guests of His Grace or no, they'd soon learn that the kitchen was her domain, thank you very much.

She loomed in the door of the kitchen, hands on hips. "Here now! What's all this?"

But then the rascal who had the brass to be wearing her very own apron turned toward the door, still busily whisking eggs in a large bowl, and saints preserve us! – it was His Grace himself!

Cook's tone changed immediately, because the Duke had always had a way with him, even from a child. Still gruff, but kindly, she exclaimed, "Your Grace! What have you gotten up to? If you and your guests wanted something, you'd only had to ask me."

The Duke smiled apologetically. "But what I wanted you could not provide, Mrs. Osbourne. Because what I wanted was to succeed in the challenge to prepare this dish myself."

Cook was bewildered. "Challenge? You mean like a bet?"

"Not a bet, a challenge," Arthur told her.

"If you say so, Your Grace." She folded her arms and looked about the room, seeing the crumbs and the pickle juice, and young people looking guilty and yet exhilarated. "Ah, well," she said tolerantly. But the Duke continued whisking the eggs, and seeing a task inexpertly performed distressed her. "Oh, do give me that, Your Grace," she said, coming forward and reaching for the bowl.

"Ah ah ah," the Duke chided, turning his back to protect his egg mixture from interference, and slopping some of it on Cook's apron. "You must allow me to do this, Mrs. Osbourne. Please, go back to bed. We're fine here."

He was the Duke. What choice did she have? Though it went to her heart to leave her realm occupied by these vandals, she nodded, said, "Yes, Your Grace," and left the room, pulling Daisy with her. In the hall, she whispered to Daisy, "Now you come fetch me the

167

minute they leave, so we can clear up the mess in time for breakfast. And what we'll do for the breakfast toast, I'm sure I don't know."

In the kitchen, the raiders reacted to Cook's departure with relieved laughter. "Thank goodness you were here, Artie!" Lord Charles said. "Otherwise, I'd think the lot of us would be roasting on spits right now. You always were her favorite, you know."

The Duke returned to his cookery experiment. Cleo coached, but held her hands behind her back, requiring him to do all the work himself. Finally, it was done.

Cleo peered at the skillet. "I think it will do," she pronounced. "You can always scrape off that burned bit."

Arthur circled the table, scooping a bit of his creation in front of each member of the party. Fortunately, the portions were small. After a great deal of chewing, Amesbury pronounced, "Quite... tolerable."

Lord Charles loyally proclaimed it as good as anything he'd eaten on the Peninsula.

"Where the food is 'dashed peculiar'," Arthur said with a laugh.

"You have the most inconvenient memory!" Charley complained.

Cleo took a bite and pronounced judgment. "It's perfectly edible," she said solemnly, "and therefore, His Grace has passed the test. As have all of you gentlemen." She bowed graciously to them. "You demonstrated your ability to find edible food to sustain yourself without assistance, in the finest tradition of primitive tribes the world over. You may all be proud of yourself."

Given permission, the gentlemen cheered and pounded on the table, while the ladies clapped their hands, the noise causing Daisy, lurking in the hall, to shrink back in alarm.

The group then settled down to a convivial and conversable meal, and it was the most pleasant meal of Arthur's memory. He looked across the table, where Cleo laughed at Lord Charles' tale of an alarming feast on the Peninsula, and capped it with a story about a goat, a nun and a bandit, a story she swore was true.

The Duke felt something turn over in his chest, a most peculiar sensation. He didn't know what it meant, but he wanted to keep looking at Miss Cooper, at her laughing eyes and shining dark hair. Looking at her made the corners of his mouth twitch, and had the width of the great table not been between them, he would have involuntarily reached out to smooth back a lock of hair that had tumbled across her brow.

Wainwright, having made vast inroads into the ale, returned to the object of tonight's party. "What about those planets, eh?" he asked. "Extraordinary things, what? 'Straordinary!"

"Not things!" Cleo said, eyes shining. "Places!"

"Exactly!" Arthur exclaimed, slapping the table. "You have it!" The assembly all looked at him in astonishment, and he stammered, "The planets. They're places. Wonderful, vast, faraway places."

"If only we could go there," said Cleo dreamily.

"Go there!" exclaimed Marianne. "Who would want to go there? Whatever would there be to go there for?"

Cleo opened her eyes wide. "Why, because no one has ever been there before, of course."

"In that case," said the comfort-loving Baron, "they're bound to be deuced uncomfortable. No good roads, not even an embassy."

"We know that," said Cleo kindly. "And of course we can't go there, but are simply wishing it were possible."

"No branches of one's bank," Wainwright went on doggedly. "No coaching inns, no tailors, b'gad!"

"Then we shall have to forego travel to other planets until they agree to provide these comforts," Arthur said, trying not to laugh. His eyes met Cleo's and he looked away hastily, knowing that if she laughed, he would too.

The party broke up now and everyone straggled off to bed. Everyone but a timid little scullery maid who hastened to fetch Mrs. Osbourne, who surveyed the devastation and grimly went to work. But as she worked, a smile crept across her face as she thought of 'His Grace and them eggs!'

Arthur retired to bed, but it was long before he slept. He stared up at the ceiling, trying to puzzle out what was happening to him. Nothing had changed, not really. Nothing but himself.

He set out in the spring to find a woman to be his duchess. And he'd succeeded in that task admirably. He had no doubt that Miss Harwell would be an excellent duchess; she was kind, good-natured, reasonably intelligent, lovely to look at, healthy, well-behaved and well-bred. But along the way, he had also found a woman he could be happy with, and unfortunately, the two were not embodied in the same woman.

Resolutely, he set himself to imagine his life with his new duchess. He saw them at the dinner table. He was perhaps telling her of his recent observations of the moons of Jupiter, first seen by Galileo. He could see Felicity listening, nodding and saying, 'how wonderful, to be sure', tolerant but entirely uncomprehending.

But the scene wavered in his mind and when it reformed, it was Cleo seated across from him, eyes shining, elbows on the table as she peppered him with questions about those same moons. How large were they, what were they made of? In fact, she might have been out in the observatory with him.

Arthur groaned. If only she weren't a thief! Or if only he weren't a duke! Oh, it was obviously impossible – a Ramsey of Winton and the drawing master's daughter! However charming, however bright and interesting, however inexplicably attractive. Anyway, he reminded himself, he was committed. The engagement had been announced and to withdraw now would be dishonorable, the act of a cad.

Rolling over, he punched his pillow, trying to create a more comfortable arrangement. Cleo would soon leave, he told himself, and he would marry Felicity, and in time he would forget about Cleo. Perhaps not forget, but at least he would think about her less and less. He would be as contented as he had ever been.

He tried to ignore the little voice telling him that to be as contented as he had ever been was no longer enough.

Cleo was too excited to sleep. What a wonderful evening! The planets! And how different the Duke seemed now. Not just a duke, a *scientist*, which Cleo was beginning to realize was a most excellent thing to be.

Cleo wondered if she could get a telescope of her own, not so enormous as the Duke's, but at least a small one. There were other planets she hadn't seen yet, that weren't in the sky tonight. According to Arthur, or rather the Duke, Mars was red and Venus was green, and Jupiter was enormous and had moons of its own. She wanted to see all that!

She felt a pang of bitter envy toward Felicity, who would soon have daily access to that telescope (and its disturbingly attractive owner) every day, and probably would never look through it unless urged to do so at an event like tonight's.

And the kitchen party! What fun that had been, more fun than Cleo could remember having since both Mama and Papa had been alive. Those barely edible eggs; who would have thought that Arthur (the Duke!) had such a willingness to attempt such an unducal thing. And when he'd looked at her, obviously trying not to laugh, just the expression on his face made it that much more difficult to stifle her own laughter. It reminded her of that time they'd met some pompous functionary in Florence and Papa had murmured through clenched teeth, "Belle, don't you dare laugh, or you'll set me off."

Cleo told herself sternly, 'you've nothing to do with dukes, my girl!', and tried to take her thoughts back to those wonderful planets. But she drifted off to sleep in the midst of a ridiculous fantasy in which she delivered a paper on some astronomical wonder to the Royal Society (as if, she thought sleepily, the Royal Society would ever permit a woman to do such a thing!), after which the Duke of Winton pressed her hand warmly and said admiringly, "Well done, Miss Cooper!" She couldn't help wishing, just a little bit, that he didn't despise her.

Felicity tucked herself into bed, thought, 'what a peculiar evening', and was instantly asleep.

***

The Duke was up early the next day, still in great perturbation of mind. He dressed hastily and donned the old brown jacket, determined on a long tramp through the woods and fields. Walk far and walk fast, that was the prescription. He set off on his walk, determined to walk the wrong woman out of his mind.

Lord Charles also rose early. He had napped most comfortably the previous day, having learned the soldier's trick of sleeping easily when sleep was permitted, and was thus quite fresh on just a few hours of sleep during the night. He was also soon out of doors, eager to roam the estate and revisit all his childhood haunts.

The other early riser was Cleo. She lay in bed for a few moments, but realized that she wanted to see the observatory in daylight, get a good sense of its fixtures and arrangements and how the telescope was moved and pointed. She was soon out in the gardens, headed toward the observatory. Lord Charles was at the far side of the garden, visiting with an elderly gardener. She called "Good morning!" with a wave and continued down the path to the observatory.

The rest of the house party slept deeply, while the staff went quietly and efficiently about its business.

Tolliver loved the early part of the morning. For the household staff, it was the most productive time of day. Without interference from The Family and their guests, tasks could be begun and carried through to completion without interruption. The house was swiftly being brought back to immaculate condition. Tolliver moved through his domain, inhaling the heady scent of beeswax, enjoying the gleaming furniture, the plumped pillows. Everything was Just So.

But as he passed through the front hall, his self-satisfied reverie was interrupted by an impatient tattoo on the front door. Callers? This early? Frowning, the butler made his stately way to the front door and opened it.

"How may I help you, sir?" But even as he spoke the words, Tolliver wondered if his unerring social instincts had failed him. Because the imperious old man at the door worn a plain black suit much like his own, the raiment of the superior servant. And the equipage being led around the corner of the manor was assuredly a humble gig.

The visitor strode past Tolliver into the manor. "Where is Miss Cooper?" he demanded. "I must speak with her immediately."

Tolliver drew himself up imposingly. "Whom shall I say is calling?" he asked, managing in the nick of time to refrain from adding another 'sir' to his address.

"Tell her it's General," the old man said impatiently. "She knows me. It's urgent."

Tolliver nodded. "I believe Miss Cooper is up, but I am not sure of her exact whereabouts. If you would come with me, please."

He led the way to the library and ushered the old man ("General?") in. "I will have Miss Cooper sent here as soon as she might be located," he said, and left, shutting the door gently behind him.

Lord Charles, entering the hall from a side door, found a conference in progress. "She's not in her room, Mister Tolliver," Mary the upstairs maid was saying.

"Nor in the breakfast room," said James the footman.

"Who's not where?" Charles asked.

The butler turned to him. "It's Miss Cooper, my lord. She has a caller, requesting urgently to speak to her."

172

"I just saw Miss Cooper," Charles said. "She was outside. I believe she was headed toward the observatory."

"Thank you, sir." Tolliver turned to James. "If you would fetch Miss Cooper, please." James hurried off. "And that will be all, Mary." Mary sketched a curtsey to Charles and left.

"What's this about a caller for Miss Cooper?" Charles asked. "Who is it?"

"He's an older gent-person, my lord," Tolliver said with a puzzled frown. "He styles himself General, but is attired as a servant. He says she knows him. I've put him in the library. I didn't know what to do. He's not the usual sort of caller. I hope it isn't trouble."

"I'll go take a look at this 'gent-person'," Charles said, and strode off to the library.

Inside the library, General paced impatiently. He turned as the door opened and a tall, well-built young man entered. The young man opened his mouth to speak, but then stopped as if struck dumb. Finally, he said, "My lord!"

"Miss Cooper? Is she coming?"

Flustered, Lord Charles stammered, "They're fetching her just now. But sir! You, here?! We thought you dead!"

General started, and stood very still. He said softly, "Do you know me, sir?"

"Know you? The man who saved my life? Rather!"

"If you know me, would you be so good as to tell me who I am?"

Charles gaped at the request. "Who you are? Don't you know?"

"If I knew, would I ask?" was the irritable rejoinder.

"But... why, you're Colonel Lord Salford, of course. Gervase, Earl of Salford. And yet... You are dead. I would have sworn. I saw it! Saw you shot in the head just as our position was overrun."

"Ah. Then perhaps you've been mistaken by a chance resemblance."

Charles ventured closer to the old man. His face cleared. "Saw you shot in the head – right there!" he exclaimed, pointing to the scar running across the side of the mystery man's forehead and vanishing into his hair. "The bullet must have creased the skull but not penetrated." He seized the old man's right hand and turned it over, pushing up the cuff to reveal another scar. "And here. You got this at Talavera."

"Indeed?" the old man said. He murmured "Salford," sampling the name, trying it on.

"You don't remember? Not at all?"

"Not at all. I've been with the Coopers, must have been ever since the injury."

"Why, this is famous!" Charles said. "You've been declared dead, you know. We must see about having you brought back to life officially."

The door opened and Cleo entered. And the Earl of Salford was once again General the butler. "Miss Cleo, you must return with me to Town at once, you're needed urgently."

"What is it, General? What's the trouble?" Cleo asked.

"If I might speak with you privately, Miss."

Impatiently, Lord Charles said, "My lord, we must get this sorted."

"That can be dealt with later," the older man said smoothly. "Now, if you please, sir," gesturing to the door.

"No, but really!" Charles exclaimed.

Salford drew himself up and directed at Charles an all too familiar glare. He barked, "I said *later*, Captain!"

Lord Charles instinctively snapped to attention. Salford jerked his head meaningfully toward the door, and Charles bowed slightly and departed without a word.

Cleo watched this byplay wide-eyed. "General? What was that all about?"

"He says he knows me," her butler said dismissively. "But never mind that now. Miss Cleo, Master Han is gone!"

"What do you mean, gone?"

"Taken the wagon and the birds and gone. He left a letter. He says he's seen Baron Marcuse and has gone after him." He handed Cleo a rumpled piece of paper. She sank into a chair and hastily scanned it.

Then she jumped to her feet. "We must go after him!"

"We must return to Town," General said. "Master Han will send a pigeon when he finds the Baron's ultimate destination. And we might hear from Mister Peter. Miss Merryhew sent for him as soon as she realized Master Han was gone, and he set out to follow him. A gypsy wagon will have been seen."

"We'll leave right away," Cleo said. "Just let me throw a few things into a bag and we'll be on our way."

She hurried out of the room and ran past a bemused Charles and up the stairs. The General followed her into the great hall. Lord Charles and Tolliver waited, hoping for an explanation of these puzzling events. "Miss Cleo will be accompanying me back to Town immediately," the General told Charles. "Please make her excuses to His Grace and tell him a family emergency." He turned to Tolliver. "Please have the horse reharnessed and brought around right away."

Tolliver looked to Lord Charles, who impatiently endorsed the request. "You heard, man, bring Lord Salford's carriage at once."

Lord Salford! Tolliver hastened away to pass the word, relieved that his social instinct had not misled him. He could spot Quality, however humble the attire.

***

Arthur approached the manor well-exercised but still in great uneasiness of mind. His long tramp had not unearthed a solution to his dilemma, but he hadn't expected it to. He knew quite well there was no solution. There was only endurance, and a hope that this inexplicable attraction was as ephemeral as it was sudden.

He resolutely avoided using the term 'love', even in the privacy of his own mind. Love was all very well on stage or within the pages of a novel, but it should have nothing to do with the manner of making family alliances, certainly not among men of his class.

Again he felt that unwilling twinge of envy for the late Miles Cooper, the man who lived as he wished, traveled where he would, and loved where he dared. And how, he reminded himself, had that turned out? With a family so impoverished that his daughter turned to crime to provide for her young brother.

No, love was a folly. He was a duke, not an artist. He had responsibilities, and the woman to whom he had bound himself was ideally suited to assist him in carrying out those responsibilities.

He mounted the front steps slowly, knowing he would shortly be sharing a breakfast parlor with the woman he had pledged himself to, and also with the woman he lo… was attracted to. He looked forward (or so he told himself) to the day when Cleo had departed from his estate and troubled his peace no more.

That reckless claim was put to the test as soon as he entered the front door.

175

Tolliver approached him with a deferential cough. "Excuse me, Your Grace," he said smoothly. "It would assist the staff to know – is Miss Cooper returning?"

Arthur frowned. "Returning? What do you mean?"

Tolliver stifled a smile. It was an object to him to apprise His Grace of information of which he might not be aware. "Why, she has left, sir. Returned to her home, as I understand it. Something in the nature of a family emergency?"

"She did? When was this?"

"They left no more than an hour since."

"Ah, did Lady Dorwood accompany her?"

"Why, no, Your Grace. Miss Cooper is traveling with Lord Salford. It was he who arrived soon after you departed for your walk, with news of an emergency."

Salford? That name was familiar. Arthur was certain he'd heard it somewhere, and recently. He stared at the floor, searching his memory. Aha! Newmarket. The dissolute young man that Justin refused to acknowledge. The man who 'ruined women for sport'!

Salford! Could he possibly be in league with Miss Cooper? But no. Arthur could not believe that of her. Miss Cooper had scruples. They might not be the same as those of society at large, but they were scruples and she abided by them. Arthur remembered the warmhearted family who could not bring themselves to abandon a wounded stranger on a battlefield. Could Cleo ally herself with a malicious scoundrel, someone who hurt others for sheer sport? Arthur knew he was unfamiliar with the finer nuances of polite society, but he also knew that his friend was very familiar indeed with the social world and its personalities. A man that Amesbury refused to so much as bow to was a very bad man. It was impossible for Cleo to be allied with such a man.

But if not his confederate, what was her position in this? Could she be his intended prey? Was the family emergency merely a ploy to lure Cleo into Salford's clutches? Or – he too had been at Newmarket. Was he onto her scheme and blackmailing her to her ruin?

Arthur looked up from his pacing. Tolliver waited with unwearying patience and well-concealed curiosity. "Send to the stable to have them saddle my horse," he said.

Tolliver lifted a finger and a footman hurried up to take the message.

"His Grace's horse," Tolliver told the footman. "Immediately."

He looked to the Duke, and received a nod. Immediately it was. The footman hurried out with the directive.

Arthur thought rapidly. If scandal was the miscreant's aim, scandal must at all costs be avoided. He said smoothly to Tolliver. "I believe there has been some sort of misunderstanding. I will follow Miss Cooper and render her assistance."

"Very good, Your Grace," Tolliver said woodenly.

In a matter of moments, the Duke's horse was being led to the front door. Tolliver, still seeking information to share with the upper servants, asked, "What message shall I give Her Grace and Her Ladyship?"

Arthur swung into the saddle and considered. He knew that after such a late night his late-rising household would arise even later than usual. "No need for messages," he decided. "I expect to be back shortly." And he was gone down the drive.

Tolliver softly closed the front door and went off to consult with Pelton on His Grace's latest mad start.

As he trotted down the long drive, Arthur wondered how he was to handle this encounter. If Cleo's ruin was the villain's aim, his very presence would scotch that notion. He hoped the blackguard didn't have the temerity to call him out, but if so Arthur thought he could acquit himself adequately, though the scandal would be enormous.

He told himself that villains were almost always cowards, and surely just knowing that his scheme had been uncovered would send Salford on his way.

Attaining the London road, Arthur urged his mount into an easy lope. Now he realized that he'd neglected to ask Tolliver what sort of equipage Salford was driving. Remembering the young man's appearance as an aspirant to fashion, Arthur considered it almost a surety that Salford would be driving a phaeton or a curricle. But he would visually inspect every vehicle he passed, even overcoming his diffidence to the extent of peering discourteously into the windows of covered carriages.

Even so, he almost rode past the parson's gig without a second glance, but once well past some instinct cause him to look back and pull his horse to a stand with a muffled oath. Because the black-clad figure he took to be a parson was actually General, the Coopers' enigmatic butler, while the 'parson's daughter' at his side was Miss Cooper herself. "Cleo!" the Duke exclaimed.

As the gig drew near, slowing at the sight of the horseman blocking the road, he raised his voice to hail it. "Miss Cooper!"

Cleo looked at him in astonishment. "Your Grace! What are you doing here?"

Arthur felt foolish and confused. "I followed you. I was led to believe you were in danger."

The gig had halted now, and the Duke leaned down to speak with the occupants.

"Danger?" Cleo asked, puzzled. "It is not I who is in danger. How came you to believe so?"

"My butler said you had left with Lord Salford, a man I know to be untrustworthy with women," the Duke explained.

"Ah!" Cleo exclaimed. "But you see, according to your brother, General here is actually Lord Salford. I suppose when he was believed dead, some other claimant took the title."

The old butler frowned. "Riddley!" he barked. "That intolerable jackanapes!"

Cleo looked at him. "General! Is that a memory?"

"I suppose it must be," he said slowly.

Cleo smiled up at the Duke, but he saw the strain in her smile. "So you see that I am in no danger, Your Grace. I apologize for leaving your house party so precipitously, but I am urgently required at home."

She obviously wanted him to let them pass. But Arthur hesitated. Her agitation was now apparent, even to him. He said carefully, "Perhaps you are not in danger, Miss Cooper, but it appears to me that you are in some form of trouble."

"And if I am?" she asked tartly.

"If you are, then I earnestly request that you allow me to assist you with it."

Startled, Cleo asked bluntly, "Why?"

Arthur didn't know how to reply. Finally, he said, "It concerns me to see you so troubled. I believe I can be of use."

General, or rather Lord Salford, interposed now. "Miss Cleo, we must be on our way."

"Let me ride with you a way," Arthur suggested. "Tell me your difficulty and let us see if we can light upon a solution to it."

Cleo and the butler exchanged a look. "Very well," she said reluctantly.

EIGHTEEN

It was just past noon when Felicity left her bedchamber and made her way to the breakfast parlor. She was still tired and wondered why. Certainly she had sustained later hours many times during the season. But that was at parties and balls, brilliantly lit, with music and laughter and chattering crowds. A late night in a dimly lit country garden was quite a different thing, she supposed, with the hooded lamps and country quiet emphasizing that one really ought to be asleep. She wondered if planet parties would be a regular feature of her new life at Winton Court, and if she would ever become accustomed to them.

In the breakfast parlor she found Mister Amesbury at table, addressing a generous plate of beef and eggs. She helped herself to some pastry and an egg and took a seat, allowing the footman to pour her cup of tea.

"Interesting evening," Amesbury offered.

"I'm sure it will make a nice conversation piece for the guests," Felicity said, "not your usual house party fare." She sipped her tea and then said with genuine puzzlement, "But how *can* he be so absorbingly interested in those faint little blots of light?!" She clapped her hand over her mouth, realizing she had betrayed herself into a criticism of her betrothed.

Justin looked up from his beef and said mildly, "Pardon? Didn't catch that."

Felicity smiled at him. Of course he'd caught that. What nice manners the man had. "Nothing," she said gratefully, and changed the subject. "Are we the first down, or the last?"

"The first, I think," Justin replied.

James the footman knew better. Mister Tolliver had told him often and often that the superior servant does not hear the Family's conversations, or those of their guests. James understood him to mean that they must at least appear to not hear the Quality talking among themselves. A superior servant spoke when directly addressed, and never entered into the conversation.

180

But James was a very young footman and Mister Tolliver wasn't there. "Oh, no sir," he said from his place at the buffet. "His Grace came down this age ago and went for his usual walk. And there was that Miss Cooper out and about on the grounds before she took off, and His Grace gone after her."

Justin looked up in astonishment. "*What* did you say?"

Now James remembered Mister Tolliver's strictures and blushed scarlet. "Nothing, sir," he stammered, adding "the tea's gone cold," before clutching the pot and fleeing the parlor.

Justin stared after him. "What the d – deuce?"

Felicity wore a puzzled frown. "Cleo 'took off'?"

"And 'His Grace gone after her'!" added Justin.

"Whatever can have happened?"

Justin scowled. All his suspicions of Miss Cooper returned with full force. "She's up to something," he said darkly.

"How can you know that?" Felicity protested.

"Because she's gone off without a word to anyone, apparently, and somehow managed to induce Arthur to follow her. It's a trick, you mark my words."

"What sort of trick?" Felicity wondered.

Justin stood and paced about the parlor. "If she can manage to get Arthur alone, she could compromise herself," he said at last. "Your dear friend, Miss Harwell, is trying to trap your fiancé into marrying her."

Felicity stared at him. "Oh, don't be absurd!" she said at last. "Whyever would she do such a thing? She knows I am to marry Arthur."

Justin waved his arms. "Look around you, and don't be so naïve. Many a chit would do the same thing for the wealth and position she would gain as the Duchess of Winton."

"Nonsense!" Felicity said stoutly. "Cleo is too principled for such a shabby trick."

"You think so? And where would she have learned those principles? From those vagabonds who raised her?"

Felicity was standing now and turned her back to him, crossing her arms. "I won't listen to such nonsense."

"You won't have to," Justin said, striding toward the door. "I'm going after them."

"Wait!" Felicity followed him. "What do you intend to do?"

181

"I intend to follow them and scotch her plan," Justin said.

"And how do you intend to do that?" Felicity asked. "If what you say is true, how does the addition of yet another bachelor prevent Cleo's compromise? Unless you intend to marry her yourself."

Justin started back, eyes wide. "Never in all the world!" he exclaimed.

Felicity was all resolution now. "We will go after them," she corrected him. "If your mad suspicions are correct, my presence will allay any compromise. And if, as I believe, Cleo has some sort of problem, then we will help her and Arthur solve it."

Justin hesitated and then nodded. "Dress for driving, then and tell anyone who asks merely that we are taking my curricle for a drive about the grounds."

Felicity flew up the stairs to fetch her bonnet and pelisse. She was quite vexed with Mister Amesbury and looked forward to his comeuppance. The very idea of Cleo dealing her such a backhanded turn! It was nonsense – wasn't it?

***

"It's my brother," Cleo told Arthur. "He's run away, and is in more danger than he knows."

"Run away?" Arthur asked. "Did he feel mistreated at home, or is he merely a boy on a spree?"

"He has an object in mind," Cleo said. "He left a note. He believes he has seen a man who stole from us in Venice and is following him. He took the gypsy wagon and his birds."

"Miss Cleo!" protested General.

Cleo waved a dismissive hand. "Oh, the Duke is aware of our pigeon scheme. No, I didn't tell him but he worked it out. And he hasn't reported us to the authorities yet, so I feel that we can trust him."

"What do you hope to do?" Arthur asked. "Will you follow him?"

"Peter is trying to follow the wagon, and I hope we will soon receive a pigeon from Han," Cleo said. "We must go home first to see if Miss Merrihew has any new information. If only Marcuse doesn't realize he's being followed!"

"Tell me about this Marcuse," Arthur urged.

"We're both getting stiff necks," Cleo complained. "Would you be willing to trade places with General?" She turned to the butler. "You do ride, don't you?"

"I suppose so," General said doubtfully. But once the transfer had taken place and Arthur was seated beside Cleo in the gig, the old butler swung easily into the saddle and sat up straight. "Ah!" he said. "This is more like!"

He moved ahead of the gig and put the Duke's horse through a series of maneuvers, before returning alongside the cart and saying, "A sweet goer, Your Grace."

The gig and outrider proceeded on its way toward London, with Salford ranging about in front of the gig. Cleo watched him in wonder. "I've never seen him so alert," she said.

"He's at home in the saddle, certainly," Arthur said. "Unsurprising, for a Peninsular man. Now, tell me about this man your brother is seeking."

"He seemed so nice," Cleo said plaintively. "We met in Venice when Papa was working on his most important project, some large frescos for the public reception areas in the palacio of a very important man. Our new acquaintance called himself Baron Marcuse, an Englishman of large substance and a great interest in art. Papa enjoyed his visits and his knowledge of art was certainly not feigned, though his background was, as we later learned."

She frowned thoughtfully and continued. "I believe that in addition having art in common, Papa was flattered to be befriended as an equal by a member of the English gentry. It had always been his intent to return to England someday and it disturbed him to think that his children wouldn't be accepted by our mother's class. He saw Marcuse's friendship as a hopeful sign that the rigid lines between classes were softening a bit."

Arthur shook his head. "I see no evidence of such a softening, I'm afraid."

"I believe you are right," Cleo said. "Certainly without Aunt Dorwood, I couldn't have expected to be accepted as I have been. But that hope made Papa vulnerable to a plausible scoundrel. A pity Mama wasn't alive then, because she had much less use for her own class. Better to spend your time with those who do things, she always said, than with those who merely live well because their ancestors once did things."

Arthur was silent at this. After days in the company of Baron Wainwright and Viscount Fenwick, he found himself in agreement with the intrepid Mrs. Cooper.

"So," Cleo continued, "when Baron Marcuse offered to haul our household goods to Sicily on his own ship, we gratefully took him up on the offer. Such a savings and perfectly safe, we thought – such a wealthy gentleman couldn't possibly be interested in our poor things. Papa even ensured that the strongbox containing his payment for the frescoes would go with Marcuse, believing it to be safer there! We went ahead of the Baron to Sicily, expecting him to join us there soon, but his ship never arrived. We eventually heard from friends back in Venice that the ship had sailed, but that was the last we ever heard of Baron Marcuse."

"Might the ship have sank?" Arthur asked.

"That's possible," Cleo admitted. "But I think it more likely that Marcuse never intended to go to Sicily. We learned from our Venetian friends that after he had departed, he was found to owe huge amounts to all the merchants in the city. Credit is so easily extended to those who are already wealthy or at least appear to be so."

"That's certainly true," Arthur agreed. "Many a man in London lives entirely on credit for years before finally getting caught out."

"Papa took the news rather well, on the whole," Cleo went on. "We'd had so many reversals of fortune in our lives, this was just another one. But Han took it very hard. The injustice of it and the man's getting away with it was something he returned to again and again. He kept saying that he wanted to make Marcuse pay, though once we got our hands on a *Debrett's* we learned that Marcuse wasn't even his name, so how could he be found?"

"And now he thinks he found him," Arthur said.

"Yes," Cleo said with a sigh. "And it's hard to blame him for wanted to settle the score, but he's only a boy, and Marcuse is a man and a ruthless one. We should have told him."

She fell silent for a long moment. Finally, Arthur prodded. "Told him?"

"Told him how dangerous Marcuse was. From our friends in Venice, we learned that after Marcuse left, several bodies were found in the canal by his palacio. Venice is a dangerous place and violence is common, but one of the bodies was a man who'd been

184

owed a great deal of money by Marcuse. He might be a murderer! But Han was young and already so angry about the theft, Papa asked me not to tell him about the bodies in the canal."

***

Lord Charles strode briskly through the parklands at Winton Court. He was returning from a long walk, though he had no intention of admitting it. Before he'd purchased his commission, he had mercilessly teased his older brother for his walking tendencies, but after years at war he was used to a more vigorous lifestyle and found himself growing irritable and out of sorts if he went too long without exercise. "Best not to let Artie know, though," he told himself. "Otherwise, he might try to interest me in mathematics as well."

The clip of hooves drew his attention to the lane, and through the trees he observed a curricle heading toward the gatehouse. Amesbury was driving and Miss Harwell sat beside him. They didn't see him as they drove past his position, being too engrossed in their own conversation. Charley walked out to the lane and watched the curricle pass through the gatehouse and turn right on the main road.

Then he walked slowly toward the manor, deep in thought. Charley had known Amesbury all his life. He was used to thinking him a rather magnificent figure, as the older man had been the polished man about Town when he was but a scrubby schoolboy. But last night at dinner, Charley hadn't missed the way Amesbury had looked at his brother's fiancée when Arthur's attention was directed elsewhere. As for Miss Harwell, his acquaintance with her was of the slightest, but he couldn't deny that she had seemed more animated just now than he had ever seen her.

Where were they going? The village would have entailed a left turn. Toward the right there was nothing of interest within a local drive. Nothing really until one came to London. Why would Amesbury and Miss Harwell be driving to London in the middle of a house party?

Of course, from London one could reach the Great North Road. Assuming one intended going north. North as in to Scotland?

Was Artie's best friend eloping with his fiancée?

Oh, surely not! Not good old Justin! But then Charley remembered those warm, hopeless glances that Amesbury had tried to hide. No longer a scrubby schoolboy, he'd been around enough to

185

know that an overpowering passion for a woman had caused more than one man to abandon long-held principles of decency and honor.

He was approaching the manor house now, but rather than going in, he went around to the stable and asked that his horse be saddled. Charley determined that the best course of action would be to take a ride, coincidentally in the same direction that Amesbury and Miss Harwell had taken. If, as was surely the case, his suspicions proved unfounded and their errand unexceptionable, no one need know that he had ever suspected an old family friend of such infamy.

And if his suspicions proved accurate? He would deal with that if the situation arose.

***

Miss Harwell was indeed quite animated, more animated than any of her court had ever seen her, since none of them had ever been privileged to witness their deity in the midst of a thundering argument.

"In all the time I've known you," she told Amesbury bitterly, "I had no notion that your opinion of women was so low, that you would believe us capable of the meanest subterfuge to capture a man with no regard for how we would make him despise us, so long as we gained access to his name and wealth."

Amesbury sighed impatiently. "My opinion extends only to this woman in particular, not to all women."

"This woman who is my friend," Felicity reminded him.

"I think your defense of Miss Cooper compliments your heart more than your head," Amesbury said carefully.

"I see!" she replied icily. "All this time you were flattering me and dancing with me and sending me flowers, and I had no notion you considered me such a shatterbrained little fool. Perhaps I am as foolish as you believe, because I never for an instant comprehended your true opinion of me."

Appalled, Justin protested, "That is not my opinion at all! You're just too… good and innocent to understand a woman of this type."

"A Dresden figurine, in fact," Felicity snapped. "To be placed on the mantelpiece and admired, but not to be taken seriously."

Justin opened his mouth and hastily shut it again. It occurred to him that if calling a young lady too good and innocent invoked such an angry response, he wasn't sure what it might be safe to say.

186

The pair rode in uncomfortable silence for some moments, before Justin said sadly, "You hate me, don't you?"

Felicity sighed. "No," she said. "I really don't." She bit down on the inside of her cheek to prevent herself from adding, "Quite the contrary."

***

As the gig made its way through the London outskirts, Arthur asked Cleo, "So what's your plan?"

Cleo clenched her clasped hands and replied, "I don't have a plan."

He spared a glance at her downturned face and looked back to the road. "You don't like not having a plan, do you?"

"I hate it!" she exclaimed with suppressed passion. "Research and planning and thinking the plan through. That's the way to do it. But there's no time for that and not enough information. All I can think is to learn which direction Han went and follow him."

Arthur nodded. "We'll have to improvise as we go, I suppose. We'll take my curricle."

Cleo shot him a surprised look. "We?"

"Of course I'm coming along," Arthur told her.

"There's no need..."

"There's every need," he said. "We're going to need to question people along the way, and it may not be fair but it is nonetheless true that innkeepers and grooms and others will be more apt to cooperate with a gentleman than with a lady. And a gentleman driving a curricle will certainly gain more ready cooperation than a lady driving a gig."

"It's nothing to do with you!" she protested.

"I'm making it my business," he said calmly. "You were my guest and now your family is in trouble."

"Noblesse oblige," Cleo snapped. Then she gasped and said, "Sorry. I'm not angry at you. And I know it will be helpful. I can usually get people to do what I want, but it's time consuming. But a duke racketing about the countryside questioning innkeepers – wouldn't that arouse comment?"

"I'll be Mister Ramsey," he said, smiling at the idea. "The useful man you originally thought me to be. And you, I think, must be my sister. My new curricle has no coat of arms, fortunately."

"Miss Ramsey," said Cleo, trying it out.

187

"We're on our way to visit an elderly relative," Arthur went on, warming to his theme. "And a young gypsy boy snatched your reticule, which would explain our interest."

"That's good!" Cleo said. "But we wouldn't want Han to be taken up by the authorities."

"Well, if he is, then he's safe," Arthur replied. "And when we're called to identify him, we can say he's not the gypsy boy we're looking for, so he wouldn't be charged."

Cleo laughed, feeling the beginnings of relief. "This is starting to sound like a plan."

***

As Arthur toiled up the stairs, he thought again what a unique family the Coopers were. Their tempestuous entry into the Hans Town residence was greeted by a flustered housekeeper, who informed them with a gasp that, "Miss Merry is on the roof."

Biting back the almost irresistible temptation to say, "Of course she is," Arthur silently followed Cleo, past the second and third floors, past the attics, and on up the narrow stairway to the roof.

Once out of the dim stairwell and onto the sunlit roof, he saw the tidy pigeon coop and realized why Miss Merryhew would wish to be here.

Cleo hurried over to her companion. "Any news?" she asked anxiously.

"A note from Peter," Merry said, "that he's traced Han to the Great North Road and is following." She looked doubtfully over Cleo's shoulder to the Duke.

Arthur stepped forward. "Miss Cooper has explained to me about Baron Marcuse, and I want to help find him. And Han, of course." Merry still looked worried. "I know about the pigeons," Arthur went on. "And I know about the bets. I've told no one and intend to tell no one."

Merry sank back into her chair, overcome. Cleo crouched beside her and patted her hand. "It's all right, Merry," she said soothingly. "I've said we're done with that and I mean it. You don't need to worry about it anymore."

"I'll go to Winton House, have the curricle harnessed and be back in a trice," Arthur said.

"And a saddle horse for me," Salford said. At Arthur's quizzical look, he added gruffly, "I'd be dead if not for that boy."

188

"Very well." Arthur turned to leave, but was interrupted when Miss Merryhew surged to her feet, pointing at the sky.

"There!" she exclaimed. "That's one of ours."

Arthur's eyes followed her pointing finger. Indeed, a pigeon was flying toward them. It looked to Arthur much like any other pigeon, and he felt a moment of skepticism. But then the bird landed outside the coop and allowed Miss Merryhew to gather it up and remove the small cylinder from its leg.

Cleo hurriedly unrolled the message and read aloud. "M left post-chaise at Stevenage. Following. H"

Arthur nodded. "I'll be back soon."

***

Winton House slept the sleep of a noble townhouse whose owners were at the country estate. So it was with the force of a hurricane that the unlooked-for Duke erupted into the house, calling for a curricle, a saddle horse, and a valise. A very junior footman played the butler's role, marshalling the house's depleted forces to comply with these demands.

Once the whirlwind had departed, the footman, the boot boy and two undermaids gathered in the servants' hall, comparing notes and trying to determine what had just happened.

"Shirts, cravats and underthings, that's what he flung into the valise," reported Sally the youngest maid. "And flung in all anyhow, not accepting any assistance."

"Ain't he supposed to be in the country?" wondered the boots. "Wot's he doin' here, anyways?"

"Think I'd ask him that?" asked Bill the under-footman loftily.

Mary was older than Sally, but more fanciful. "It was a duel, that's what it were!" she suggested excitedly. "And here's His Grace havin' to fly the country, a'cos he's killed his man!"

"None of that kind o' talk!" Bill said sharply. "Happen Lem will know what it's about, him driving the curricle. Don't you go talking nonsense, Mary, and sure not outside the House. What do ye all have to do, then? Get back about your work."

The gathering broke up, with some grumbling about Bill's taking too much on himself. His sudden field promotion to temporary butler had gone to his head, the others thought, and he was giving himself airs.

***

189

Arthur had just entered the Cooper townhouse when Cleo hurried down the stairs, carrying her bandbox and a roll of paper. "A young lady ready when the carriage arrives!" he exclaimed, much struck. "I hadn't thought it possible."

Cleo gave him an amused look. "Are you calling me unwomanly, Your Grace?"

"Oh, not at all!" Arthur stammered. He would have extended his apology, but Cleo waved it away.

"Look at this," she said, unrolling the paper. "Han left it. Marcuse to the life. The hair is different than I recall and the clothes are of the current style, so this must be based on Marcuse as Han saw him just now."

The paper was a marvelously rendered pencil portrait. Arthur studied it carefully. "This will certainly make it easier to ask after the man," he said. "Description can be so imprecise, but this – the nose, the eyebrows, the chin. If someone saw this man today, they would remember. I fancy I've seen him somewhere myself. Not someone I've met, but perhaps seen in passing." He rolled up the drawing. "Shall we go?"

"To Stevenage," Cleo concurred, and they left the hall to find Salford mounted and waiting for them.

Lem the groom held the curricle reins, and Arthur and Cleo settled themselves in the carriage. Lem moved to take the groom's spot, but Arthur handed him a coin. "We won't be needed you more today," he said. "You may take a hackney back to Winton House."

The Duke drove off with the old man riding alongside. Lem watched them off, scratching his head in perplexity. He looked at the coin, flung it in the air and caught it. Take a hackney back to the House? He could think of better ways to spend this. Nice walking weather anyway. He set off on foot back to Mayfair.

***

As they entered the settled areas of London, Justin and Felicity were still squabbling. The current bone of contention was where to go next. The Cooper townhouse in Hans Town? Winton House in Mayfair?

Suddenly Justin drew his team to a halt. "Isn't that Lem from Arthur's stables?" he asked, pointing at a figure striding jauntily down the street. Raising his voice, he called, "Lem!"

190

The groom turned at the sound of the call and swept off his cap. "Mister Justin, sir! Fancy seeing you 'ere!"

"We're looking for the Duke," Justin said hurriedly. "Have you seen him?"

"Haven't I just?" Lem said. "Brought the curricle as ordered, we picks up the young lady and then he sends me off home. Driving hisself, he is, with naught but a valise and a bandbox."

"Which way did they go?" Justin asked.

"Why, north, sir, to be sure. Great North Road, I hears the young lady say."

Justin was about to question the groom further, but he was interrupted by a silvery laugh. He turned to Felicity, who was smiling ruefully.

"How provoking of them to start without us," she said gaily. "They must have known we'd be right along. How I shall scold them! Thank you, Lem. Come, Mister Amesbury, we must hurry."

Puzzled, but following Felicity's lead, Justin nodded to Lem and gave the horses their office to proceed. Once they'd moved out of earshot however, he complained, "I intended to learn more from Lem."

"We know the road that they've taken," Felicity said reasonably. "What more could he have told us? If our object is to scotch a scandal, we mustn't allow the servants to realize we don't know where they've gone or why. No, we must present the appearance of a joint expedition."

"You have a point," Justin admitted. "But what the deuce are they doing? How did Arthur get roped into such a mad start?"

"To learn that, we must catch up with them," Felicity pointed out. She refused to speak aloud the fear in her heart. Going north with a valise and a bandbox – could it indeed be that they were eloping? How would it feel, she wondered, to learn that her best friend had eloped with her fiancé? Why, she would be heartbroken! But no, she had to admit after a moment's reflection. Her heart would not be broken. She would certainly be angry, but it would be due to the public humiliation of such an event.

Felicity stole a glance at the man beside her, and felt a sudden irrational wish that it was she and Mister Amesbury who were eloping. Not that she would do anything so wildly improper,

191

however romantic it might be. But if she were to elope, though of course she would not, she would want it to be with Justin.

What a coil! Felicity foresaw grief and scandal, whatever the outcome of today's events.

NINETEEN

At the first toll, Arthur and Cleo got a shock. Why yes, the toll man said, he had seen a lad driving a gypsy wagon that morning. "Same as I told the Bow Street Runner," he said chattily. "Must have been about ten when he come through. Seemed a pleasant enough lad and paid the toll with no argumentation. What's 'e done then?"

"Why, nothing that we know of," stammered Cleo. "We were just… curious."

The barrier up, Arthur drove through to prevent further quizzing. Once down the road, he and Cleo exchanged worried glances. "A Bow Street Runner?" Arthur asked. "What's that brother of yours gotten himself into?"

"I have no notion!" Cleo said. "Could someone have caught on to the pigeon scheme?"

They rode in worried silence for several minutes. Then Arthur said thoughtfully, "The pigeons were in aid of a weather experiment of mine."

Cleo blinked. "They were?"

"Yes," Arthur said, expanding his fable. "They were bringing me information on temperature, wind speed and weather conditions from various locations around the country at the same moment, for an analysis of weather patterns."

"This is for the Runner?"

"Of course."

Cleo thought it over. "I must say, it does sounds like something you would do."

"It's something I will do!" Arthur said, warming to the notion. "Imagine how beneficial it would be to have advance warning of changes in the weather." He turned to Cleo. "Can you drive a curricle?"

"Adequately, I suppose," she said. "I wouldn't back myself in a curricle race, or some difficult driving."

The reins were thrust into her hands, and she found herself driving the curricle, while Arthur burrowed in his pockets for his small notebook and pencil stub. He wrote busily for several moments and then restowed his writing material. "I didn't want to lose the weather experiment idea," he said apologetically. "If you would hand me the reins – "

"I'll drive for a bit, if you don't mind," Cleo replied. "It gives me something to do beside fret."

"I am confident we will see this through," Arthur assured her.

***

Charley kept his distance but kept the curricle in sight. He couldn't believe it. The Great North Road! What could Justin and Miss Harwell be doing other than eloping? Should he confront them now? Filled with indecision, he continued to follow.

***

At Stevenage, Arthur and Cleo stopped at the posting inn at sunset. Here their inquiries met a blank wall. The innkeeper was out and would not return for several hours, they were told, and as for the post boys who might have arrived with any post-chaise, they would be off duty.

"Whatever shall we do?" Cleo asked.

"We will have dinner," Arthur said. "It's been long since breakfast, and one must eat, after all." He turned to the bar man who had disclaimed all knowledge of the post chaise and ordered a simple meal and a private parlor. "And I will want to see the innkeeper as soon as he returns," he said.

When the food arrived, Cleo picked at her slice of partridge, worrying. "What shall we do now?" she wondered.

"We must hope the innkeeper has information for us," Arthur said.

General strode in then. He'd taking the curricle and saddle horse to the stables upon their arrival. "I've been scouting the area, hoping that Master Han left a sign of some sort, but there's nothing I could see with darkness coming on."

"Where could he be?" asked Cleo plaintively.

A clatter in the front hall told of new arrivals. The sound of voices filtered into the parlor, a man's voice sharply questioning the bar man. Cleo and Arthur exchanged puzzled looks. Arthur was just thinking the voice sounded familiar, when the door to the parlor was flung open and Justin entered.

"Aha!" Justin exclaimed.

194

Felicity was right behind him. "Oh, don't be absurd," she said crossly. "Aha, indeed!" Then she took in the sight of the inhabitants of the room and faltered. "Arthur? Cleo?" Then she saw the old man in the corner constructing a sandwich for himself. "General?"

Arthur stood up. "What are you doing here?" he asked.

"We followed you," Justin said significantly, throwing a dark look at Cleo. "The question is, what are *you* doing here?"

"We're looking for my brother," Cleo said with a nice appearance of calm. "And he is following a scoundrel who stole from us in Venice."

"There!" said Felicity. "So you're not eloping."

"Of course we're not eloping," Cleo said indignantly.

"How could you possibly think such a thing?" Arthur asked.

"Ask your friend!" Felicity said, turning her back on Justin and crossing her arms.

"I didn't suspect you of eloping," Justin tried to explain. "Not deliberately."

Arthur looked thoughtful. "My social education has indeed been faulty," he said. "Because I had no notion there was such a thing as an accidental elopement."

"No?" said the exasperated Justin. "Clever chits have been known before this to lure eligible men into compromising positions, forcing them into marriage, and here I find you in a private inn parlor with Miss Cooper – "

"– and her butler!" finished Cleo with a chuckle.

Arthur met Cleo's eyes and couldn't keep a quick spurt of laughter from escaping before clamping his lips tight.

Felicity turned back to the group, eying Justin ominously. "Can you not simply admit that you were wrong?" she asked with dangerous sweetness.

Justin threw up his hands. "Very well. I was wrong."

"And I was right!" Felicity said triumphantly. "Arthur and Cleo are here on some mission and we will help them with it."

"Of course we will," said Justin with a sigh.

Heavy boots sounded in the hall and a voice said, "In here?" before the door was flung open again.

At the table, Cleo murmured to Arthur, "If this is a private parlor what must the public room be like?"

Charley strode into the parlor, his eyes lighting on Justin and Felicity just inside the door. "There you are!" he exclaimed. "Now you can explain to me what kind of cad elopes with his best friend's fiancée."

"Eloping?!" Justin said, stunned. "We're not eloping!"

From the table, Cleo added helpfully, "Nor are we."

"In fact," Arthur summed up, "no one is eloping."

"Artie?!" said Charley.

"Stand down, Captain," said Salford, bringing his sandwich to the table and taking a seat.

"Sir!" Charley replied.

Justin stared at the militant young man who'd once been his young admirer. "How could you even think such a thing of me?" he asked.

"I don't think you have any standing to ask such a question," Arthur pointed out.

Cleo intervened. "You must be famished," she said sympathetically. "Such a long way from Winton Court. Please, help yourself to supper and join us."

The sight of the sumptuous spread did much to lower the room's emotional temperature. "I confess to being quite sharp-set," Felicity admitted.

Soon six people sat around the table, doing justice to the partridge and pigeon pie and hearing the tale of romantic far-off Venice and the dastardly Baron Marcuse.

"What a shame!" cried Felicity sympathetically.

"Are you certain the blackguard was English?" Justin wondered.

"We would need to find him to determine that, though he certainly convinced my father," Cleo said. The drawing was produced and passed around the table.

Justin gave a start of surprise when the paper reached him. "Why it's Twomey!" he exclaimed. "You remember, Arthur, Marcus Twomey. Twomey's Gallery? The art dealer?"

Arthur thought back. "I recall accompanying you to the gallery, but I didn't actually meet Twomey himself."

"Oh, that's right. Well, it's him, I'm sure of it. To the life."

"Then we have a name!" Cleo exclaimed. "What an enormous help!"

***

196

The innkeeper, returning weary from a visit to his sister, she having just delivered her eighth, wanted nothing more than a pint of his best and a chance to put his feet up, but the nodcock he'd left in charge informed him impressively that their private parlor was currently in the hands of a group of people he characterized as mad gentryfolk.

"Rest easy, Joe," the innkeeper said. "Gentry's ways is not our ways, but we are well compensated to put up with their wild starts and eccentricities. Why I remember when young Viscount –. But never mind that. Have they been fed? Do they need rooms?"

"Supper they has had, but as for rooms, I dunno," Joe told him.

"I'll see to it, then."

The innkeeper knocked briskly on the parlor door, and entered. "Will you ladies and gentlemen be requiring anything else? I'm sorry I wasn't here to tend to your needs and hope you've been seen to properly."

"We've been well taken care of," said a mild young man who the innkeeper immediately recognized, he told Joe later, as every inch a lord. "But now we require information. Are you acquainted with Marcus Twomey?"

"Well," the innkeeper said doubtfully, "not to say acquainted, though he's been in here a time or two. Lives just out of town, he does."

"Excellent! So you can give us directions."

"That I can do."

Having given directions to Twomey's residence, the innkeeper bowed himself out, leaving the party to debate their course of action.

Suggestions became increasingly fantastical, before the Duke rapped on the table for attention. "We can't know what we are to find there, so the obvious course of action is simply to go. Justin, you know Twomey, so we should be admitted. Our actions must be dictated by circumstances."

"I could call tomorrow, I suppose…" Justin said.

"We go now!" insisted Cleo. "We have no idea where Han is or what danger he might be in."

Justin balked at the impropriety of calling on a mere acquaintance in the evening with no prior appointment, but he was overruled. Felicity told him there was a time and a place for the niceties, but this was neither the time or the place.

197

Salford addressed Lord Charles. "Captain, you and I should reconnoiter outside the residence in question. Half-moon is surely enough light for a Peninsular man."

"Quite enough," Charley agreed.

"It's the four of us, then," Arthur said. "We'll be calling about a painting, that should get us into Twomey's presence. Then we must play it by ear."

Cleo sighed. "I so dislike not having a plan."

Marcus Twomey lived in a gentleman's residence a mile outside Stevenage. A small handsome manor set in its own grounds, it didn't seem at all a den of villainy. The two curricles arrived shortly after dark, and the party approached the front door. Cleo felt a moment of reassurance at the thought that two soldiers were out there in the dark somewhere.

Amesbury presented his card to the dour retainer who opened the door, and asked that he and the Duke of Winton be announced to Mister Twomey. The title acted like a charm, and the retainer tried to present a display of affability as the quartet was ushered into a parlor.

"We've interrupted his dinner, I'll be bound," said Justin when they were alone.

"Not if he keeps country hours," replied Arthur idly.

Marcus Twomey was a large, fair, and florid man, slightly running to fat. He entered the parlor uttering effusive welcomes, seeing the call not as an unmannerly intrusion but as potential customers. "Ah, Mister Amesbury!" he said. "Did the dear Countess appreciate the painting you selected for her?"

"Indeed she did," Amesbury said. "She tells me she wished she'd thought to take a pot shot at the original painting years ago."

"And Your Grace," Twomey turned to Arthur. "I understand from my staff that you too made a purchase from us. I apologize for not attending to you personally, but I was only informed of your visit later. I do hope you will return. An appreciation of art is the true hallmark of the civilized man, is it not?"

Before Arthur could respond to this excess of amiability, Cleo rose from the settee where she and Felicity had been sitting. "That's him," she said baldly.

Twomey turned to her and even by candlelight, the visitors could see that he paled alarmingly.

"My dear young lady," he faltered. "I fear you have me at a disadvantage."

"Oh, you've put on some flesh since last we met," Cleo said. "But I would recognize you anywhere – Baron Marcuse."

"Baron – " Twomey gave a poor imitation of a laugh and spread his hands. "You have obviously mistaken me for someone else. My name is Twomey and my title is a plain Mister."

The Duke said severely, "Miss Cooper has made the charge that you are the so-called Baron Marcuse who stole from her family in Venice. How do you respond to that?"

"W-why, that I've never met this Miss… Cooper, is it? – in my life, nor her brother either!"

"Oh, that was a mistake," said Arthur, shaking his head. "If you've never met Miss Cooper, how is it that you know she has a brother?"

"You said family," said Twomey, harassed, "so I naturally assumed…"

"Family doesn't always mean brother," Arthur said. "Mother, father, sister…"

Grinning, Justin joined in, "Aunts and uncles, cousins and grandparents."

"And yet you immediately went to 'brother'," Arthur concluded.

Cleo leaned forward. "Where is Han, you rascal?!"

"I really have no notion what you're going on about," Twomey said fretfully, moving to the secretary in the corner and rummaging in the drawers.

But when he straightened and turned, he had in his hand a pistol which he pointed in the direction of his inconvenient guests.

Both Arthur and Justin moved when they recognized the weapon, and they moved without thought, instinctively. And they positioned themselves so that Arthur stood between Cleo and Twomey, while Justin stood between Felicity and the danger.

The significance of the acts struck them both at the same time.

"Arthur?" said Justin.

At the same moment, Arthur said, "Justin?"

From the settee, Felicity was heard to say, "Justin!" softly.

Arthur turned to Cleo and grinned. "I believe what we have here is a revelatory moment," he said.

She smiled at him. "Perhaps we do," she said gently.

"I say, Arthur!" protested Justin. "If a man won't shield his own fiancée..."

"Had I tried, I would have been knocked down by you hastening to perform that office," Arthur pointed out. "Why the deuce didn't you tell me when the season began that your affections ran in that direction?"

"Because I didn't know!" He turned to Felicity. "It was only once you became betrothed that I realized what I had lost," he told her.

Felicity turned the ring on her finger, and asked Arthur with a twinkle, "Should I hand this directly to Cleo or would you like to give it to her?"

"I believe it is customary to get an acceptance of an offer before the presentation of a ring," Cleo reminded them all.

Arthur's face fell. "And you wouldn't accept?" he asked sadly. "You don't love me?"

"I didn't say that..." Cleo stammered, confused.

Felicity advised, "This is where 'sir, this is all so sudden' becomes useful."

"Excuse me!" The quartet jumped at the exclamation from Twomey. They looked back at him. "Remember me? The man with the gun?"

"Of course, how rude of us," Arthur said. "Please, do carry on."

"Yes," growled Justin. "Tell us how you intend to dispose of four of us, including a duke and an earl's son. You'll catch cold at that, I'll be bound. With the innkeeper at Stevenage knowing where we were going."

Twomey was becoming agitated. "Bob!" he called.

The dour retainer entered the room and gaped at the tableau he saw there.

"I need some assistance here, Bob," Twomey grated.

But Bob was backing out fast. "I don't think so, guvnor," he said. "Pop a gypsy lad into the cellar, that I will do and no one the wiser, but I'm not massacreeing no dooks, I tell you that flat." And he was gone.

Twomey looked back at his guests, waving the pistol at them in a manner he probably hoped was menacing. "You all just hold it there," he blustered. "Hold it there and let me think."

Justin smiled nastily at him. "You expect us to hold it there while you shoot us one at a time? Twiddle our thumbs perhaps while you reload?"

"Just... just stay back!" Twomey said.

But while he was focused intently on the threatening-looking Amesbury, Arthur quietly stepped forward and neatly grabbed his wrist and forced it toward the sky. The pistol discharged into the ceiling. Arthur smiled at Twomey. "Unarmed now," he observed, and planted a fist flush into Twomey's face. Twomey went down like a felled tree.

"Oh, well done, Artie!" said a new voice. Everyone but the unconscious Twomey turned to see Lord Charles and Lord Salford entered, pushing Bob between them.

"We caught this fellow trying to make a surreptitious exit," Salford said.

"Splendid," said Arthur. "I'm sure he would be willing to testify against his master, for a consideration. In the meantime, perhaps he should be tied up." He looked down at the man at his feet. "And this fellow as well."

"We must find the cellar!" Cleo said. "You heard this fellow, he put Han in the cellar."

The party spread out to search. It was Arthur who found the heavy door in the kitchen, secured with a heavy bolt. He called the others, who hurried into the kitchen. Faint thumping was heard through the door, and when the bolt was drawn Han tumbled into the room, mussed and with several bruises and with his gypsy disguise in great disarray.

"Cleo, how famous!" Han gasped. "I'd managed to get out of the ropes, but this door defeated me."

"Why is he dressed so oddly?" Felicity murmured to Justin.

"No idea," he murmured back.

"But come down and see," Han went on. "Papa's paintings are down here."

The outing had assumed the aspect of a treasure hunt. Everyone availed themselves of candles and descended to the cellar to view the lost paintings of Miles Cooper.

Looking at the crates and the paintings stacked against the wall, Cleo said with satisfaction, "They're all here."

But Arthur looked closely at the uncrated paintings and made a discovery. "Not all of them," he said. "Because I have one. I bought a painting called The Hunter at Twomey's Gallery – "

"With Orion!" said Han.

"I'm in receipt of stolen property," said Arthur. "As much as I admire the painting, I see that I must return it to you."

Cleo and Han exchanged looks. Cleo said, "Consider it a gift from us, in appreciation for all your help."

Justin brushed dust from his sleeve. "Let's return upstairs and find a way out of this coil," he suggested. "We have recovered stolen property, two thieves and kidnappers tied up upstairs, and we'll not return to Winton Court tonight."

Upstairs the quartet joined Salford and Charley, who were guarding the prisoners. "What shall we do with them?" asked Charley.

"We must turn them over to the authorities," said Arthur, who had somehow become the leader of the expedition.

"'Ere now, wot's all this?"

The group moved to the entry hall, to find a tubby man with lank hair and a knowing eye looking them over. He removed a well-thumbed notebook from a capacious pocket and flipped it open. "Acting on information received," he said officiously, "I 'ave come to this address to investigate reports of a kidnapping in progress."

Arthur looked closely at the newcomer. He moved toward him and murmured, "Barton?"

"'At's roight, yer worship," said the man loudly. "Horton. Lucius P. Horton of Bow Street, at yer honor's sairvice."

Cleo bit her lip to hide a smile and hurried forward. "Bow Street! Thank goodness, did Miss Merrihew call you in?"

"Indeed she did, Miss. 'Ave you any information for Bow Street about the miscreants in question?"

"Why yes, we have them in here," Cleo informed him. "Trussed up and ready to be turned over to the authorities."

Barton, or rather Horton, followed them into the parlor and inspected their handiwork. He whistled appreciatively. "Normally I don't 'old with gentry a takin' of the law into their own 'ands, but I must say ye've made neat work of it."

"You can charge them with kidnapping this lad," said Arthur, indicating Han. "And also of theft of a large number of very valuable art pieces."

"That I'll do," Horton said. "I'll just take them off yer 'ands now and deliver them to the local magistrate. Your honors can make your affy-davys at your convenience." He murmured to Arthur, "And see that the lad is cleaned up afore makin' a statement, so that his essentially noble nature is apparent to their excellencies."

Salford and Charley helped Horton load his prisoners into his wagon, and the party watched him drive off. Then they returned to the empty house and looked at one another.

"What do we do now?" Felicity asked.

"Scandal is inevitable, I'm afraid," Justin said.

"We brush through with a high hand," said their new commander, the Duke of Winton. "Tonight we rest at the inn, where the ladies may share a room to satisfy the proprieties, and tomorrow we return to Winton Court."

"And tell them what?" Cleo asked curiously.

"Keep it simple," said the Duke. "Your brother ran away and we went to fetch him."

"Ran away?" protested Han. "I was on a mission!"

"You ran away," Arthur said severely. "We went to fetch you and along the way managed to assist in the apprehension of thieves."

"And we're back to where we began and you marry Felicity?" Justin asked. "I can't agree to that!"

"Of course not," Arthur said. "We will send two new announcements to the Gazette, announcing your engagement to Miss Harwell, and mine to Miss Cooper."

"And you still haven't asked me," Cleo complained.

"Honestly, Arthur," Justin said. "I despair of you. You can't announce your engagement to a lady you haven't proposed to."

"As you haven't proposed to Miss Harwell yet, I don't see that you have cause to criticize," Arthur told him.

"Why you great looby, how can I propose to a woman you are engaged to?!" Justin shouted.

Cleo and Felicity exchanged looks. It was time for the women to take charge. Felicity stepped up to Arthur. Removing her ring, she placed it in his hand, saying sweetly, "Your Grace, while I recognize the honor of your proposal, I must inform you that we would not suit." Then she grinned at him and said, "We really would not, you know. You are far too adventurous."

Arthur closed his hand over the ring. "I honor your honesty," he said formally, "and feel certain that you are right." He turned to Justin. "There! Now propose to the lady!"

Justin grasped Felicity's hand and pulled her from the room. Arthur turned to Cleo. She blushed, feeling the interested eyes of her brother, her butler, and her future brother-in-law watching curiously.

The Earl of Salford exchanged a significant look with Lord Charles and then turned to Han. "Master Han," he said smoothly, "I am not at all easy in my mind about your father's paintings. We should examine the cellar before we leave here, searching for any evidence of damp."

"Damp!" exclaimed Lord Charles. "No indeed, fatal to paintings, damp. We must go at once!"

Pushing Han before them, the two soldiers left the room. And Arthur and Cleo were alone.

Arthur cleared his throat nervously. He told himself that this was his second proposal, after all; he ought to be an old hand at this. And yet, he instinctively felt that a proposal to Cleo required a very different formulation than that to Felicity. Aha! He had it!

"Miss Cooper," he said formally. "Will you come adventuring with me?"

She smiled!

"Why yes," said Cleo. "I do believe I shall."

She was extraordinarily close to him. Then he realized that this was because he had taken her by the shoulders and pulled her into his arms. Without conscious thought, Arthur lowered his lips to hers. Arms came around his neck and she was kissing him back, and it wasn't awkward at all, it was... exhilarating!

Breathless minutes later, Cleo's head was nestled on his shoulder and she murmured, "So this is what love feels like."

"What does it feel like?" asked Arthur the scientist.

"I don't have a plan," Cleo said, grinning up at him, "but I don't care!"

"Of course not," Arthur told her. "Do you know why?"

"Why?"

"Because this is *living*." And he kissed her again.

EPILOGUE

SIX MONTHS LATER –

The dock was a bustle of activity as the research vessel The Seeker prepared to get underway. Onboard, naturalists and astronomers jealously tended to the stowing of their equipment, hampering the work of the ship's crew. On the dock, a distinguished group had gathered to see off the latest venture of the Duke of Winton, and bid farewell to the Duke and his new Duchess as they sailed to the antipodes.

Society was still talking about the brace of marriages that had baffled the *ton* that summer. For the Duke's original fiancée, Miss Harwell that was, had married the Duke's great friend Mister Amesbury, and society gossips were entirely unable to determine who had jilted whom. Hard feelings, if any, were well concealed, as the two couples had married in a joint ceremony at Saint George's, Hanover Square. The Amesburys and Wintons were invited everywhere in hopes of unraveling the mystery, but a mystery it remained.

Mrs. Amesbury remained the queen of society and seemed divinely happy, despite letting a duke slip through her fingers. The new Duchess was an unaccountable little creature and one wondered what to make of her. She and her husband were seen less in society than the Amesburys, being thoroughly occupied with the design and outfitting of the Duke's new research vessel.

The Dowager Duchess shivered in her furs. "Why are they leaving in the winter? It seems so unaccountable of them," she complained.

"It will be summer where they're going, Mama," Lord Charles explained.

"That's what Arthur said, but it sounds highly improbable to me."

"You're just concerned that another one of your babies is leaving for foreign lands," Charley teased.

"I'm not concerned at all," the Dowager corrected him. "Since I'm sure dear Cleo will take excellent care of him. She is the most sensible girl!"

Peter stood with Miss Merrihew and the Earl of Salford. The Earl had been recognized officially as himself and regained his title and estates, to the chagrin of the churlish cousin who had been in possession of them so unworthily for several years.

"Where will you go now, Peter dear?" Merry asked.

"Go?" Peter said. "I'm going nowhere. I am quite comfortably established and intend to go on as I began."

"Do you really think that's wise?" Salford asked.

Peter laughed. "I'd wondered that until Duffy Wainwright returned to town. I'd used my supposed school friendship with him as my way into the acquaintance of his older brother the Baron. I thought sure that Duffy's return would put paid to my term as a gentleman, but once I met Duffy and asked him 'do you remember' about a variety of predictable schoolboy pranks, the young nodcock became convinced that we had indeed been boyhood friends. Well, that settled it. The thing's too easy! Here I stay."

Mister Morton stood beside Han and Lady Dorwood on the dock and watched the ship's preparations with yearning. "I don't understand how you can bear to remain behind and miss the experience of exotic lands," he told Han.

Han shook his head. "You must understand that for me England is an exotic foreign land, and now that I'm here I want to explore and experience it."

Morton looked thoughtful. "Exotic England. Hmm. There might be inspiration there."

For Mister Morton was now a published author and the toast of the literary salons. His *Tales Of The Levant*, with illustrations by Hannibal Cooper, was a stunning success. Lord Byron had many imitators, but Morton had written a parody all unaware and his opus had been released at just the right moment, when society which had worshipped the erratic lord for too long had at last decided it could tolerate no more of his arrogance, his rudeness, and his outrages against propriety. Society hastened to buy Morton's work and revel in its masterful send-up of the Byronic mystique. The news that the book's beautifully hilarious illustrations were the product of a thirteen year old boy merely made the work that much more thrilling.

Nor was Han the only Cooper to achieve artistic accolades. As promised, Mister Lawrence sponsored an exhibit at the Royal Academy of the newly discovered work of the late Miles Cooper, and Han and Cleo's father at last gained the recognition that had eluded him all his life.

With the Duke's assistance, Cleo had used 'Papa's legacy' (actually the gains from her pigeon scheme) to purchase for Han the Grange, the Bufford family residence where Mama had grown up, and which Uncle William had lost gambling. The estate was in poor condition, but with the attention of the able young steward Arthur hired, it was expected to be in good heart and a profitable gentleman's residence by the time Han was old enough to take possession of it.

In a move that many considered an excess of amiability, the Coopers offered the use of the Grange's dower house to Lady Sylvia. She accepted with as much grace as her personality would permit, which is to say none at all. Lady Dorwood's fondness for her young niece and nephew was now without limit.

From the deck of the Seeker, Cleo looked down at her brother and waved and smiled. She had every right to feel proud of herself, she concluded. She came to England and accomplished all she set out to do, and even more that she had not thought of. The fact that she was now a duchess and the wife of one of the richest men in England crossed her mind but seldom; of greater satisfaction was that she had found a man who suited her as ideally as Papa had suited Mama. That had been entirely unexpected and completely delightful.

She turned to her husband and smiled at him. "Happy?" he asked.

"Completely," she said. "I don't know how I would do at being a duchess who was merely a duchess. But as a scientist's wife, there will always be some new experience just around the corner."

"Not just new experiences," Arthur told her. "Adventures!"

Cleo gasped and pointed to the dock. "Arthur! Lord Salford is holding Merry's hand!"

"Let him," said Arthur, and kissed her.

207

THE END

####

ABOUT THE AUTHOR

Joyce Harmon has been from one side of the galaxy to the other (slight exaggeration) and seen a lot of strange stuff (very true). Since retiring from the Navy, she has worked as a winery tour guide, a journalist for a local newspaper, selling collectibles on eBay, and making candles - and always, always, a writer. She shares her rural Virginia home with two haughty and indolent cats and one clever, busy dog, and is haunted by a noisy crowd of characters, all clamoring to be written down and set loose into the world. She accommodates them as quickly as she can. She is the author of the Passatonnack Winery mysteries, *Died On The Vine* and *Bidding On Death*. *A Feather To Fly With* is her first Regency romance, and is followed by the novella *Regency Road Trip,* and the novel length Regencies, *Katherine, When She Smiled* and *The World's a Stage.*